JUNE 0'|

THE BLUE CHILD SERIES:
On the Mountain

Dedicated to Jeanne Lohmann, medicine woman to miracles

Jeanne Lohmann told me I was a poet and writer and with her naming, I became one. She is my mentor and proof of the generosity of the universe, that help comes. Jeanne is a wise elder who helps me find my voice, as she does for so many writers. Together we edited this book in the rich territory of loving companionship. Enjoy Jeanne's books of poetry and prose: *Gathering a Life; A Journey of Recovery, Between Silence and Answer, Granite Under Water, Flying Horses, The Light of Invisible Bodies, Dancing in the Kitchen, Calls from a Lighted House,* and *Shaking the Tree.* The most recent book is *As if Words.*

Dedicated to Judith Bouffiou, midwife to possibilities

Judith Bouffiou is a gentle, loyal friend. Over the decades she has pushed and prodded me toward my best and highest possibilities. For those who find their way to Judith's basement, the world opens.

Acknowledgements

My son, John O'Brien, has always brought the most amazing gifts to my life. His generosity of spirit, the power of his personality, the originality of his thought inspire and support me. John reminds me of the power of bloodlines. There have been a few men in our family with his strength of will. John is one of them. My father was another. John is the published author of *A New World Series*. His support of my writing, and the support of my brother, Bill Park, have helped keep me on track.

I am grateful to have been born into a family that believes in visions and miracles, and who trust their dreams. My father, William Nelson Park, Sr., and my mother, Doris Park, were powerful spiritual people. They knew the call of the soul whether it came on the night wind, in the behavior of the deer, or an impelling vision. I am grateful for what they taught about nature. They knew the animals, the water, the forest in the old way, not only as a source of food, but as spirit-filled creation to be loved and respected. My family also believes in the importance of an individual's life-work, that it is an expression of sacred spirit, the making of soul. Within this matrix, I keep writing.

My grandmother worked with plant medicines, as did her mother. To this rich tradition other plant medicine people have contributed. Elise Krohn, herbalist and native food specialist, has taught me much. She is a gifted writer about plants, tradition and place: *Wild Rose and Western Red Cedar*, and *Feeding the People, Feeding the Spirit*. Joyce Netishen is another herbalist and maker of plant medicines who enriches my life. Find her at firerosefarm.com. However, any errors about plants and medicine are all my own.

I want also to thank my friends and fellow poets, Linda

Strever and Shelley Kirk-Rudeen, for thoughtful discussion about the book, its characters and the implications of their journey.

Culture creates reality, pre-programs experience, determines its proofs.   Once the matrix is set, it is only in dreams or at the periphery of sound and sight that other possibilities present. Occasionally they come in spiritual experiences induced by extreme states. Ancient ceremony carefully executed is the exception.

On the Mountain

Chapter One

Cultural reality is a flat world with edges. Occasionally, in the upper rooms of the soul, gravity fails, momentum is impeded, space and time collapse. The pieces can't be recollected. Don't tell anyone who doesn't already know.

It is not yet dawn. Ruby is waiting in her car for the first light of day, listening to the rush of water down the steep crevasse in the mountainside. Other than the water, it is silent. The birds are still asleep; the morning breeze hasn't begun to stir. She is waiting for the mountain to speak, or the water. Waiting to learn why she is here. It is in moments like this – waiting – that she wishes the spirits spoke more plainly. But, of course, they don't. Ordinary language like ordinary thought has limited value in the spirit world.

When Ruby wakes, as she did this morning, with an impelling urge and a clear vision about where she is supposed to be, she goes, doesn't sink back into the tempting warmth of her bed. The one time she did – a wind storm heaving the trees around her house as if they were kelp beneath the sea in a December tide – everything went wrong. She badly burned her palm building the morning fire, and, turning to get a bandage, tripped over the edge of the rug and fell hard. She knew better than to resist and wasn't surprised that all day she felt emotionally flat, disconnected. No matter what the weather, she never refused again.

So, here she is. When she woke this morning with the familiar pull, she flipped the down comforter off her sleepy body and left the bed's warmth. The urge was so strong her hands shook as she pulled on canvas pants and a thick wool sweater. Quickly she grabbed water, stuffed some nuts in a bag, got her warmest coat, a blanket and pulled on her boots – out the door in less than fifteen minutes.

Backing out of the driveway her headlights illuminated an owl sitting on the bird feeder. Ruby smiled. A little early for the owl to catch a bird for breakfast, but perhaps she missed last night's meal and was anxious to eat. Suddenly she'd swooped toward the car, landing on the stones beside the passenger window. Startled, and no longer amused, Ruby gave her the attention she was due. The owl looked through the window and tilted her head. Her behavior was almost plain English. After all the spirit bird of Ruby's grandfather is the owl. Clearly, it signaled that today's trip would be different.

As she watched the owl, an image had formed in Ruby's mind. It was of the road at the very top of the mountain, right beneath the peak. The image meant that today's destination would be the place where the road ended and the hiking trails that network the Olympic Mountains began.

It is a spooky place, this entrance to the wilderness – one of those places guaranteed to raise the hair on your arms and speed your heartbeat – and it is rugged, a place where only pickup trucks and SUVs can go. Hiking trails thread the rugged mountain range of the Olympic Peninsula. These are not family friendly trails. Moss hides slippery beds of shale. Many of them parallel deep ravines and are too narrow for a misstep. They are wet and treacherous. Rocks that seem stable have been loosened by water freezing and melting over and over. Trees not quite uprooted lean on their neighbors, waiting for the next wind. Ruby knows she is supposed to be here but has no idea why, so she waits.

Though Ruby loves the mountains, she has never walked far enough into them to require she stay overnight. There are many spirits who live there – not all of whom are human friends. Ruby has experienced their power, has seen and heard them – shapes and shadows among the trees, voices she can almost understand. Then there are a few war veterans, the ones who withdrew here decades ago, chose the forest and the mountains far away from war, its reminders. They live in caves and tree houses, live off the land. Neither veteran nor beast welcomes company. But it is not really these that make Ruby unwilling to spend the night except in her car. She is puzzled by her behavior but not given to introspection; she makes sure she is in the car or off the mountain by night.

Ruby watches the light move through the stages from dark to dawn, waits to learn why she is here. The night is still deep gray, so dark the mountains and the trees aren't yet outlined against a lighter sky. In an hour or so everything – trees, rocks – all will be dark blue as if the air is filled with a thicker substance. The eye will not be able to differentiate the hard matter of trees from spirit forms that seem just as likely to take shape as stones. Ruby's grandfather, not one to wait for sunrise, used to say that this is the hour for prayer, for deep listening. That is what Ruby is doing now.

It had taken an hour to make this trip. Each winter the melting snow streams across the road leaving exposed stones and deep ditches. But last winter's heavy snows and lashing rain were exceptional. Boulders tumbled down the mountain and the earth above the road slipped. Mudslides left little room to squeeze past. In some places the road has fallen away. It is just as well that Ruby could not see what she knew was there beyond the headlight's reach: the steep drops below, those places where the road was still crumbling, the oozing, unstable ground. It is ironic – Ruby loves the mountains but is terrified of heights.

The pre-dawn wash of deep blue begins. She is parked in the only place possible – a small round space where the road ends and where hikers, when there are any, leave their cars. She's turned the car around facing toward the road she's just traveled. The area is small and is surrounded by forest. The last portion of the road arriving at this cul de sac is actually a bridge. Under it, a waterfall. On each side of the wide creek are cliffs cut by the cascading channel. On Ruby's right, somewhat behind the car, is the trail. Ruby cannot see it but she knows where it is. Movement catches Ruby's eye. Slowly she turns her head to see what it is, but it is still too dark. Ruby puts a hand on the long stick beside her, not as a weapon, but seeking comfort as from an old friend.

The staff stretches from floorboard to roof. It is always in the car for use in forays into the woods. Taller than Ruby with a curve at the top it helps steady her crawl over logs, tests the ground for pits left by roots of overturned trees, steadies her over terrain thick with undergrowth. It is Vine Maple – flexible, strong and light.

Many years ago it was gathered in early summer after the leaves were fully matured and the sap high in the plant. Ruby collected it from a small hill above a wide creek, the perfect place for gathering canes for elders and a staff like the specimen beside her. As the trees grow on the side of a steep hill first they jut outward before reaching upward for the light. The result is a natural curve on one end. It was the work of a morning to find the right length and curve for her purposes. For hours Ruby ran her hand along the root of each tree where it disappeared into the soft hillside before she found the perfect curve, the long, straight length. With a small handsaw, she cut the tree from the root.

It is a long process to finish a staff, to season it so the flexibility is not lost. Prepared carefully it will bend against the body's weight and not break. Under the shade of its sisters and using a sharp knife, she scraped the thin bark away exposing the white wood beneath, promising the spirit of the tree to grow in its place, promising to remember the tree in its summer glory. Above the creek she ate lunch – last night's stew – poured coffee from the thermos – the first meal of the day. Satisfied with the day's work, she lay back against the bank she'd exploited, sipped the coffee and studied the dappled light, the creek – details that would keep the place alive inside her.

At home Ruby sanded the Vine Maple smooth, and placed it in the storage room to dry so that it wouldn't split. There it stayed for six months before she finished it. A staff like hers, spiritually prepared, forms a relationship with its maker. Ruby's obligation is to listen; it's to support. Red wool is wrapped around its top, two deer hooves hanging. The bottom is worn rough and brown from its bite into the thick mulch and mud of the forest as she searched for medicine plants. There are scars left by stones as it anchored the crossing of a rushing creek or the climb down a steep hill that Ruby wouldn't have dared without its support. Otherwise it is still white and as lovely as the mountain's peak. At the end of her strength Ruby places her back against a tree and slides to the ground, still clutching the leaves of Skunk Cabbage.

The old woman makes a sound like bass strings on a big instrument. In response, creatures emerge from the trees and gather in the center of the clearing where there is a flurry of activity. Ruby takes this opportunity to spread the funky leaves inside her clothes across her sacrum; she folds the long tips around her hips. Several go inside her sweater over each shoulder. They will prevent the spasms that would otherwise follow.

There is humming behind Ruby and to her right. Ruby turns to find one of the Old Ones standing nearby, a darker shape against the trees. He is the one who followed her to gather the Skunk Cabbage. Is he there to protect her? Surely they know she is in no shape to run. Ruby wonders why she didn't know he was present by his smell. Perhaps it is the Skunk Cabbage or that she has been with them all day and stopped noticing.

Like tanning hides in the traditional way, soaking them in water and brains, after several hours the rotten smell permeates the skin and clothes, disappears. This memory of hides takes Ruby to a warmer place, to the edge of a green river in late spring. Hides, elk and deer, dozens of them, are spread on ropes between trees waiting their turn to become clothes, blankets, drums. More hides are in the river and tied to posts to keep the strong current from carrying them away, the river beginning the process of removing the hair making the women's work easier. Other hides soak in tubs to become buckskin. Buckskin, the end product so different from the making: soft, warm, smoky. Ruby remembers the laughter of the women – of her grandmother – making fun of a hunter whose aim went wild leaving a hole in the middle of an otherwise perfect hide. The sweat lodge at the end of the day, cleansing them from the work, unknotting tired arms. The warmth of the hot stones, warmth of women's laughter. Warmth. Remembering, Ruby drifts to the edge of sleep.

It is the itch of the Skunk Cabbage leaves against her hip that pulls Ruby back to the present. She places her hand on the ground to shift her weight and is startled instantly awake. Under her hand is something cold and very slimy from which every cell in her body recoils. Her brain begins to work and pieces together the evidence, or more accurately, it offers memories of fishing with her grandfather when she was a child. Not on a fishing boat in the dangerous waters of the Pacific, he didn't take that risk. Instead they'd fished from a sand spit near the house where a small river emptied into the sea. They sat in the early morning with poles. She'd caught small fish on worms until she was older and he taught her to cast. Her chunky child's body wrapped in a slicker, wrapped in the warmth of his soft voice – it was those things rather than catching fish that pulled her to join him. But she had been reluctant to handle the fish they caught and he had insisted that if she was going to fish, going to eat what she caught, she had to have a little respect, at least enough to hold its living fishy body. So, either there is a fish lying by her hand or she has truly lost her mind.

Food. They are trying to feed her. She is moved by their effort, and chagrined by their choice. The fish is raw. Raw fish is a delicacy to some people but not Ruby. Even people who do like it raw don't bite into a whole raw uncleaned fish. But there isn't really any choice. Ruby needs food. She picks it up and steels her mind so that she won't gag. The creature inches closer and squats. A vibration begins in Ruby's chest. The Old One is talking in their humming, murmuring way. Gentleness fills her, gratitude deep and inexpressible. Not just for the generosity of the fish, but for life itself even though she is exhausted and unnerved by the unfamiliar feeling of powerlessness. Maybe it is a side-effect of exhaustion. Maybe it is what is left when everything is stripped away. Love. Awe. Gratitude.

Holding the fish against her leg, using her fingernails Ruby scrapes the scales off. The small scales and the shape of the fish say it is probably a trout from one of the lakes nearby.

Mindful that the fish has not been cleaned of intestines, she bites into its back. No go. It is too tough. She saws the fish back and forth trying to break through the flesh. Gags, tries again. The taste is wretched and the slime worse. So much for gratitude.

This is not working. Ruby longs for her knife. She places the fish beside her on one of the Skunk Cabbage leaves and leans back against the tree again. The creature crouches beside her, picks it up. When he lays it back down again, Ruby is able to slip her hand into its empty cavity. The fish has been cleaned. She puts the thin pieces along the open sides into her mouth and sucks the soft flesh. Bites off small hunks, rolls them around her tongue. The fish is no longer disgusting. Hunger takes over and Ruby relishes the raw bloody flavor, sucks and chews the fish to bone. Fish is smeared on her face and hands, drips off her chin, soaks into her pants. No wonder she cannot smell the Old Ones. She smells of the day's sweat, Skunk Cabbage and now fish – aroma strong enough to overwhelm any other.

The scuffling sounds in the meadow stop. The creature near Ruby grunts, murmurs and one of the others answers. Against the protest of bone and muscle, she stands and heads toward the group. Don't ask how she knows this is what they want. Perhaps, they are guiding her by sound which she appreciates for surely they must know she doesn't want to be touched.

She stumbles over a branch. When she regains her balance, the Old One near her tugs the hem of her coat and pulls gently. He is leading her though the dark, not quite touching her, but almost. Ruby shrinks inside her clothes, irrationally trying to distance herself from his hand. She knows by the effort they are making to keep her alive that they don't intend to kill her. She knows the young one's help is probably necessary to keep her from tripping, that he is being practical and possibly kind. But Ruby is exhausted. Silent tears drip down her face following the deep creases between nose and mouth, drip off her chin mixing their chemistry with the muck already on her sweater.

Near the middle of the clearing where the group of Old Ones stand are two fallen fir trees lying side by side. The trees must have fallen many years ago as they are dry and limbless. Between them is enough space for Ruby to lie down, a place to spend the night sheltered from the wind. Perhaps, if she digs a burrow in the debris between them, she will live. She tucks the remainder of the Bear Medicine inside her shirt and more around her hip. The heat of her body – such as it is – will release the medicine of the leaves; they are anti-inflammatory and will bring warming blood to the surface of her skin. By morning, the leaves will be dry and crackly. They will break into fragments inside her clothes. But by then, the medicine will have done its work. Ruby releases long gray hair from its knot on the back of her neck, tucks it inside her collar and zips her coat to the chin to hold her body's heat.

The Old Ones step aside and wait quietly. Ruby crawls over the tree, pushes rocks and sticks aside. Before curling up she glances at the mountain looming above. She is facing the peak; the bright star is still above. It is beautiful. Curling up Ruby gathers debris with which to cover – but it isn't necessary. Two of the Old Ones gently spread a light substance from shoulder to feet. Touching it with her fingertips she recognizes bark, not the hard slabs of the outer tree but the soft inner bark of cedar pulled in long strips from the living tree and pounded into fibers, soft enough to make shirts and capes, warm like down and also made water repellant by the resin in the tree – an important quality in a wet climate. The cedar covering her however is not the soft result of careful work. It is rough, the hurry-up job of need. When did the Old Ones prepare it? They couldn't have planned to spend the night here. They clearly are frustrated by Ruby's slow pace and surely intended to be further along the trail by now.

The cedar smells delicious – like home – and is a soft, warm nest. The clean scent almost dispels Skunk Cabbage and fish. There is nothing sweeter than cedar newly stripped from the tree. Clean and cleansing. *Cedar*, the mother tree – clothes, shelter, canoes, oars, mats – and when you have wandered into trouble, she will make you new again.

Wrapped in leaves, covered by cedar, a wonderful lethargy settles inside Ruby; she wonders again why the creatures are urging her up the mountain; why they are working so hard to make sure she lives to get there, and, ultimately, why her. She wonders about what the Old Ones really are, tries to recall more of what her grandmother said about them. The sleeping bag and the blanket back in the car belong to another world.

The sound of the murmuring Old Ones is distant. The space between the logs is a silent, safe chamber. Fear is gone. Whether this is the result of exhaustion or the work of the Old Ones, Ruby doesn't know. Grateful, whatever the cause, she drifts toward sleep. Sometime in the night she hears the soft sound of weeping. The sound is coming from the mountain. Ruby snuggles deeper inside the cedar and falls down the long tunnel to sleep.

Chapter Two

Nature reflects all realities – the one we know, and all the others.
Where does night go when the sun rises? Who listens when trees
mourn? Is the river the water flowing, or is it a spirit who carries the
water from its home in the mountains and sings it to the sea? Are you
weeping, or has "the cry" come upon you?

It is early when Ruby wakes like a diver rising from a great depth to the loud grunts and rumbles of the creatures. The star-sprinkled sky above is clear. No sounds of weeping, the star at the top of the mountain gone. So is the ache in her hip.

A piece of red meat lies on the smaller of the two logs. Venison, red and dense. It is the back-strap from along the backbone of a deer, tender enough to eat raw. Delicious.

Ruby sits on one of the logs wrapped in the insulating cedar and eats the meat. When she is finished, she disentangles herself from the soft bark ready to start the day, but feels the intense prickle on her back of someone watching. Turning, she finds the old woman standing across the meadow, its upper end. She is half-hidden, nearly camouflaged in the brush and trees where, just beneath the peak, the trees are stunted by the icy wind of winter blasting across the bare stones. The intensity of her gaze is nothing Ruby has ever experienced. The impact penetrates the skin, moves inside Ruby's body probing the organs. It is like a small, winged creature on an errand. It flutters along the outline of Ruby's lungs, across the curve of liver and into her abdomen. It is so visceral Ruby feels nauseated. Panic buds, but Ruby moves it aside to allow the old woman's examination – as if she had a choice – hoping it is soon satisfied.

The old woman's attention moves up Ruby's spine, pauses behind her heart. The bird-like flutter becomes stronger, takes up the rhythm of Ruby's heartbeat. The creature and Ruby's heart move as one, except, instead of one beat, there are two. Just as Ruby is unsure how much more she can take, the old woman retreats, moves to her throat and then withdraws. Bent, hands on her knees, Ruby struggles not to lose her breakfast. Shaking and gasping, she finally manages one deep steadying breath and then another. She looks toward the old woman but she is gone. Ruby turns toward the trail below.

This experience together with the internal, visceral way the Old Ones communicate is invasive like nothing Ruby has ever known. The Old Ones don't seem to be confined to their own bodies; perhaps this kind of "visitation" is normal to them, but Ruby hopes she doesn't have to suffer it again. It is raw and disorienting. She feels scoured. There are no signs that the Old Ones have taken control of her thoughts or decisions, unless it is in her agreement to follow them at all, and that decision, at least, seems only an extension of how Ruby is, what she has always done – that she comes when called. But if Ruby had anticipated these events, she would not have. The old woman's purpose, like the purpose of the journey itself, is mystifying and disturbing.

The sun is shining though it is too late in the season to be warming, particularly under the old-growth trees. Ruby and the Old Ones are climbing higher. Earlier this morning, just after first-light, they had taken a trail branching west and Ruby's heart sank. The linking trails of the Peninsula can be chosen for short or longer treks, tailored for length and difficulty. The choice of the western trail was discouraging. Once begun there is no shorter, easier option. They are headed into the interior of the national forest – the wildest, most rugged part.

Ruby has been anticipating the end of the journey in an event that signals it is over, that the purpose of the Old Ones is completed. She hopes that when it is she can find her way back down the trail, but the choice of the western fork opens the possibility of a one-way trip. It is not that she can't find the way back, but that the deeper into the forest they go, the less likely it is she can make her way alone and without food. Of course, it is possible that the Old Ones will escort her back to the car, or give her supplies. They don't seem to be without compassion. Or it is possible that once whatever they need her for is accomplished, she'll be on her own.

Last night when she heard the weeping she'd thought for a moment that perhaps she was meant to help someone lost, hurt or in trouble – something pragmatic.   But the voice had that echoing quality of the spirit and Ruby abandoned the hope of an ordinary resolution.   But now that they are traveling further around the mountainside, now that they have taken the western fork, Ruby resigns herself – again – to a deepening mystery.

Ruby has always believed that she is living the reason she was born.   Through her eccentric grandmother and grandfather, she knows teachings that few remember, but it is not hers to teach the young.   Hers is to do what she can't avoid anyway – go when called, gather plants and make medicine, weave, dream.   When she moved across the width of the Peninsula she assumed – to the extent she thought about it at all – that this place – the earth or the water or the plants – on the southern arm of Puget Sound must need what she represents – a teaching, a medicine, a bloodline.   Hers is to live in the between places, to keep a spiritual door open.   In fact, her understanding – again via her grandmother – is that she is a door.   It never occurred to Ruby that she had a literal task to accomplish or a role to serve the people like her younger sister, Grace.

Now she wonders, already feels a growing distance from her blue kitchen – its perfect pots of steel and zinc and clay, the long wood spoons carved by her grandfather, jars and sacks and boxes – not for cooking but for making medicine.   Across the end of the room hang the plants she uses most and those that are her favorites – Nettle, Pipsissewa, Yarrow.   She can feel the familiar dry leaves between her fingers, hear their subliminal song.   And the red and white weaving on the loom in front of the fireplace – but these, the core of her life, are dreamlike, almost as if they belong to someone else.

Ruby and the Old Ones are moving fast, slower than yesterday but still the pace strains Ruby's strength and stamina. As she did then, she stops for water at every creek.   Her clothes are dry, but her skin itches from the dried flakes of Skunk Cabbage and from the bits of cedar that penetrated the fabric. Pants and shirt are stiff with mud and sticky with last night's meal.

Just as yesterday, the old woman sets a steady pace. She is largely quiet and when there is the grunt and murmur of conversation, it is among the others. It is she who determines when it is time to stop and when to move on. From this Ruby gathers there is a hierarchy in the group and the old woman is its leader. Her broad hairy back is fast becoming Ruby's guide just as she imagines it is for the others, though what comfort and direct help Ruby has received has been from the young one.

Back on the trail, Ruby gathers the soft tips of fir branches. At this time of year they are not the soft taste treat of spring, but they are still lemony. They will boost her energy and clear the dreadful taste in her mouth left from last night's fish.

The group walks in silence. Seen from a distance, someone might at first think them a group of determined hikers but a second look and the observer would blink or rub their eyes, maybe even look for a place to hide. Up ahead is a rill, just a trickle of water lit by sun. Kneeling Ruby splashes water on her face, washes the sleep from her eyes, the residue of the meat from her hands. If she finds a larger pool in the sun she promises herself a bath no matter how much the creatures protest. She feels more secure today – at least for the moment. The Old Ones evidently need her. She is provided shelter, food; the pace is adjusted to her abilities. Not for a moment though does Ruby believe the journey is for her benefit.

Sitting beside the tiny trickle, Ruby lifts her face to the early light, fills her lungs with the cold, clean air. She bends to watch the changing colors of the water, listen to the early morning silence of the old forest, delights in a tiny pool of water nestled between rocks. Violets, long past their bloom, form a carpet at the edge, their round sweet shape a homey comfort – though their spiritual power is not for the easily rattled person. *Violet* appears and disappears, announces a crossing. Ruby pulls on its power.

The peace is shattered as a hand enters her field of vision. It is the young creature who supplied the fish the night before and the venison this morning. Kneeling he puts a small root on the rock, but it is his hand that rivets her attention. The color is light gray with a few very dark hairs. His complete otherness startles Ruby, sends a chill up her spine.

His hand is thick, the fingers long and round, not the hairiness of an ape, nor is his hand shaped like one. If you'd asked Ruby, she would have guessed his hands were furry, but they aren't. They look much like hers. Ruby bonds studying his hand – the soft curve of his relaxed fingers, the heavy nails at their tips, the open palm – studies him as she would an unfamiliar flower, or a track in the dirt. The pulse of his heart in a blue vein is strong and steady. Absorbed, Ruby reaches her finger toward his wrist – and catches herself just in time to stop. She is startled by how close they are and embarrassed by the impersonality of her examination. He is entirely motionless kneeling in the dirt.

It occurs to Ruby that he has arranged this up-close encounter. The young one is the only one of the creatures who approaches her. It is he who brings her food. Ruby wonders if he is trying to break the barrier of separation between them from the natural curiosity of the young, or by assignment. Maybe the Old Ones instructed him to gain her cooperation, or perhaps his work is only to make sure she survives.

Ruby sits resting on her heels, turns her attention from the young one's hand to the root he laid on the stone. It is *Licorice Fern* – return from the edge, go inside. Ruby pulls up her sleeve, looks at the inside of her arm. Yes, it is mottled with long red welts. A histamine reaction, probably a response to distressed nerves, the cedar, the Bear Medicine. The question Ruby had last evening about whether the Old Ones use medicine plants or not is answered. She chews the sweet, peppery root slowly to let the medicine do its work.

Ruby and the Old Ones take up their positions and follow the trail curving around the broad bulk of the mountain.

In mid-afternoon, they arrive at a wide treeless place. It is not a meadow but a sloping band of rough stone opening the view westward to valley after valley, overlapping hills and tall rugged peaks each vying in stature with the other. Endless, yet only a small portion of the total wilderness, a world apart.

As she looks across the forbidding terrain high clouds above separate. Ruby stands in a pool of pale yellow light, but in the west the clouds are thick and low with the telltale blue of rain. In these mountains rain is the norm. It comes in off the ocean sometimes in sheets and buckets, sometimes as mist seeming to both rise from the earth and fall from the sky – fog so thick the ground is hidden, or it drifts in skeins that diffuse the light and make everything surreal. The advancing clouds predict days – and, at this time of year, possibly weeks, of saturating weather. The root system of trees will be undermined, boulders will break free. In places the trail will become a channel of water; in others it will disappear except as a break through the forest. And if it comes as snow, already overdue, it may fall steadily for weeks without break.

But, at the moment, the view is beautiful: the green of trees, the blue distance, the white snow on the peaks. The size of this roadless wilderness is the explanation for why people can live here for a lifetime and never be seen. The beauty says why they might want to – but the skills required to live in this wilderness continuously and in winter are more than those of anyone Ruby knows. For the moment, the pool of light and the beauty before her are everything she needs.

There is a humming in her chest, and Ruby understands the communication. It is time to move on. The Old Ones leave the trail, skirting the open area. They pick their way through the trees and rejoin the trail on the other side. Back within the shelter of the trees, the metallic smell in the air says tonight will be cold. Maybe the rain will hold off. Ruby hopes so. Cold as crystal nights are, the rain at this altitude will be little more than icy – it might as well be snow. She is glad for the insulated, waterproof jacket she wears. Grateful for the hat of Canadian wool. Unprocessed, it still contains the natural lanolin making it additionally warm and water resistant. The second evening on the mountain will begin soon. Famished and feeling weak from so much strenuous activity, Ruby hopes dinner is not raw fish again.

It is. Several small fish, already cleaned, lie beside her when she rises from a stream. Ruby promptly sits down to eat. She is tidier than last night, spreads a cedar branch over her lap to protect her already filthy pants. Like last night she eats all the fish, sucks the bones. Finished, she washes her face and hands, wipes them on green boughs to remove the fishy smell.

Hunger satisfied, she looks around to see what the Old Ones plan next – if they are preparing to spend the night here or if they are to walk further. But the Old Ones are nowhere to be seen. She hears no humming, no grunts, feels nothing in the center of her chest, nor any sense of someone or something nearby. She is alone. While she ate, the creatures slipped silently away; absorbed in satisfying her hunger, she didn't notice. They have followed, guided and herded her since she got out of the car; they pushed the pace, fussed when she took too long, and communicated in a hundred ways the urgency of their destination. Now they are, quite simply, gone. Ruby sits against a fat alder to think and wait. An hour passes. Nothing. Did they expect her to catch up when she finished eating? Surely they did not expect her to manage the slippery fish while walking. Unsure, she continues to wait, but the light is failing and night is not far away.

Ruby can be still for long periods waiting for the exact best time to collect a plant, or for an animal to lose its shyness, but with a cold night falling the need for action looms. Perhaps she should follow them after all. She looks for tracks and finds none. In a forest of undergrowth and brush, tracks are difficult to find, but there should be partial prints here and there in damp places. Ruby tries to remember what their feet look like and cannot. She could follow the trail and hope to find them, the warm cedar bed they provided the previous night. But if she can't, night will find her unprepared. She turns her attention to locating a protected place to sleep. She cannot be distracted by tracks – or their absence. The Old Ones are gone. She is on her own. Why, she cannot imagine.

Around her are tall upright trees, no fallen giants to snuggle between as she had last night. She decides to leave the trail, to look for shelter nearby. To her right is a small steep hill. The forest is brushy with Salal grown tall reaching for the sun. The dark green waxy leaves hide treacherous footing. The forest floor is covered by ground hugging creepers, twisting roots, deep moss. What appears to be solid surface sinks into deep holes between roots and stones. Lichen and moss are a thin skim over slick stones. Each step would have to be tested as if walking on thin ice. Again, Ruby wishes for her staff. It would dig deep to the solid places, brace her against what she cannot see. Without it, and with the shadows growing long, she dares not go in that direction. To the left there is less Salal and more space between the trees. It is the direction she chooses. Occasionally she scuffs her feet in long swaths to leave a trail on the forest floor; a precaution. She doesn't plan to go far and besides, Ruby never gets lost.

Up a small hill to the right Ruby spots the telltale red of an old cedar stump. She clambers up, but the tree fell so many years ago it has disintegrated into a rough mound of colorful cedar dust. Beside it is a flat gray stone, an opportunity for rest. Ruby zips her coat tight, pulls the wool hat close around her ears. It is getting colder. Because of the dense canopy, the forest is park-like; each tree long ago earned its place in the sun and it has been a long time since one gave up its spot to winter wind.

Beside her, the smell of the cedar is strong. So is the presence of the trees. They are aware of her but give no direction or answers. The desire to drift is strong, to merge with the trees, the mountain. But the cold that will come tonight will turn this dream-like state into nightmare.

Her drifting, dreamy state reminds Ruby of a day long ago. It was in late spring and she was in the mountains on the coastal side. She'd come upon a meadow where she had never been. The meadow was nothing unusual – grass, flowers and an oak tree in the exact center, a good place to eat lunch. In the warming sun of the meadow and with a full stomach, Ruby went to sleep. When she woke, the meadow was immersed in an opalescent shimmer of light. It was hard to focus. Nothing had changed – the tree was in the same place, her backpack on the ground – except for the shimmer and the complete absence of sound. She could see the flutter of birds in nearby trees but couldn't hear their twittering song, not the buzz of bees or the breeze in the tops of the evergreens. The leaves of the oak tree, the blades of grass were completely still. She was warm, a little bit sweaty from sleep and yet she shivered.

Ruby knew there were spirits who capture people in other dimensions and hold them. She knew she was in one. Ruby closed her eyes, grasped the cedar bracelet placed on her wrist by her grandfather and thought hard about the day he'd put it there. She began to hum what she remembered of the song he sometimes sang. With a loud crack a branch of the oak landed at her feet; the shimmer disappeared from the light. She could hear birds and bees again. Ruby grabbed her backpack and hurried from the meadow into the forest. When she arrived home that evening, her grandfather took her into the long room at the end of the house where he carved. He taught her the exact verses of his medicine song, the rhythm of its drumming. He told her she would be the one who inherited his medicine gear and his drum when he died. Today is not like that but it is similar. There is a watching presence that is not the mountain, not the trees. It is something different and more powerful.

The mist becomes light rain. Ruby breaks from her torpor, leaves the flat stone and walks on. She rounds the hill to see if on the western side the trees have been more susceptible to the storms coming off the sea. Instead there is an old burn, the fire from a lightning strike. The trees are tall white ghosts. Between them stand their bushy progeny, and nothing else. Ruby turns back, briefly considers digging at the base of one of the trees to create a den, but in this rain she could wind up in an icy bowl. It is then, with startling recognition, that Ruby realizes she does not know in what direction the trail is. The reliable sense of direction on which she has always depended has deserted her. It has disappeared as abruptly as the Old Ones. The scuff marks she made earlier aren't visible either. In the fog and misting rain everything is confusing..

Ruby – who never gets lost – is. The light is almost gone. If she had the equipment from the car, she'd be fine, but alone and without it she is not sure. The Old Ones have to know she is missing, and yet she still hears nothing. She could yell and see if they respond, but given the sense of something watching, it seems the wrong thing to do.

Ruby needs help. She leans her forehead against the nearest cedar, her hands cushioning her face. She presses her body against the comfort of its cold surface. She needs to clear her mind. How could the Old Ones bring her this far and then abandon her? They'd seem so determined on some errand or destination. Why make sure she was fed, had medicine and then leave her to possible hypothermia?

Ruby is not familiar with feeling helpless. The mountains and the forest are her second home. She should know what to do. Why doesn't she? Yes, she is under the influence of a powerful spirit but still she should not be confused or lost. Ruby senses there is a key in what is happening and it is hers to discover. The trembling of her old body stops. Her breath mingles with the scent of cedar. From nearby branches hang long pale streamers of moss. *Usnea*, a powerful broad-spectrum antibiotic and the spiritual food for winters that last too long, for arduous journeys. Grateful tears form in her eyes. An old friend is here.

She hears her grandfather's song in the background of her mind but it will not break the power that has caught her as it did so many years ago, though it does stop the churning of her thoughts. No, his song is not the answer. But something is there, something behind the song itself. An idea is struggling to surface. And then, like a cork, it pops to the surface. She will sing in the language of the Old Ones – as nearly as she can. She will try.

Stepping away from the tree, she takes a deep,

shuddering, cedar-scented breath. The sound is a groan more than anything else. Not an expression of frustration, nor even fear, though there is a hint of supplication. It is a spiritual asking, a searching, a sending out.

Ruby abandons herself to the effort and her voice grows louder. It curls between trees, skitters along the ground, bounds from the stones and reverberates up the mountain. It breaks apart. Some tones find their way down the canyons, some higher vibrations hover over the water and move it in little circles as if multiple small stones had been dropped. This is no scream but neither are there any words. Instead there is a pouring out of intensity beyond ordinary emotion. What began as a call for help becomes a reach for something much greater, for help beyond the moment. There is ecstasy, a willingness to expend all in the expression of something unidentifiable and completely essential, an abandonment of self. Ruby is lost in sound, becomes sound; some tiny part of her mind knows what began as an experiment has become something else.

But the experiment works. Striding through the trees comes the young creature who seems to be assigned to Ruby's care. He is humming loudly. He is mimicking Ruby's voice, picking up her lower tones, giving them cadence and form. To Ruby's surprise she does not stop. It is as if her calling, once begun, has developed its own will. Ruby and the Old One stand fifty yards apart facing each other, lost in a song so raw it might be the mountain groaning, or the starlight moving across the galaxy.

The Old One varies the tones creating fractals of Ruby's earlier feelings. She follows. Together they fill the forest with variations. They vibrate together, combined voices creating overtones. And now Ruby hears their song echoing back, falling down the mountain from all its stony places. She cannot tell the difference between her voice, the Old One's and the mountain singing. The jelly inside her cells, her muscles and bones melt into the vibration of sound, rearrange and settle again. A tiny part of her brain can still think; it wonders if the music reaches across the entire mountain range, if the ducks and the seals are listening. And then, Ruby leaves her body altogether. She is aware only of a loose sort of Rubyness in a cloud of blue sparks. Still she sings. The voice of the Old One drops lower and slows.

He falls silent, his eyes fixed on Ruby. Ruby is silent too. Back in her body, she is still vibrating. Trees, Salal, even the Old One – everything is outlined in a rim of light. The Old One straightens, turns into the deep gloom of early night in the direction from which he came. Ruby follows. She feels so light she can barely feel her feet in contact with the ground. It is at least a mile back to the trail where the group waits. Soft murmuring between the old woman and the young one is the only reaction to her return, or is it their return? Ruby doesn't know. She isn't sure they abandoned her on purpose, but she suspects they did. Her sense of direction returns and she is no longer confused, but something is profoundly different.

Beside the trail the Old Ones begin to make a bed. Two of them drag a half dozen long bark slabs from somewhere up the trail. Fir, from the look of it, weathered. The young one and another that has not been part of the group before prop the slabs on the downhill side of a wide tree a few feet from the trail. The one who is new to the group is small, almost human-size but from something about her manner she seems quite old. Her hair is a paler gray; she is slightly hunched at the shoulders. Or perhaps the clue to her age is in the deference given her by the young one. He is watching her gestures, anticipating her wishes. With the crook of her finger she motions toward the placement of a slab at the edge of the arrangement and he exchanges it for a thicker piece. If she is humming it is too softly to hear. Ruby watches distracted by the white aura around the trees, the Old Ones, everything.

The young one and another move stones to anchor the edges of the shelter. The whole is surprisingly stable and roomy. The young one stoops to spread the cedar inside. Clearly this is tonight's bed. It is a common sense solution – one Ruby should have thought of when she was looking for a place to sleep. Though she wouldn't have had the insulating cedar, the protection of the bark would have been sufficient. Ruby believes that the Old Ones deliberately blocked all options except calling them in their own language. It is the first indication of their power to control her mind and their willingness to do so.

Unlike last night, she does not drift quickly into sleep. She lies thinking about their singing – if that's the right word – between her and the young one. The Old Ones created a crisis with only one solution – the use of their vibrational language. They must want to communicate, perhaps something about the reason they called her. But do they also know that the experience has left her vision altered? Probably.

Finally, she succumbs to emotional and physical exhaustion. Late in the night, Ruby wakes. She is fully alert, her heart pounding. Footsteps, carefully placed, slow, soft, but with the weight of a man. Someone is near. It is not the Old Ones – she never hears their footsteps – and it is not an animal. Only a human would move with such methodical caution.

Whoever it is knows how to walk with remarkable quiet. The steps come closer, inches from the lean-to. He sniffs and Ruby almost laughs. With her rank smell, hiding would be impossible – sweat, fish, skunk cabbage and fear. He moves several steps away and now she can see him as a dark shape between the fir slabs. He sits down beside the trail, no snap of twigs or crunch of stones.

The lean-to is flimsy. A yank on the bark planks and it would tumble apart leaving Ruby exposed, her nest destroyed. Ruby wonders if the Old Ones have left again, if she should prepare to defend herself. Her palm curves around a stone. A nearby rustle, a soft grunt. The Old Ones are close after all.

The man rises. "Sorry," he says. In a hoarse, guttural whisper, he adds, "I don't know how you came to be with them, but I wish you well." His footsteps leave going back up the trail from the direction he came. Ruby wonders if he is one of the men who lives in the wilderness, one of the eccentric veterans. What kind of damage makes his isolation necessary? Or perhaps it is hard won wisdom. The night is quiet again for a moment and then there is a low drumming sound, the one that only a big drum makes, one from a thick elk hide. It sounds like a heartbeat, like Ruby's heart beating. The old woman would certainly know its exact rhythm. Ruby sleeps.

The next morning the tracks where the man stood are as close to the lean-to as Ruby thought. The edge of the print is softened. Not hiking boots, but footwear made of soft hide. Not moccasins of suede for there is no definition in the print of toe and heel so they are not the soft deerskin favored by summer's Pow Wow dancers, worthless in this wet, rugged environment. His prints suggest heavy rawhide meant for endurance, much like him, Ruby guessed. He'd wished her well.

Chapter Three

Effort at the edge is prayer, an invitation. The answer does not come in common language, images or in natural law. It may be as subtle as the breeze, or as shocking as the cedar tree walking. Keep what you see to yourself.

Agnes is restless all night twisting in the heavy red and blue Pendleton blankets that keep her warm in the wet, coastal chill of the Northwest winter. Her sleep is light weaving the night-sounds into dreams. In the background is the distinctive sound of her grandfather's drum. The dreamer dreams; the dream-maker watches over her uneasy sleep. When the phone wakes her, the dream fades quickly but Agnes knows the message will bring trouble, someone's need predicted by her restless sleep. She lies for a moment listening to the late night – or is it early morning. She is reluctant to answer the intrusion into the peace of her solitary life.

Agnes is an extreme introvert more at home alone in the sloughs and the forest behind her cabin than with other people. She has no friends other than a few cousins who aren't offended by her failure to stay in touch. The extended family, reaching from Canada to the high desert in Oregon, don't expect her at celebrations or even funerals.

The isolation of her cabin reflects her nature. It is located just where the river spreads into a broad estuary mixing fresh water with salt, where it empties into the Pacific Ocean. No one lives near this wet and often flooded place. No one but Agnes.

The road that leads to Agnes' cabin is gravel and dirt. It connects to the coastal highway, a long stretch of Highway 101 where there are no towns or even stores. It is all marsh and brackish pools, more water than solid ground. Agnes is isolated further by the fact that the road – one she built – from the highway to her cabin leads only to the cabin and stops there. She doesn't mind the long periods when the road is impassable, when she cannot leave nor anyone arrive. In fact, it is flooded now but still passable with the pickup truck sitting behind the cabin on its big mud-gripping tires.

She walks through the cabin with toes curled away from the icy floor. Only a wood fire can cut the seeping cold of winter's chill in such a wet climate. Agnes didn't light one last night, not even to cook. Instead she sat in the dark drinking swamp tea left from the morning and chewed on strips of elk jerky trying to draw together the threads of her impressions – a uneasy sense of being watched – the same sense as when she is in the forest and a hidden predator is watching her tracking them. By the time she'd gone to bed last night she was still puzzled and becoming wary as well.

Drawing a long wool wrap around her she curls into the big square chair by the cold stove, tucks the ends around her toes and finally picks up the phone steeling herself for what she knows will be trouble. On the other end Grace's voice is low and urgent, "Thank God! I was afraid you'd be in the forest or on the water."

It is early winter but Grace knows there is still time to gather the roots from high on the mountainside, roots that are Agnes' favorite winter medicine. She knows Agnes spends long hours in a kayak on the estuary, paddling up the river, or along the ocean's shore collecting kelp and gathering clams. Grace's voice is usually a low lazy alto, but now it is almost unrecognizable – the pitch is too high, her words tumble over each other. Even in the heat of anger or passionate debate Grace is self-possessed. She is as brave as eagles but right now she sounds scared. Agnes does not herself feel safe in a world that frightens Grace.

"Where are you? What's wrong?" Agnes asks.

"When I got home last night there was a note taped to the door, a warning. I ignored it, thought it was the usual political nonsense, but now I don't think so." Grace is a woman who steps into a fight rather than away from one. Agnes can't imagine a note that Grace wouldn't see as a challenge.

At the same time Agnes is relieved to hear that Grace is at home and not two states away at a conference or visiting family on the back reaches of one of the big reservations across the mountains. If Grace is at home, she is within the reach of a several-hour drive rather than far away advocating for issues critical to Indian survival. Grace is beautiful, sensual and articulate but also cynical; she says Indians have to work twice as hard now that they no longer pluck the heart strings of an easily bored America. Or elicit the condescending good will of liberals who grieve for Indians past and do little for Indians present; those who buy feathers but don't want to hear the startling infant mortality rate. It is in the world of advocacy for Indian rights that Grace lives.

Agnes and Grace could not be more different. Agnes cannot be bothered with the economic and legal problems associated with tribal treaties – government control of Indian trust funds, access to plants and animals necessary to practice ancient traditions, protection of sacred sites – all those rights so dear to Grace's heart. While Grace is a formidable and aggressive foe, Agnes retreats and lives as she wishes though she knows she might be the last generation that can. But despite their extremes of personality, Agnes and Grace are close. In fact, they are cousins, taught to think of one another as sisters, raised together by the same maternal grandmother. Grace knows she only has to ask and Agnes will come.

"What did it say? Read it to me." Agnes asks. What could be so bad? Grace has been threatened before even from within the Indian community itself. Battles between Indian families can last for generations – who signed the treaty, who supported a compromise to benefit their family, different ideas of when to hold and when to relent. These enmities may also be about access to hereditary rights – songs, names, spiritual power. Internal tribal politics could be training ground for international ambassadors to the Middle East.

But Grace cuts to the bottom line. "Come now. I am at the old house. Something has been outside for hours. It doesn't knock on the door and it doesn't leave. I've done everything I know to do and it makes no difference." Agnes is startled. Both women were trained by their grandmother and what she taught them should suffice to keep Grace safe. In fact, the knowledge of how to keep herself safe by what their grandmother taught is one reason Grace could feel so confident in her work. Something is very wrong.

"Bring grandpa's medicine drum," Grace adds.

"I'm on my way," Agnes answers, but Grace is no longer there.

Agnes rises from her warm nest calming her anxious heart. It will take hours to get to Grace no matter how much Agnes rushes or how much Grace needs her. Grace lives between an apartment in Portland and the house where both girls grew up. Their grandmother, Marianne, left the house in her will to both girls equally but Agnes chose not to live there, but tonight that is where Grace is, and where Agnes must go.

People in the village visited the old woman everyday – dropping by to talk about their troubles or to bring fresh fish or meat. Or bring Mountain Huckleberries, tiny black sweet berries gathered high in the mountains – a labor of love, a generous gift. But there was a not-so-hidden motive in the gift of berries. On Thursday mornings Marianne cooked pies, the week's supply for her family – huckleberry, blackberry and cherry latticed with flakey crust made of fat – bear, elk and even pig ordered from the market in town. So on Thursday a steady stream of people from the village arrived at her door. Marianne laughed at the number of small emergencies that developed among her neighbors on Thursdays. Without knocking they entered through the kitchen shyly sniffing out the days offerings.

Marianne loved the people in the village, people connected to her though generations of mutual help, shared beliefs and by blood, so she enjoyed dishing hot pie onto clean white saucers, offering a pitcher of cream. Pie on Thursday was one of her contributions to the social fabric that sustained the community and affirmed the place of each. It was the time to gossip – who is pregnant, who is ill – a time for slow, thoughtful discussion of an innovation, a problem, or the kitchen might rock with raucous laughter.

When the old woman died the traffic pattern of the

villagers didn't change much, or at least they didn't change if someone was at home, even though there was no pie anymore. Without the joy of Marianne's pie, they still came to exchange news but now it was with Grace and about issues that reach beyond the village – less fish in the river because of the silt from over-logging, and on the other end of things – how to keep the young people from moving away so they can learn about the tides and currents, the songs for the river and the ocean, the fish – teachings always just one generation from disappearing forever. The result was too much social contact for Agnes though it suited Grace's extroverted nature.

The house has a core of kitchen, living room and five bedrooms. It was built by Marianne's grandfather and expanded by her husband. The old sections of the house include a long room paralleling the south wall but separated from the rest by a breezeway. It was primarily a carving shed where Marianne's grandfather and father carved cedar ceremonial posts, masks, rattles, and sometimes coffins. Sometimes when all the aunts, uncles and cousins came, the room was used for makeshift beds, too.

At one end is a small room, six feet by six. No one was allowed to enter except Marianne, and, when they were alive, her grandfather and father. The room was a place with the sole purpose of housing ceremonial regalia that belonged to the spirit that is descendant in Marianne's family, items so sacred they could only be touched by the few who are trained to care for them.

Agnes saw the regalia only once. Shortly after she came to live with Marianne and not long before Marianne's father died, a few old people gathered in the long carving room one night. They drummed and sang for a long time. Grace and Agnes sat in chairs placed behind a wide-backed old woman so Agnes didn't see much of what happened, but afterwards Agnes stopped dreaming of the car wreck in which her mother died – the endless loop of the black stones and the ocean's blowing froth rushing closer and closer, her mother's long scream, and, worst of all, the wait for her mother's voice afterwards.

That long night left its mark on Agnes. After the crash, she sat silent and still in the wet sand and the cold wind off the ocean. At sunrise, Henry, who had delivered the newspapers to the reservation for the previous twenty years, saw the wreckage below. It was not the first time that the beauty of his long morning drive following the narrow curving road above the beach was marred by the human debris of a tragic night. The road was slick with ocean spray; its curves sharp. Raccoons, or other animals, on their way to feast at low tide startled the unwary driver.

Nevertheless the shock of the overturned car made his stomach plummet. He assumed there were no survivors – the car was upside down in the rocks. Reluctantly he climbed down the embankment to make sure. When he spotted the child, her unblinking black eyes wide and her usually sunny face frozen, he groaned. He recognized her and knew that grief was on its way to Marianne. He hefted the silent child from the cold beach and walked back uphill to his car, shoved the newspapers aside on the car's seat and drove to the nearest house. After he called the police he braced himself to do what he must. He drove to Marianne's house delivering a child in shock, delivering the news of the death of Marianne's youngest daughter.

After the night of drums and songs Agnes slept and over the following weeks began to speak again. She was moved to Grace's bed and began to sleep through the night. Grace's warmth and the deep breath of her sleep became a mantra of safety for Agnes though she was never the laughing child she'd once been.

Now Agnes gathers what she needs for the trip north along the old coastal road. Her cabin is one large room with a separate bedroom off the kitchen, but across an open breezeway is another room for the storage of drying plants, a place to store fish and elk she canned or dried earlier in the year, paddles for the kayak, winter clothes. It is there she heads to collect more dried elk, salmon, her warmest jacket.

Once in the breezeway Agnes is struck by the absolute silence – no restless ducks in the reeds, no sound of lapping water or the call of a coyote. No sound of deer sloshing across the watery meadow. No raccoon waddled around the cabin's corner. It is not the silence of a predator on the move. Not the silence of hunkering prey. It is predator of a different kind, not wolf, cougar or bear. Agnes waits for the silence to break in a rustle of feathers, a caressing breeze off the water – but it doesn't happen.

Nature is Agnes' closest companion. She knows its language – the stance of the grazing deer, the splash of a fish, the distance and pitch of the coyote's cry. She interprets these to guide not only her day – whether to travel on the water, stay out of the forest – but her life. It is how she chose where to build the cabin; its layout strung along the bottom of the estuary. Marianne taught her daughters that listening and watching is a spiritual responsibility, that witnessing what is revealed was an old idea of the people.

Witnessing is not passive. It is one's own spirit seeing beyond the surface, focusing, interpreting. The spirit's arena is an exchange chosen partly by its spirit nature and partly by the individual's choices. The spirit will call more of what the individual offers even if that is gossip, violence or drunkenness. Agnes is witness to nature. She lives within its matrix; depends on it to feed the body, the spirit and to protect her. Grace is advocate for the people. Allies, spiritual and political, surround her efforts sufficient for her safety. At least they did until now.

Quickly Agnes moves into the storage room, puts dried meat in a bag, collects her coat, a thick sweater, a blanket and places them in the cab of her pickup. From her room she gets a duffel bag that is always packed. In it are a towel and soap, a toothbrush, small jar of bear fat and a change of the silk underwear she has learned to love for the soft layer it provides between her skin and the rough wool that makes up most of her wardrobe. It is her secret luxury. A secret except from Grace who bought her the first tempting set of underpants and tank top, brought them all the way back from a conference in

Denver.

Agnes stops the pickup where the road is closest to the water. The tide is in and the estuary is full from the reed-lined edges near the cabin to the banks of sand and sea grass on the far side near the dunes. The tall dunes bank the transition of river to sea making the estuary broad and rich. Hundreds of migrating birds rest there twice each year, their soft night voices providing a reassuring lullaby. In the estuary otters, protected from the wind, search for shellfish. At low tide the deer cross the silt high-stepping in deep mud, or swim the estuary's width looking like sleek seals, their heads barely above the water.

This wet place is not for people from Chicago or Dallas. They grow irritable in the long months without sun, the seeping damp, the tall brooding trees, the mildew in their shoes. But to Agnes this is paradise. She loves this place of transition of land and sea, fresh water and salt, where the division of day and night is not clearly marked. It is a place of water in all its forms – mist, fog, rain, ocean spray, and howling storms straight from a thousand miles of open sea.

Agnes can't wait for any further sign. The silence, the watching presence is the only communication she will have – something unfamiliar, dangerous and powerful. She heads for the highway and turns north. Tonight there is no visible moon. Clouds hide the stars. It is so dark the lights of the truck barely illuminate the pavement. Like a cat, Agnes has excellent night vision, but tonight darkness is a heavy blanket compressing her breath. Even the engine of the truck seems muffled and distant, monotonous but not soothing.

Agnes feels disembodied, ethereal. She knows that the feeling is someone or something trying to lure her off the road and block her reaching Grace. But Agnes knows this road well – the creeks, waterfalls, the meadows. She knows its twists and curves, including the one that took her mother's life. She will not drive off the road. She will not be tricked.

The road north along the coast is not designed with tourists in mind. It doesn't dutifully hover along the beautiful shore except in short sections. There are few tourist destinations except campgrounds for campers and tents. The motels are graceless cubicles lined up along the road. If the road is not built for tourists neither was it built for straightforward, efficient travel. It was shaped by old realities and is traveled by ghosts.

The road curves inland to the hills and passes through small timber towns, or, to be more accurate, towns that were once timber towns. It jogs toward the sea and follows the sensuous curves of rivers to one or more of the protected bays scattered along the coast. It follows these for a distance and then loops back again toward the forested hills.

The changes in direction from hills and mountains to sea seem capricious, but are not. There was once logic to the pattern. The road was built to transport trees, to connect sawmills to ships waiting in the ports. Sawmills that no longer exist except as piles of rotting sawdust and ponds filled with debris. The remains of busy ports are seen in old posts standing where once there were wharves, from where ships transported lumber to hungry markets in Seattle or San Francisco.

It is a road that follows rivers made shallow with silt washed from hills and mountains stripped of roots and moss that hold the earth in place. A road that leads to broad bays made shallow for the same reason. The twists and turns follow the path the trees once traveled, the work of loggers and the goals of lumber barons.

The roads served this purpose snaking over the coastal side of the Olympic Range until two decades ago when the old forests were depleted except for the central mountains protected as a national park. Over this designation and its protection legal wars still rage fierce and full of cunning. The last of the timber barons and their attorneys hang on to a way of life that is finished; if they have their way, they will destroy this vast wilderness on the way out.

Ahead is a smear of lights, one of the small dying towns. A service station, a store, a restaurant with the predictable menu of fried steak and gravy, a church and a bar lined up along the road reflect the essential services of people learning to need very little. The men who once rose early to be in the woods by first light sleep late. They once worked at sawmills where acres and acres of logs piled three stories high waited. Rough men with heavy shoulders to heft the big saws, coarse hands thick with scars and calluses, yet they were nimble too, prancing on suddenly dislodged logs, agile men who learned to race a falling tree, or prance from the path of a "widow-maker" as a dead limb was shaken loose by the vibration of trees hitting the ground. Cables used to drag trees from their fallen places broke and whipped their metal ropes sending men diving for cover. They worked fast among unstable logs on ground littered with limbs and brush ripped and smashed by machines. Death was not uncommon.

These are men familiar on the peninsula. Their rough arrogance has become bewilderment. A life once fueled by adrenaline has become a slow journey into depression. The bars that once dampened the day's fear, bars noisy with laughter and dark humor, are quiet. The alcohol still flows but now as a companion to deep silent anger. They draw unemployment, hunt deer and elk to put meat on the table, and they drink.

Depression is palpable in little towns like the one Agnes enters. The political posturing in courts about the fate of the trees is real for the men who have not imagined an alternative. This is as far west as land allows. There are no new beginnings, no places left to start over. The American solution of moving west, the mindset that there is always more has met the sea.

On the outskirts of the town a dog walks unevenly toward the road from the recessed doorway of an abandoned building. Brindle with a square snout, he moves in a slow sideways shuffle as if his hip has been broken. He looks toward Agnes' approaching pickup, his bright yellow eyes caught in the light. He stretches his bristled head toward the sky and howls, his mouth forming a perfect "O." Agnes shivers. Maybe the dog is nothing more than a broken animal whose fate is to help carry the pain of the town. Or perhaps, he was roused by something evil afoot tonight.

On the other side of town rain begins to pour. The entire

peninsula is one of the wettest places on earth but more so on the coastal side beginning with the hills at the edge of the sea and reaching into the mountains where clouds are trapped against the spine of the Olympics. Mist hovers in trees like winter's breath, or is as thick as soup in small valleys. Wet, low clouds hide the beaches and seem inseparable from the rumbling sea.

Or, like now, rain streams as water will from a woven net lifted from the ocean onto the deck of a fishing boat. Hard rain in cascades and sheets that washes old logs, deadfall trees, fallen limbs and boulders down creeks and rivers tangling them in creeks and gullies. Massive roots, the monuments of ancient trees that record in their rings hundreds of years of the land's history, are rolled and lifted from their homes to join the rush to the nearest ravine. On a rare sunny day the power of the water is hard to imagine but after a week of water flooding from the sky it is easy. The Peninsula is a watery domain.

The rain blurs the windshield; it turns the highway into a reflective sheet of moving water. The lights of the truck make long strobes of light against the falling rain. Agnes slows her speed and focuses on the shimmering image of the pavement. She knows this weather and these roads, knows enough to take her time. Yet it is time she feels she doesn't have. Grace must realize that it will take Agnes hours to arrive and yet her voice had been urgent as if she needed help right now. Fear takes hold in Agnes heart, fear that already Grace might be injured. If it is an ordinary threat why hadn't Grace called the tribal police just down the road? Agnes knows the answer – the threat is not ordinary. Besides, Grace never travels unarmed. Agnes tries to remember one of the medicine songs of her grandfather but cannot. She can hear the beat of the drum, but not the song. Nevertheless, she sends a prayer through the night.

For some reason a different image of Grace comes to mind. Last March, Grace talked Agnes into going to a Pow Wow, something Agnes never does. It is a Pow Wow so far off the beaten path that few people go except the descendants of one family. The shelter for the dance is an old, very small longhouse. Because there are no crowds and Grace wanted it so badly, Agnes went.

They drove over the mountains to the high desert. The smell of sage was strong and sharp in the long yellow slant of early light. Agnes reveled in the transition from the lush landscape of the western side of the mountains to its stark contrast on the eastern side where there is little rainfall, where the bones of the earth show through. Agnes blanked out the rich farms along the river that cover old village sites and burial grounds. Instead she saw only what she chose – the red and black rim-rock, the soft blue desert flowers on the slopes. Not seeing farms, condos and warehouses was a way to see the spirit of the land as it has always been.

With a bed and propane stove in the back of Grace's van they had everything they needed for a couple of days. The sisters laughed as Agnes teased Grace about the rush to get there. Grace is beautiful, irresistible. Men stop talking when she arrives; they follow her as if in a trance, as if they have no choice. The more charming assert themselves early.

They parked next to a rocky creek under a cottonwood tree near the longhouse. Almost as soon as they were out of the van a man broke away from a small group and approached laughing: "I knew the creator would send me a gift today! A fine woman or a good horse!" Wide smile, long hair in wrapped braids he sauntered over, or perhaps it was a strut. He walked right past Agnes, of course – no surprise to either woman – aimed like an arrow for Grace. Grace gave him a small smile, stepped around him without breaking her stride headed for the old house. Her hips had a tiny sway but the motion was magnified in the rhythm of her shawl and long hair. Her poise and understated response have the impact of an aphrodisiac.

On the dance floor, at the food stands, men find her. Old men, young men, traditional dancers and urban radicals. The men who know her watch the others. Like Agnes, they are amused in an affectionate sort of way. They know Grace's availability depends altogether on her mood. If a frustrated suitor grows rowdy, friends materialize. Grace also carries a small pistol of high caliber in a small buckskin bag. Grace is a complex woman.

The trip was the last time Grace and Agnes visited other than by phone. Why has this memory of warmth and sun come now? Then she remembers. On the trip over the mountains just as they topped the crest and dropped onto the drier side of the Cascade Range, Grace grew silent. Agnes knew Grace's silences and waited. What followed might be the whole purpose of Grace's determined effort to get Agnes on the road and, sure enough, Grace began to talk. She said that at one of the annual tribal ceremonies the month before, the elders gave a warning. They said that someone was awakening an old spirit dormant since the times of disruption when tribes were moved by the government from their homes to almost uninhabitable lands, the times when the children were stolen and placed in boarding schools.

Someone or something had called a spirit that had been put to sleep generations ago, put to sleep because it was too powerful in the presence of so much anger and grief; yes, it could be used against the invading enemy but the chaos it would also cause would be deep and permanent. Long ago the elders had hidden this old medicine; they'd contained it in a cave in the southwest, and concealed the entrance. Now someone is trying to break the bonds that hold it.

The elders live in isolation even from each other. They watch the sunrise and the night sky to see what is coming, to read the signs, so they can help the people. Once each year they gather for four days to talk. When they have reached agreement they tell a trusted few what they have seen. Grace is one of the people they trust.

Grace said it is uncanny to watch the elders gather because there is never a pre-determined day to meet though there is a time of year. They have no phones or other way to communicate yet they all arrive on the same day. Old cars and pickups make their way down the steep switchbacks to an old house beside the river. Before the first car has come to a halt, the adult children of the elders move into action. Two piles of firewood in the yard are lit. Jars of elk and salmon are opened, cooking begins. On one fire a big zinc pot of coffee is set to boil. Other pots hold potatoes and eels. One large room is set aside for the elders so they can talk privately. Blankets are stacked at the end of each couch so they can sleep when they are tired. For four days, their murmurs continue.

Agnes has never been there and this was the first year Grace passed on the message that was given. When asked why, Grace told her what the elders instructed, "Tell your sister." Grace didn't know if she should also have told Ruby. Because of the decades of difference in age, Grace and Agnes sometimes forget that Ruby is also a sister. They think of her as an elder. Anything, but an equal.

Now, the wet road turns from hovering beneath the foothills back toward the ocean where the rain falls even harder and the road is narrower. Trees, bent and twisted by the wind off the sea, grow thick; younger trees cluster at their feet creating an impenetrable curtain caught in the lights of the truck. Ditches are filled to pavement's edge with water running fast towards the nearest canyon. Old cattails, stiff with autumn's chill, lie across the banks and clog the ditches. If the rain continues at this rate the road will flood and Grace will be beyond Agnes' reach.

Agnes is bent forward, her face nearer the windshield in order to see through the sheets of rain. Just ahead is a sharp, downhill curve. Agnes brakes gently and that is when it happens. Careful as Agnes is, still the pickup hydroplanes veering toward the ditch in seeming slow motion. The lights pan trees, cattails, running water. At the edge of the ditch the sodden earth gives. Agnes accelerates hard, twisting the wheel back toward the road, knowing that once in the ditch or mired in the mud, her journey toward Grace is over. Tires spin, mud makes a wet arc behind the truck. Above the sound of spinning wheels and racing engine, the beat of Agnes' grandfather's song fills the truck. Agnes' spirit reaches for help but oddly it is Ruby who comes to mind, not her grandmother, nor her grandfather.

Seconds seem like minutes, and then the miracle - one of the back tires catches on a bed of fallen cattails. Agnes feels the traction and presses the accelerator harder. The truck fishtails loose from the mud, swerves across the road towards the opposite ditch. Agnes pumps the brakes and the truck halts crossways the road. Resting her head on the steering wheel, Agnes waits for her heart to slow. Shaking, she is grateful for the help of cattails.

Cattails protect and contain. Made into traditional mats they were hung on walls to protect from winter drafts; they covered floors to keep feet warm, provided beds and doors and baskets. Marianne taught her granddaughters when collecting plants to leave no sign of their presence when finished – arrive, gather and leave without trace. But tonight that is not possible. Instead, cattails were drafted into a new role, were left in a muddy mess of broken stems. Still, Agnes will never see them in the same way again.

Agnes raises her head, determined to drive more carefully and slowly. Her love of Grace cannot be allowed to determine her pace. It feels like folly not to rush when Grace's need is so immediate, but, as she'd just experienced, it is greater folly to do so. She backs up, rights the truck in the road and drives on ready for a longer journey.

But at the bottom of the hill, around a curve Agnes brakes. There before her is what she feared most: the road is blocked by a wide pool. A creek, ordinarily small and docile, now fills its small ravine. On the upper side of the road, it makes a waterfall over a pile of jammed logs, but more importantly on the other side is a pile of limbs and debris blocking the water's flow and creating the pool. Agnes gives little thought to the fact that if she hadn't hydroplaned on the other side of the curve she might have plowed straight into the water. As it is she stops inches from its edge appalled at the magnitude of the obstacle. Agnes cannot believe how difficult the simple journey north has become.

She takes a deep steadying breath and studies the water.

She guesses it to be over her head in the middle. How deep it would become depends on how high the pile is on the downstream side but from the swift movement of the water on the surface Agnes guesses it has already topped the jam. For a moment she considers swimming across and walking, but in this weather there will be no cars to give her a ride and it is a further three hours to the old house. If she is going to make it to Grace, she has to drive; the pool has to give.

Agnes is strong. She has always been. It was Agnes who helped her grandfather heft the completed carvings into the dented and scarred bed of his pickup. And when Marianne was old, it was Agnes who chopped the winter's wood. She built her own cabin with help only in raising the rafters and the upper beams. It took all spring and summer but by October everything was in place. She can walk long distances in the mountains without fatigue. She kayaks the ocean. Agnes is strong enough to contemplate unjamming the logs on the downstream side.

Sometimes in a flood-created dam like the one confronting Agnes, only one or two large limbs are the key to the entire dam. Once those are dislodged everything breaks free, limbs fly into the air, logs shift and twist underwater and the entire pool rushes downstream. If that happens, success can also mean death.

Using her flashlight, Agnes can see nothing atop the water that will easily dislodge the dam. It appears that unjamming it can only be done from under water, if it can be done at all. Agnes is no stranger to cold water. When she was a small child, Marianne, like most traditional grandmothers, taught her the gift of winter water. Endurance is not the goal. Instead of shrinking to the smallest possible stoic dot, Marianne taught Agnes and Grace to embrace the cold before entering the water. Expand, become permeable. In this way the hard taskmaster of endurance is avoided, the doorkeeper to shivering, teeth-chattering misery. Marianne said, "Open the place in yourself where the stars are." The result is soaring spiritual ecstasy.

But tonight the purpose is not spiritual. There will be no ecstasy. Agnes strips off her clothes and stores them and her boots in the pickup. Wearing only tights and an undershirt to protect her skin from the debris in the water, she wades in – and then she stops. Something is wrong. She listens. At first she hears only the splash of water flowing over the logs, the rain against the truck and the pavement, its splash on the pool's surface. And then the chitter of an owl.

Chapter Four

*Go deep as your culture allows and still you will not reach the spirit
who acts through you, the one that chooses you, breaks you so that you
can do the work. Don't allow your culture to over correct your
wounds lest you are made too clean of everything important.*

Ruby has grown thin with effort. Her pants hang slack
on her body; the Velcro belt cinched to its limit. Even her feet
slip inside her shoes. In the last few years Ruby lost her
plumpness, the soft roundness of cheek and hips. Now the wiry
tensile strength of her aging body has changed again. She is
thin, seemingly fragile. But her back is still reasonably straight;
her pace steady, dogged. The arthritis in her hip has eased. Her
coarse hair slips from its bun, strands hang against her sweat
dampened face. She has moved inward searching out those
places where endurance waits for need.

The food the Old Ones provide is sufficient. The meat is
rich with the nutrients of grazing deer, fat wild fish but there is
nothing of plants or carbohydrates except the occasional
medicinal root. Ruby does what she can digging plantain roots,
wild ginger. Both grow beside the water, but these are not
enough to supplement her diet or add calories. They provide
other support however – *Wild Ginger*, sweet and powerful, a
woman's plant for tapping intuition. *Plantain* – the work of the
snake climbing to its highest place.

Since the musical encounter with the young creature, she
is sustained by something else as well. The rime of light at the
edge of everything is no longer disorienting. Her depth
perception is no longer disturbed. She is not afraid of falling
where roots and stones protrude. As her body grows lighter, so
does her spirit. Each moment is its own entirety. Radical
acceptance, a bit like psychosis. Or spirit travel.

Ruby listens to the murmur of the Old Ones, listens to
their moods, tries to understand the meaning. Sometimes she
hums, too. When she does the young one moves closer and
listens carefully.

Today is the third day since leaving home. In the late afternoon the group stops within the shelter of the trees at the edge of a large meadow slanting upward. The Old Ones are uneasy. Several stand behind trees searching the meadow methodically. Others spread out along the tree-line sniffing the air, peering at the ground. Humming softly, the old woman squats in a brushy tangle, her head dropped to her chest. Those scouting the tree-line return, stand beside her and wait. She seems almost asleep, then raises her head and rises. Still, she hesitates. Powerful as the Old Ones are, what could they fear? Ruby understands from their grumbling rumbles that they do not like open places. But, still.

An hour passes, then another. Finally, the old woman steps out and the others follow. This time, Ruby is last in line. The Old Ones do not adjust to her slower pace. They move rapidly over the meadow. Given their obvious anxiety, Ruby wonders why they haven't followed the tree-line.

From the drying leaves of the plants Ruby knows how beautiful the sloping meadow must be in spring when all the flowers are in bloom – *Arnica, Bear Root, Balsam*. She is tempted to dawdle, dig the roots, but the Old Ones are moving too fast. Ahead is a long spine of stones bisecting the meadow from her right near the peak and ending at a cliff on her left. The cliff is the answer to why the Old Ones did not cross inside the tree-line, the reason they opted for the treacherous crossing of open space.

The ridge of rough rocks reaching across the meadow's center is difficult going. What the Old Ones made look like easy passage with their long strides, is not. Each step is a choice to be made carefully. By the time Ruby is near the top, the Old Ones are out of sight but she can see where the path enters the trees. And, she can also see the bigger obstacle hidden by the stony ridge.

Between Ruby and the trees is a bed of shale. Shale beds are smooth flat stones sitting atop one another in multiple layers with little offering of traction. It is the nature of shale beds to slide unpredictably. On a bed this broad, it would be doubly likely that Ruby's weight would initiate an unstoppable slide sending her down its length and over the cliff. Because shale is sharp, if she falls, even if she is able to get up again, the result would be bloody. Why would a hiking trail lead across such danger?

Looking around, Ruby sees the answer. As the trail leaves the trees it wanders further up the mountain crossing a portion of the meadow where there is little shale. It appears the Old Ones opted for the shale and less time in the open instead of the major route. Ruby determines to take the longer path, but as she turns upward, the rumbling growls of the Old Ones in the trees beyond are clear warning. Nevertheless, the shale is too dangerous. Ruby ignores the Old Ones and continues upward only to stop again as their rumbling grows louder and becomes a cacophony of sound, loud drums and even trumpets. For a moment, Ruby's mind is blank, washed by sound seeming to come from all directions. She can also feel the old woman moving inside her body. Though she cannot see the Old Ones they are obviously spread out along the tree-line from where they are giving her specific, emphatic instruction.

Ruby doesn't like shale, but, her years in the mountains have taught her something about it – if she steps onto the outer edge of her foot instead of the sole and tests each step before placing her full weight, she might make it across without incident. Focus, concentration. Ruby's scalp prickles and her stomach tightens. With a deep breathe she takes her first step. Silence from the trees. Approval.

Inch by inch she crosses, places her weight slowly on the outer edge of one foot, waits to see if the rocks hold and then lifts the other. This works until she is halfway across and steps onto a stone the size and shape of a dinner plate. It begins to slide. She extends the other leg for balance, shifts further onto the outer edge of her foot to give the stone an opportunity to bite into its neighbors. It does. Her progress across continues to be punctuated every few steps with similar short slides. Ruby begins to feel confident, but wonders if the Old Ones know how dangerous this is.

And then it happens.   At first it is just another small slippage of one slick stone above another. She shifts her weight but, instead of stabilizing, she continues moving inexorably and in slow motion. First the left foot slides a few inches and as Ruby shifts her weight, the right one does. Ruby knows rock slides can stop just as suddenly as they start. She keeps her balance evenly on each foot, knees slightly bent and waits. The world becomes very small – shifting weight, sliding stones. Suddenly everything slides faster, not just the rocks where she is, but everything below and above as well. The entire bed is in motion. Ruby shifts rapidly from foot to foot – almost hopping – in order to stay upright. But with the rapidly gaining speed of the stones, she begins to flail and nearly topples onto her face. Overcompensating, like a cartoon figure, or an off-balance lumberman on a floating log, she flails in the other direction. Back and forth in slow motion. Strategy is abandoned.

Ruby rushes to that small area in the center of her being where her grandfather's song lives.   Its instant, powerful response fills her mind. It does not help her regain control, but instead, as she continues to slide, an idea comes.   If she can regain even a small fraction of balance, it may be enough to leap in the direction of solid ground. If she can leap once maybe she can do it again, and again. Like running on wet stones in a creek, never standing still long enough to slip, moving light and fast. She anchors her will, hopes her feet will follow, and leaps. Or tries. The distance gained is not much but she leaps again and again, each time with better result.

She keeps her eyes on the trees and toward stable ground, but in her periphery she cannot help but see how quickly the cliff grows closer.   Barely feeling the stones beneath her feet, Ruby reaches deeper with each effort.   She is running, running towards the trees. The awful rumble and clatter of the mountain in motion fills her ears. It is twenty feet from the cliff's edge and ten to the safe ground beyond the slide. The outcome is uncertain.   If she is close enough to the trees when she reaches the cliff perhaps she can grab a root or a limb. Her grandfather's medicine song grows louder.   The rime of light surrounding everything spreads across. The shale shimmers. Ruby cannot see trees, solid ground or even the cliff. Still she runs.

Suddenly, Ruby feels her wrist become entangled, but in what she doesn't know. She prepares herself for a hard landing on sharp rocks, a last painful breath. But that doesn't happen. Instead, she lands on her back at the base of a tree in a bed of Salal. The shock is so great she wonders if she has slipped over the cliff, if she is dead. Her grandfather's song recedes. The thick shimmering light thins.

So does the sound of the stones in motion. Silence again. Turning her head a mere fraction to get her bearings, she sees the thick calves of three Old Ones standing beside her. The ache of her wrist and its red mark answers what happened. Grasping her arm, they plucked her to safety. Why they waited until the last possible moment, she doesn't know. Exasperated, irritated, she grumbles in complaint. There is no answer.

Ruby's legs shake with exhaustion, and she is confused. If she'd taken the route she wanted, rescue wouldn't have been necessary. A few bloody spots on her socks are witness to the sharpness of shale, but nothing is broken. No doubt she will be very sore tomorrow, but she has to admit she suffered no harm.

The Old Ones stride back into the trees along the path, but Ruby does not follow. She is uneasy and distrustful. She wants to understand what happened. Granted the Old Ones do not appear to like open places, but that does not explain why they would not allow her to take the longer route.

Ruby climbs from the Salal and finds her feet, slowly straightens her already stiffening body, pauses for one last look back at the path above the slide. There she now sees what the Old Ones saw. A man is sitting in the shadow of a large boulder beside the trail. He is motionless. If she is not wrong, he is the man who sat beside her bed several nights ago, the one the Old Ones sent away with a few grunts. Is he following them? Is he only curious? If so, his curiosity had nearly fatal results. Futile thoughts, Ruby turns to follow the Old Ones into the trees.

But not all the Old Ones are gone. Beside one tree is the old woman who dragged the slabs of bark down the trail, the one who joined the group the same night the man came. Her eyes are fixed on him. With a murmur she directs Ruby to move behind her. Ruby does, but, just as the old woman is doing, she keeps her eyes on the man. The woman begins to hum, a seemingly gentle sound initially, but one that has undertones of anger. Ruby feels the sound vibrating in the earth beneath her feet. Within seconds the trembling of the ground is so strong she reaches for the stability of the tree beside her. The shimmer of light grows stronger until, as before on the shale, Ruby can barely see through it.

The boulder beneath which the man sits shatters, and he scrambles away. The broken stone crashes across the shale but this time the motion in not limited to the shale. The whole hillside is in motion – an avalanche of rock and dirt mixes with the bed and all thunder off the edge of the cliff. The trail tumbles too.   Through the vibrating light, Ruby has a last glimpse of the man. He is running down the trail on the other side, a step ahead of its crumbling. He won't be using the trail again, nor will anyone else – including Ruby. Sound and light fill the space between them. She can see him but now they are on different sides of the divide.

It is clear how far beyond the borders of the ordinary world Ruby is. And how long she has been there – at least since the light first appeared after she and the young one sang. She knows the borderland, has wandered there for intervals.   She knows the shimmer of light is a sure signal of the passage, that its presence is not always reassuring. When she was young and caught in the power in the meadow, she'd known it as an enemy claiming her life. Not this time. She doesn't know why the Old Ones brought her here. She's not even quite sure where "here" is. She doesn't know why one moment they risk her life and the next they save it. What she does believe is that they have a purpose for the journey and that their intent is not evil. Before the earth is still again, the old woman turns into the forest and Ruby follows. The path behind them is closed.

It is dusk. No food since morning. The shimmering outline has become a pastel corona, the trees softly lit. Water in a tiny spring ripples pink, pale green and turquoise; gentle sounds tell stories of remembered winters. At the edge of hearing is the bell-like voice of the mountain singing of ice and stars. Though Ruby is exhausted she is also filled with peace. Questions subside. At least for the moment. She hums with the mountain, following with her own lower notes.

The Old Ones turn along a creek's path. Inside a circle of cedars is a sunken place. In its round shape they put the shredded cedar and Ruby gladly climbs under. The circle is a cedar nursery. The central tree is long gone, leaving a depression where its roots were. Around it are the children. A sacred place, the root of the mother, her nest. No fish, no deer.

Ruby dreams. The mountain sings to the night sky. Fog forms, grows thick. Song and fog wash down the mountainside looking for Ruby. They coalesce into a woman standing beside her bed; entwined in the song is weeping. Over the woman's heart is a sapphire blue light. It is unclear if the woman and the mountain are the same but it is clear that the woman is sad. More than sad; she is grieving.

Ruby is cold, digs into the cedar needles beneath, pulls the cedar around her shoulders and drifts back into sleep. If the woman has something to say, she will return. And there she is again, still weeping. The blue sapphire becomes a star. The woman opens her hands and similar lights fill her palms, but Ruby's attention is caught by the light over the woman's heart. It explodes filling the circle of cedars with blue shards. Ruby is unsure if she is still in the dream or not.

The next morning Ruby wakes late. Sun has dispelled the fog. In the silence, the Old Ones are a watchful presence. Even though Ruby sees the welcome venison on a nearby limb, she sits for a moment, thinks about yesterday and about the dream. The further she travels, the stranger the journey becomes. The woman in the dream has a reason for arriving, a reason for her tears. Ruby recalls the terrifying events on the rock slide. Perhaps, the Old Ones did not want her to encounter the man. Or perhaps they intended to close the trail between her and home.

Nearby the humming of the young creature in charge of Ruby's care arouses her with soft grunts. Ruby's first steps are mere hobbles of stiff ankles and sore muscles. Venison resting on a cedar frond is welcome; beside it is the hairy root of *Osha*. It is one of the plants Ruby was tempted to dig yesterday and she is glad to see it.   Its sweet, spicy taste, loved by bears, is delicious. Purifying, vivifying, clarifying. It will not explain the mystery of what the Old Ones want or the reason for the weeping woman, but it will pull her spirit from yesterday's shocks.

The day never really warms. Ruby's fingers are icy with their frequent use as a cup to drink. The Osha helps but a midday meal helps even more – fish. The trail winds up and down hills and little valleys. In late afternoon it makes an abrupt turn downhill toward another small valley, one near the bottom of the mountain. The days of effort and shock have taken Ruby around and down only one of the many mountains of this immense forest. She sincerely hopes that it is the only one the Old Ones intend to traverse, but she is learning to keep her hopes in check.

Near the valley, the trail is narrowed by a high dirt bank on one side. The bank is soaked with miniature springs and trickling waterfalls. Maidenhair Fern with their long umber stems wave in the currents of air from the water's movement. She loves saturated banks with muted light. *Maidenhair* – not a plant for uncertain women. The trail drops steeply. The dripping water forms a small rill.

At the bottom of the valley the trail twists sharply to the left. The trees thin, allowing the long rays of the declining sun to penetrate. As if lighting a stage set for performance, the sun scatters the last of its yellow light on a big oval pool. Reeds and long grass grow along the edges at one end, giving it a marshy look. In the center, the water must be deep because there it is dark. At the end nearest, it is shallow and forms a basin. Or a bathtub. Evidently others have had the same idea – stones make three broad steps into the pool.

It is early to call it a day, but Ruby hopes it ends here. A bath would be a miracle of sensual pleasure. Clean clothes are another. The bits of cedar from the bed that have worked their way inside the fabric of Ruby's sweater and pants are sharp splinters. Her thick socks, soaked again and again in the mud beside the creeks, are abrasive with dirt. As if in answer to her unspoken need, the Old Ones scatter across the clearing, signal that the day's trek is over. Except for the old woman who leads. She sits on the far side of the pool, and, as she often does, tilts her head toward the mountain, listening. With a gesture she sends two of the Old Ones back up the trail. Surely they cannot still be worried about the man. Surely he cannot have worked his way through the canyons around the slide and have already arrived.

Wet clothes will mean a very cold night, but Ruby cannot pass the opportunity to be clean again. Surveying this lovely park-like place of giant trees, Ruby sees the rest of the miracle - a cabin. It is one of the rustic shelters dotting the trails, insurance for hikers against sudden storms. There will be wood for a fire to dry her clothes and possibly soap. Ruby heads toward the cabin to see what riches it holds.

The steps to the cabin are stumps that lead to a small roofed porch of rough planks warped and gray with age. On one side of the door is a short stack of firewood – dry cedar sticks, branches. The door is swollen with moisture, but Ruby gives it a shove with her shoulder and it yields. Inside, two bunks are bolted to the wall. They are made of heavy wire mesh inside a wooden frame meant to be softened by a sleeping bag. At one end, there is a stack of faded green blankets, the kind found in military surplus stores. Against the back wall is a wood stove with a small black door used to feed the fire. On an open shelf above are candles, a pan and a pot, a kettle, salt – and a big bar of white soap. Ruby builds a fire in the wood stove and the room begins to heat. Ruby warms, but not for long. The pool waits.

Outside, the sun no longer casts its yellow light but the

pool, the tall trees, the smell of wood smoke are surely the template for heaven. Beside the pool Ruby strips. First she dips her hair in the cold water, soaps, rinses. The coldness of the water on her scalp makes her dizzy, but she continues until her hair squeaks with cleanliness. She ties it back into a rough knot so its length is out of her way, scoops silt from the pool's bottom to scrub away the caked grime from face, feet, torso. The frigid water first numbs her skin and then it begins to burn. The euphoria of sustained immersion in very cold water is welcome.

Still nude Ruby addresses her clothes. The wool sweater cannot be safely washed in such a rough manner, but underwear and pants go into the pool for a good stomp in the silt to break up the grime. When they are thoroughly saturated, Ruby whips the pants against a tree to loosen crusted dirt and fish scales. Another immersion and then the soap, with the stone steps as wash board. One more soak to remove soap and silt and the job is complete. The socks she washes more gently so they can be saved. While she has a spare pair in her coat pocket, she wants to save these as long as possible. Good socks without holes are essential. Otherwise blisters will stop her almost as completely as a broken bone. Ruby can do little about the filth of the sweater, but she can dilute its smell by layering it in mint for the night. She wraps a blanket around her waist, gathers the wild mint beside the pool.

Inside the cabin Ruby hangs the clothes to dry. Before the fire, she loosens her thick, gray hair to let it dry and then wraps in a blanket to make another trip outside. She dips water from the pool for the hot tea she intends to savor, gathers wild ginger and huckleberry leaf to add to the mint. She packs a white cup with the leaves, covers them with hot water and sets a saucer atop the cup. As it steeps she wraps mint inside the sweater. Between the steeping tea and the bruised leaves the cabin is fragrant with medicine.

Later, Ruby sits on the porch leaning against a post, cup in hand. The tightness in her muscles from yesterday's effort drains away. Draped in the fan of her long hair and the blanket, she dozes. Shuffling near the steps announces the arrival of her cedar bed. Beside it is a large pile of venison. Ruby didn't know how hungry she was until she smells its rich, raw scent. Inside, she cuts the meat into small pieces and places it in water to make soup, adds salt from the air-tight container on the shelf. While it cooks she spreads blankets on the wire bed, the cedar on top.

Ruby anchors one of the candles in a cup filled with dirt, and lights it. Beside it are a book and a pencil with a dull knife-sharpened end. The book is for campers to make notes about their experience, notes for those coming next, a way to leave something of themselves in the mountains. Ruby opens it, runs her fingers over the writing. She is curious about the people who slept here, but it is curiosity she cannot satisfy. Ruby cannot read. Or write, though she draws beautifully.

Marianne, Ruby's grandmother, did not send her to school. Grace and Agnes went, but not Ruby. The education of the younger two consisted of school through grade six – long enough to read, write, acquire a sense of the world. Most afternoons when they returned home, school continued, but it was school designed by Marianne. Elders arrived to take them to the beach to teach them the names of birds and shellfish; into the woods to identify roots, gather bark and leaves. They were taught the tides, the winds, the clouds, the seasons. Their teachers taught them the story of how things came to be. In the evenings around the fire, only Indian was spoken so they were fluent in their own tongue – a sure way to anchor imbedded values. When they were older, others dropped by to talk about the treaties and tell them about Washington DC. Marianne watched the girls to see where their interests, and their future, lay. Agnes withdrew into nature; Grace became a warrior.

But Ruby's education was different. In fact, she cannot say that she had one. From as far back as she can remember, she lived with Marianne and has known what she knows now. She does not remember another mother like Agnes does. Marianne's eldest daughter disappeared many years ago and Ruby assumes she is that daughter's child though she does not remember anyone saying so. Once, in answer to Grace's question, Marianne said that Ruby had always lived with her – and in a tone of voice that did not invite discussion. Ruby's mind skitters away from these thoughts.

With a candle nearby, she opens the book to its first blank page. She wants to say something about the pool, the cabin, her gratitude for the water, to say something to others who might come. Even though the path is closed behind her, she imagines someone will come again.

Ruby does not expect to be coming back from wherever it is that she is going. Her suspicion that the journey is to be one-way seems verified not only by the destruction of the path, but by the direction chosen by the Old Ones at each junction, one leading deeper into the forest. With the onset of winter, this can only mean one thing. So, Ruby wants to say something, leave a message, for those she is leaving. This is as close as she dares to think about her sisters and the possibility she will not see them again.

Taking up the whole of one white page she draws a heart shaped leaf, ginger. Peeking from beneath one leaf is its shy flower, a flower never seen from above, a showy performance only for those who know where to look. She draws the long curving veins of the leaves. A simple plant with strong medicine, it grew thick on the south side of her grandmother's house and was one of Marianne's favorites. Ruby's brown hand rests on the picture. She is remembering a home saturated with love and old wisdom, one that held Ruby's strangeness lightly.

The smell of soup interrupts Ruby's memories. Famished, she eats it all. After she finishes, she pours the last of the tea and heads for the porch one more time before bed. It is very dark and she can see little except the shine of the water. She settles her sore back against a post and sips the strong, warm tea. Ruby is thinking about her grandfather, remembering the time he told her not to spend the night in the mountains. It was the same night that he placed the cedar bracelet on her wrist, so "you remember the way home again." It was an odd order to give. Almost everyone in the village spent nights in the mountains, in hunting camps, or gathering berries and roots or bark. She didn't feel deprived by his instruction and never disobeyed it, probably because night in the mountains made her uneasy. Now, after so many years she is wondering what her grandfather feared. Or knew. Ruby has never thought about these things before. Never asked these questions.

Movement. A rustle in the dark at the end of the porch breaks into her thoughts. Ruby turns expecting to see the familiar shape of the young one, but the figure is larger. It is the old woman who leads. As if she has been waiting for Ruby to appear, the Old One moves along the edge of the porch to stand beside her. The cabin, perched high in order to remain accessible in deep snow, almost reaches the Old One's waist making her only a little taller than Ruby. Waiting, Ruby sips the last of her tea. She is resigned to closer contact, but it is contact too intimate for a woman of Ruby's privacy. She hopes she is better prepared than on previous occasions: when the old woman probed her body, when she was lost in the forest. Both times she was overwhelmed, but tonight she knows what's coming. Or hopes she does. She also hopes to learn why she is here.

Ruby doesn't flinch when the old woman raises her hand to touch her, the big hand gently cupping ear, cheek. It isn't a caress – or at least, not only a caress. Predictably, the Old One begins to rumble and murmur, a hum like the soft burr of bees. Ruby concentrates her attention in her chest, tries to understand. The music the old woman makes enters the space around heart, lungs. To Ruby's relief it is not the fluttering, bird-like creature of yesterday, the entering of her body to explore organs and spine.

Instead, inside Ruby's skull is a single loud pop. Areas of her brain become warm. Ruby worries that she will lose consciousness, but she doesn't. It is as if two tracks of experience are operating inside her mind – one is hers and one originates from the Old One. Ruby tries to relax into the old woman's efforts.

Images begin to form, but they are not only visual. Each is imbedded with information. Some overlap. And with each, is feeling – love, fear – all with a dozen different subtleties. Ruby realizes that the old woman is introducing herself. Not by name but by describing her nature and her purpose – which appear to be essentially the same.

The image of forest enters Ruby's mind. Simple overview. Ruby suspects the Old One is testing her understanding. Ruby wonders if her mind is as foreign to the old woman as the old woman's is to her. Or is it that the simple scene presented is more complex than Ruby sees? Ruby looks again closely and sees variations of color that she had never seen before even though she is so attuned to color she can spot the strongest plant in a field of its neighbors. Then the vibrations of the mind meet her heart and Ruby knows she is seeing love. The old woman loves the forest, the mountains. Ruby understands this. She does too.

But there is more. This is home, the old woman's home. It has been her home for thousands of years, maybe longer. This area is the home of her people, the home of the Old Ones. There is something more, bigger. The weeping woman Ruby saw in the circle of cedars appears enveloped in blue light with the shape of a star over her heart. The woman has a soft smile but the intensity of her eyes is anything but soft. Her combined sadness and power add a third thread to Ruby's internal experience.

The Old One continues. There is a problem. In fact, there is a crisis and Ruby is the solution – if there is one. They are traveling as quickly as possible given Ruby's age and human limits. Even so, it might be too late. Ruby hears the weeping become deeper, sees a darkened room, and then a star-filled sky. She does not know what to make of this, other than the need is desperate and the problem sweeping in its scope – at least it is to the Old Ones.

The old woman stops humming. The images in Ruby's mind clear and the strumming vibration in her chest subsides.

The porch, the post, the night air return. Ruby is back in the ordinary world. Though it is reassuring in some ways, she also feels empty – as if sight were suddenly deprived of color. She knows this is how the Old Ones perceive humanness, somewhat like a world without color.

Before the contact with the old woman breaks completely, Ruby looks her fully in the face. Her eyes are long dark ovals shot through with rays from the almost invisible pupil. Just beneath her eyes is the straight ridge of her cheekbone. Deep creases cross her brow. She is beautiful, exotic. The old woman turns her head and breaks contact. The conversation is over. She leaves and disappears into the night.

Much as Ruby's tired muscles long for warmth and the comfort of a bed she is reluctant to go inside. The cabin seems confining without the sound of the wind in the hovering trees, the rich scent of the earth, nevertheless, she nestles into the soft cedar and drifts into sleep. Sometimes during the night Ruby surfaces from a dream. The old woman is singing. In the dream she weaves a net silvered with moonlight and the collected light of stars. Sparks rest at the intersecting threads. Ruby feels the song enter her body, muscles relax, cells strengthen.

The next morning, Ruby welcomes the dry, clean clothes. She washes the dishes, gathers the used plants to deposit under the trees. The remaining warmth in the cabin is pleasant, but Ruby will not miss the walls. She wonders if she is becoming like the Old Ones. Or the veteran – the man with elk skin boots. The absence of walls must be one thing he learned to love quickly. Even so, he must have a shelter from the long freeze of winter, the soaking rains, a place to store food.

Outside, ready to leave, the Old Ones are gathered near the trail. They seem restless. The sounds they make are like metallic wires in a strong wind. Ruby looks back at the cabin and the pool. It rained during the night. The scene is pristine, as if they were never there.

The direction continues west. Steep switchbacks pass microcosms in the plunge to the bottom: dry rock and lichen, deep moss with tiny bright-colored spores. A cliff drops into a ravine filled with broken trees from an old burn. Above, a red-tailed hawk coasts.

Ruby pauses to enjoy the beauty; she feels as if she too could fly, become the hawk, glide the length of the ravine, balance motionless on the currents of air. She feels the lift under her feathers, sees the broad perspective of hills and valleys, feels the freedom, the lightness of severing her tether to the ground. In the back of Ruby's mind is a warning. She knows this feeling, this hypnosis, knows its danger. But instead of stepping back from the edge, she moves closer.

Ruby has a strong spirit, but she also has two major vulnerabilities. One is that she does not spend the night in the open in the mountains – at least not until now. The beach, prairie, desert – yes – but not the mountains. The other is that she fears heights. They terrify her, yet they also have a hypnotic effect – as they do now.

Even steep-sided back roads can wrack her with unpredictable and immobilizing terror – or entice her to the edge. Ruby knows she is not suicidal, yet there is something mesmerizing about great heights with steep drops. When she is in the mountains or traveling a road with deep ravines, she knows not to look down. If she does, the result is unpredictable – temptation or terror. She remembers tumbling down a hillside, banging into boulders, before she stopped bruised and scraped against a small maple. She does not remember actually stepping off the edge. Only the fall.

An Old One touches her shoulder. Another has looped a finger under the edge of her sweater, pulling lightly as one does with a small child. Grounded once again, Ruby sees her toes are at the cliff's edge. Her heart pounds in her ears. She is dizzy. For a moment she doesn't know whether to give in to the temptation to fall. The decision is made by the finger hooked under her clothes, as it pulls gently. Ruby steps back. The Old Ones turn to the downward path as if nothing has happened. Ruby is shaking. She is also embarrassed by her weakness, its power. She doesn't know its cause or origin, just that it has always been.

The drop below is mirrored on the right side of the trail with a tall shoulder reaching up the mountain, not quite vertical but steep enough to form a waterfall dropping in three sections, each with its own pool. The spray from the nearest makes the path muddy and in one place it has even formed a small pool on the path itself. Still shaken, Ruby bends to cling to waist-high ferns at the pool's inner edge – even though it means getting wet – in order to inch safely around. Between her and the outer edge of the path Ruby sees a pair of feet, thick and broad. As frightened as she is, she still has room to be surprised by the high graceful arch. It is the young one. Evidently, the Old Ones do not intend to risk her near the edge again. They may act matter-of-fact about her vertigo and the terror of a few moments ago, but they are also taking precautions. Cold water drips from Ruby's hair and inside her collar.

Nearer the valley, the steep drop becomes a gentle slope. There the trail turns south where there is a rough log bridge. It crosses a creek made deep by the waterfalls above. But the path the Old Ones take does not approach the bridge. Instead, in long, rapid strides, they turn aside and step into the water. Ruby is surprised to see the water comes only to their ankles. When she arrives the reason is evident. In the water are three flat-topped stones, spaced so the Old Ones can cross without the need to swim. The stones, though very large, seem intentionally placed for this purpose.

On the other side the Old Ones push through the tall brush clogging the entrance to a small ravine. Behind, she hears the odd metallic sound the Old Ones made this morning. She looks back to see three squatting beside the water. They are smoothing the moss and mud clear of prints, though who might follow Ruby can't imagine. But the Old Ones are cautious in everything they do – crossing the meadow, sending scouts back up the trail at day's end. Perhaps they don't usually follow the trails that humans use. Maybe, like Ruby, they were called, called from their safe places to collect her.

Movement catches Ruby's eye. Between branches, she

sees the man squatting on the bridge peering between its rails. His clothes have the soft folds of deerskin. His hair is gray. A long, thick braid hangs over his shoulder. At first, the Old Ones don't seem to be aware of him. Then one wheels away from the group, charges toward the bridge. Noise like trumpets booms through the air, bounces off stones. The man leaps off the bridge, runs fast in the other direction. He is the same man as the one above the shale bed. He must know the mountains well to have arrived so quickly.

Ruby guesses that the men who live in the mountains and the Old Ones know each other. Perhaps they have some unspoken agreement of non-interference, of living in separate, overlapping spheres. Or maybe the men have little significance for the Old Ones. Even if this man lives to be very old, he will be a brief moment in the age of the Old Ones. Still, they seem upset with his persistent interest. Ruby wonders about her sister's friend who visits the Old Ones from time to time. Why do they come to him? Why does he want them to?

The man intrigues Ruby, the extreme life he has chosen, how he survives. His aloneness she understands, his seeming lack of need for companionship. For her, nature is – almost – enough. There are times when she wants to see her sisters, when she visits the longhouse near her cabin. Still, she understands the sufficiency of solitude.

The Old Ones fan out through the trees walking in long strides. Ruby follows behind the young one. His bulk pushes the bushes apart and makes a short-lived path before the branches swing back. The opening is enough for Ruby to follow, but there will be no evidence of their passing.

For the next three days Ruby and the Old Ones travel the pathless wilderness. Wrapped in the cedar, she sleeps at the base of trees, eats birds or other meat left for her. No more fish. Perhaps there are fewer in the high streams. Her weight has stabilized, digestion accommodated to raw food. She doesn't eat as much as she did the first few days.

It seems like she has been traveling in the mountains forever, and will forever. She can understand most of what the creatures "say." And the few times she has tried to say something to them, they seem to understand. In truth, there is little to communicate. The Old Ones focus on the path ahead. Behind them several always erase trace of their passing.

Among the Old Ones Ruby can now distinguish individuals. She can almost say she has a relationship of sorts with the young one. He is attentive, focused, gentle. The old woman seems removed, her attention on some bigger picture. During moments of rest, she usually stares at the peaks. Or she stands separate, sometimes half hidden by trees, watching Ruby. The small elderly woman who brought the back so many nights ago is alert, watchful. Birdlike. Ruby still doesn't know if they sleep at night, or where they go when they fade into the trees at dusk. She knows some stay close because their soft rumbles sometimes wake her. Once, she woke to high ringing tones almost beyond hearing. It is a sound that travels a very long distance. Ruby still doesn't know where they are going, or why, but, after the "conversation" with the old woman, she trusts them again, even though she is still partly persuaded that she will not be returning home again.

Late on the third day, they are following a deep valley that winds away from the base of one mountain and curves toward the base of another. The Old Ones are forced into single file as they approach the second mountain. The old woman veers northwest and then seems to disappear into a black stone wall. As Ruby gets closer, she sees that it is not a wall, but a place where two huge slabs of stone overlap. The gap between is only wide enough for the bulk of each in single file. Just before scooting though the opening, Ruby looks behind, sees what she expects – one of the creatures is hidden in the trees watching the trail behind.

On the other side of the crevice is what seems to be an animal trail but instead of meandering as animal trails are apt to, it goes straight up the side of the mountain. A hard two hours later, they arrive at a saddle formed between the stony peak directly above and the mountain's jutting shoulder to the south. The saddle is small, a smooth dip with room for only

five or six. Trees surround it, but the saddle itself is bare earth
and small stones. There the trail ends. This is not what Ruby
expected. Why have they worked so hard to arrive at a dead
end?

Moving further into the small area, Ruby gasps and
drops to the ground. Her heart thudding in her ears, her body
hugging the dirt, Ruby looks again. At the far edge of the
saddle is a sheer cliff. To anyone but Ruby the scene might be
wonderfully   breath-taking.   She   has   an   unobstructed,
panoramic view to the northwest. Fading into the blue distance,
mountains overlap with broad valleys, deep ravines, meadows
and rivers.

Ruby is not near enough to the cliff to see how tall it is,
but she knows it must fall nearly the entire height of the
mountain. The Old Ones must have known how she would
react. They must know, given that they have been inside her
mind, given the event of a few days ago at the top of the ravine.
Too petrified to move anything except her eyes and sprawled
on the ground where she collapsed, Ruby looks around to see
where they are.

What she sees instead is that the path doesn't actually
end. Far worse, on her right the cliff extends up the mountain
to the sharp planes at the top. The path – such as it is – leads to
a ledge breaking across the smooth surface of the immense cliff.
Ruby isn't sure what the right word is, but "cliff" seems too
small to describe what she sees. To the west, the mountain
presents a smooth, glistening black face. It appears to have
broken apart in an ancient upheaval sending a portion of its
western side into the valley below. If so, the break must have
been along an existing fault line because, from what Ruby can
see, it is featureless except for one place where the wall bulges
and the ledge disappears. There are no sheltering trees or
brush. Nothing to break a fall. Though only a goat is more
sure-footed than the Old Ones, Ruby does not know how they
manage.

Even though the path doesn't end at the saddle as Ruby
initially thought, it ends for her. Even if she persuaded herself

to crawl onto the ledge, huddle against the cliff – at some point she would freeze unable to go forward or backward. If it is the intention of the Old Ones that she follow them onto the ledge, her terror is the fatal flaw in their plan. Nothing – no matter how strong their need or how much she wants to help – will be enough.

The young one sits beside Ruby, touches the back of her hand with one finger. His touch is gentle, his fingertip soft. Inside her panic, Ruby is sad to disappoint him, but this is the one thing she cannot do. Overwhelmed, Ruby cries. The young one hums, a barely audible sound. He is trying to reassure her, but it's no use. The old woman squats on Ruby's other side. The others gather filling the small area. No persuasion is enough, no manipulation of her feelings, no fear-induced survival response. If they try to force her, she will leap into the air and certain death rather than attempt the mountain's chiseled black path. Ruby's body hugs the safety of the earth.

The Old Ones begin to hum in an undulating chorus. Several voices break away in deep explosions of sound. Others create the high vibration Ruby has heard only when the Old Ones are distressed. Initially it penetrates her chest in the usual way, but she buries her face in her arms, tries to shut them out. The sounds grow in volume, much louder than Ruby has heard before. They reach up the mountainside and into the valley below, expand, first toward the west, and then north and south. Singing fills the sky. The song is magnified in echoes, in layers of sound. The ground shakes, rocks fall. Ruby feels as if she is disintegrating.

The old woman stands and the young one follows. They aren't touching her, but Ruby is being lifted into the air, carried toward the ledge. There is nothing voluntary about this, no decision made. Ruby doesn't struggle. She can't. Intention doesn't translate into action. Terror grows, horror takes root, panic blooms. Ruby manages to lift her hands to her heart in supplication, but the Old Ones ignore her mute plea. She is hyperventilating, her vision blurred. The old woman touches Ruby's trembling face, turns it towards her, locks her gaze onto

Ruby's, and steps to the ledge.

The old woman radiates peace, but her intention does not reach Ruby. The song reaches higher pitch, becomes even louder and then settles into a pattern of long notes similar to those of the mountain singing. Ruby shatters. Cells loosen their hold. The old woman walks backward. Ruby does not know how she is propelled forward as her feet are nowhere near the earth. The young one touches her elbow. Step by step the little group advances onto the narrow path. Everything disappears. There is no precipice. No mountain. No path. No Ruby.

Reaching the bulging curve of stone that Ruby saw from the saddle, the path narrows. Even the old woman is careful, shuffling around its bulk. The young one's grip on Ruby's elbow tightens. But once around and only twenty feet further, the ledge straightens again, and ends. Where it stops is a deep recess. Porch-like, it opens to an enormous cave. As the old woman, Ruby and the young one step across the threshold, all sound stops. The woman steps aside. The hand leaves Ruby's elbow. Stunned, she collapses to the floor of a cave. It is filled with blue light.

Chapter Five

You are an actor in a story – a metaphor – one given by your culture
when you were born. Behind the "you" that wakes in your bed each
morning, drinks a cup of tea, smiles at your children, is another. Place
a bowl of milk under the next full moon. Invite her inside the house.
Don't be surprised if she comes armed with arrows, spear, rifle.

Ruby slumps on the cold stone floor, body limp and boneless, empty of thought or feeling. Though the floor is rigid, she has no desire to move. Only the rhythm of her breath assures her that body and spirit are united. She isn't sure she cares.

Ruby has changed. She is lighter, not only by weight. Her mind is not fixed to its usual patterns. What she feels is the result of hardship and shock, and also the intrusion by the Old Ones into thought and emotion. When the old woman entered Ruby's mind that night at the cabin, when they forced her along the ledge – each time she became less the Ruby she knows. The hypnotic effect of the Old Ones, their songs, the ways they immobilize her resistance, persuade her over and over to adapt – each contribute their part.

The icy stone numbs Ruby's arms and hips, her feet. Numbness moves toward pain. With a deep shuddering breath, she struggles to sit, surprised again at how light she feels, how distant – as if she might float un-embodied out the cave's entrance and toward the western sea following the song the Old Ones sang to bring her to the cave.

Not that she can see anything in the west, not the mountains she knows are there, not clouds. While she lay nearly unconscious on the cave's black stone floor, the snow that had threatened for several days arrived. Where the ledge ends is a thick curtain of white falling snow. By dusk the moving wall of snow fades. Nothing is left but the cave, its invisible ceiling far above, the curving walls. The only sound is the brush of Ruby's clothes when she moves.

Ruby's first thought is a warning – the interior cold she

feels, a sign of hypothermia. A second thought following fast on the heels of the first, is, again, that she does not care – the absence of struggle, the ethereal peace brought by shock and the intense cold are appealing.

The young one finally breaks the still tableau to lay meat beside her. Ruby doesn't respond; food has no appeal. Instead, she stares blankly as if still able to see the falling snow. Only when the young one places the meat in her hand, lifts it to her nostrils so she can smell it – only then do her eyes shift to take in the Old Ones.

Nibbling the meat, she looks around the cave. It is dimly lit by a source she doesn't see. The blue color is similar to the sapphire of the weeping woman, the one from Ruby's dream, the one she saw in the old woman's mind. But it seems to blur as well as reveal. Edges don't quite end so much as fade.

The Old Ones move to the far side of the cave to what seems to be a bench. Ruby scoots to the other side searching for one on the opposite wall. When she finds it, she climbs onto its surface and promptly lies down. It is far too cold for safe sleep, but nevertheless that is what Ruby intends. She doesn't stir when the young one tucks the cedar around her. Tender as he is, Ruby will not forget the ruthlessness of the Old Ones when her will and theirs clashed.

Ruby wakes the next morning still deeply cold. Though cold penetrates the core of her body where warmth ought to be, her hands and feet are not numb. She doesn't shiver, pull her coat tight or her hat down over her ears. Snow still falls, sealing her senses within the cave. From its brightness she knows it is well past dawn. She has slept for many hours. The blue light is not as strong as it was last evening. It and the light from the opening are too muted to reveal the entire cave.

As she suspected, across the cave is a bench. It is a little wider than the one on which she sits. Like the ledge, the cave's floor and walls appear to be carved. The shine on the walls, the blue color and the thick snow curtain make the cave surreal.

Ruby naps through the day. Once when she wakes she finds the body of a bird beside her. From the shape and size and its dark meat, she assumes it is dove, though where the Old Ones would find one anywhere nearby and in winter is a mystery. Even though she is not hungry, she eats it, chews the tiny bones. She sleeps and wakes all afternoon. At last she stretches and rubs sleep from her eyes. She thinks about what has happened. Is the trust she feels for the Old Ones at times, and the lack of it at others, irrelevant? Is she just a tool, one the Old Ones need? Is what they do for her, and to her, pragmatic from their point of view?

At the back of the cave is an opening, and from it a subtle blue light brightens. The color deepens and spreads. As the light strengthens, the contrast between the lit opening and the outer cave becomes so strong that the place where Ruby sits seems dim. The blue light, however, does not make her vision clearer. Just as was true last night, it mutes and distorts.

There must be an inner cave beyond the doorway. From it comes the swelling slow beat of a drum that fills Ruby's chest and picks up the beat of her heart. Drum and heartbeat meld into a single rhythm. Ruby is being summoned.

Between the outer and inner cave is a short tunnel of five or six feet. It rises high overhead, plenty of space for easy entry by the Old Ones. The drum slows its beat, and with it the rhythm of Ruby's heart. She steps through the entrance into a room filled with thick, blue color. The cave is large, though not as big as the outer cave, and shadowy. Without the black bowls of cedar oil – some on the floor and some in niches – all with lighted wicks – Ruby would see little. Even so, it is difficult. In the blue light, the flickering lamps give the impression of starlight on water. *Cedar* loves the water, is immune from rot. One generation to the next, it clears what is murky.

On the back wall, the one opposite Ruby, are more openings that branch in different directions. In the mountain's height and its immense base is room for a honey-comb of chambers. It is big enough to hide caves, rivers, secrets.

In the center, is a tall, narrow platform with a bundle on top. Near Ruby, to her right, stands the old woman. She sees another woman – the small one to whom everyone defers –

sitting against the far wall between two more openings. Her head is bowed as if in prayer or deep thought. She is humming. The young one sits very still at the far end of the platform, his eyes fixed on Ruby.

The pounding beat of the drum stops. Mixed with the low hum is the high-pitched, almost inaudible, monotone of the mountain. While the mixed sound is not loud, the effect makes it difficult to think. The young one rises, walks toward Ruby, takes her hand between his long fingers, and leads her to stand beside the bundle.

The platform is four or five feet long, several feet high and carved from the same stone as the cave. Ruby bends to get a better look at the bundle, and then gasps. The bundle is a child. She is suffused with blue light, not a reflection of the blue light in the cave, but illuminated from within. Like the weeping woman in Ruby's dream, over the child's heart is a small dot of cobalt. Her hair is a cloud of dark curls. She is beautiful, but she is either deeply asleep or unconscious. Ruby's shock is mind-stopping and it is as if she, the Old Ones, the cave and the child could be a sleeper's dream. A bubble floating between stars.

If the child is breathing, her breath is very shallow. Perhaps four years old, the child's features – high straight cheekbones, eyebrows thick and dark – are strong for someone so young. Her arched nose is broad at its tip, the nostrils sculpted. Her hands are tangled in the loose garment she wears. The little girl has the plump look of health, and no visible injuries, so why does Ruby have the distinct feeling that the child is in danger, perhaps dying?

Ruby's questions mushroom outward reaching for answers, find the music. The response from the Old Ones is immediate. The young one takes Ruby's hand and leads her back to the wall, presses on her shoulders, asks her to sit. Ruby knows what is coming. She tries to prepare. The old woman approaches, moves inside Ruby's mind.

Ruby becomes a small point at the base of her skull, watching. Images open in layers like the bloom of a many-petaled flower. In spite of Ruby's intention to cooperate, when her consciousness becomes overwhelmed by that of the old woman's, she pushes back. But the old woman is insistent, pushes hard against Ruby's resistance. Everything disappears.

Ruby has no internal filter sufficient to slow down the flow. No place to hide. Seeking something solid, she leans against the wall, turns her face and presses against its cold, smooth surface. The old woman slows the flood. Ruby can see again - the cave, the blue light. Then, like waves on the shore, more images roll in. Tears of distress roll down Ruby's cheeks. There is nothing else can do to help herself

The old woman's message is emphatic but confusing. The child is a star child. Her arrival was delayed because something sinister trails her. She needs to get off the mountain quickly, but cannot without help. Ruby's help. And she needs a home. Ruby's home. A protest stirs at the back of Ruby's mind. She doesn't know how to care for a small child. Ruby manages to turn her face from the wall looking to the old woman for answers. None are given.

A star child. What is a star child? Arrived from where? And of equal importance, threatened by what? The old woman places her hand on the child's chest. The cobalt light explodes outward. It reaches the rough stone roof and the cave's curved back. The intense color surrounds Ruby, the child and the Old Ones. "Star," Ruby is told, is both a place and a dimension. Ruby takes this to mean the spirit world. The child was to have arrived when Ruby first moved to Puget Sound. Ruby was always intended as the child's home. "Always" is communicated by the expanse of time it takes the cedar to grow from seedling to maturity. This doesn't make sense to Ruby. While she is old, she is certainly not as old as a tree. The cobalt explosion retreats to a star-like spark again.

The child is in danger. She could be destroyed by an enemy following her. Once she is off the mountain she will be safer. Ruby wonders how she can protect the child when the Old Ones cannot. The old woman answers, "You will have help. But it will not be easy." Images shift. Ruby sees an intense struggle, a battle of spirits. She cannot see the enemy, only the struggle. The old woman fills Ruby with a sense of urgency, "We must move fast."

With a loud crack, she leaves Ruby's mind, pulls Ruby to her feet, beckons her to stand beside the child. The cobalt spark on the child's chest is alluring. Slowly, just as the old woman had, Ruby reaches, extends a finger, touches the blue light. A pulse rushes up Ruby's arm and explodes in her chest. Love fills Ruby's heart.

The drum beat begins again. The child's heart rate increases, Ruby's slows. Ruby and the child breathe together. At the back of the cave, the blue light gathers in spirals of tiny flames like butterflies. The cobalt spark over the child's heart grows stronger. Her skin darkens.

Ruby falls in love. It is the first time. Even the love for her sisters doesn't touch what she feels now. Tears drip down the folds of her face. She studies the beautiful child, measures the steady breath. Ruby doesn't have the remotest idea about how to take care of a child, much less a star child – whatever that means – nor how to get her safely off the mountain. But she is willing. Even determined. Then, Ruby remembers the ledge.

Ruby spends the night in the inner cave. She sleeps on the bare stone by the wall. The small elderly woman moves only to trim the wicks, fills the oil from a container she carries on a rope at her waist, sometimes adding herbs. The scent in the air is subtle – cedar, but also the musky smell of *Mugwort* – ancient plant – draws the poison, sweetens love. No food arrives and Ruby doesn't want any. Inside the envelope of extreme cold she doesn't need it. The cold itself is food. At least for a while.

The light from the outer cave tells Ruby it is morning. Overnight the intense cobalt light above the child's heart has diminished to the small size of an alder cone. Nevertheless, as if it is her natural pigment, the color of her skin is still blue. Her slow breath both reassures and worries Ruby – the child is alive but still deeply unconscious.

Watching the child, Ruby understands why the Old Ones were so impatient with her pace. It appears that somehow her presence, the attunement of her heartbeat with the child's, has stabilized the little girl, steadied her heart, made her inhalations deeper and more regular. Ruby is puzzled. Why does the child need to move so quickly off the mountain? Ruby scrubs her memory to remember exactly what the old woman said. Very little, really. But she did say there was an enemy. Is this the reason the Old Ones were so watchful? Perhaps they were adamant that the man not follow because of the attention he brought to the group.

These questions are over-shadowed by more basic ones. Where did the child come from? Why is she in an icy cave inside the mountain? Who is she? She certainly is not an ordinary human child though in most respects she looks like one. The color over her heart is similar to the woman in Ruby's dream, the one she saw in the mind of the old woman. And why a star child? Ruby has no answers.

The woman at the back of the cave begins to hum. Again, the mountain responds with its high-pitched tone. Ruby knows something is about to happen. Through the entrance comes the old woman followed by others who join their voices to that of the singing woman. Without so much as a glance at Ruby, the old woman lifts the child, cradles her in her arms. The Old One's face is both tender and tense. Then, seemingly satisfied, she turns to leave. Sound stops. The small woman at the back of the cave rises and extinguishes each lamp one by one. She leaves only one small light near the door and exits as well. Everyone is gone except Ruby.

Puzzled, apprehensive, Ruby rises to follow. But instead of a crowded outer cave, she finds it empty except for the small woman. She looks back at Ruby, holds her eye for a moment and then steps outside onto the ledge, disappears around the corner. Ruby is shocked. The Old Ones are gone. They took the child. Ruby is alone inside the cave.

To the extent that Ruby has allowed herself to think about the ledge, she assumed that when it was time to leave the

Old Ones would carry her in the same way as before. Terrifying as that was it is the only way Ruby can leave. Now they are gone and she is trapped.

As the journey progressed, Ruby came to believe it was one-way, but inside the inner cave she learned from the old woman that she was to take the child off the mountain. A return trip was implied. Ruby's mind searches for understanding. Are they coming back?

When the Old Ones left her in the forest, it was to force her to discover their language in her own voice. Lost, filled with confusion and dismay, memories of her grandfather's song had surfaced and brought the answer. Immediately, the young one came. The crisis the Old Ones created brought Ruby the solution they wanted.

Are they doing the same now? But Ruby knows she cannot lift herself as the Old Ones did. She doesn't have their power. Surely they do not want Ruby to traverse the ledge by herself. She cannot. But, Ruby also does not want to be separated from the child. If Ruby did not feel so compelled to be with the star child, she might resign herself to death. She might let the cold and the mountain take her. The mountain, the cold and the cave seem to be all the reality she knows. All she remembers. Except for the child.

Ruby is not a person given to crisis. She is ordinarily puzzled by the intensity of others. Her sister, Grace, who is so passionate about her work, is a mystery. Ruby understands that what Grace does is important, accepts Grace's calling, but her sustained passion is foreign. Ruby is more like Agnes, though without her mother's death in the car accident, who knows how Agnes might be. Nevertheless, Agnes and Ruby are withdrawn, quiet. So, Ruby's powerful feelings of the last few days are worlds away from her usual, emotionally-remote state. Confusion, terror. And now this need to be with the child. Ruby is exhausted.

Overnight, the snow stopped. The clouds lifted. Nevertheless, outside the cave's mouth is a white world. Fog is arriving inland from the coast. Not the heavy blanket that hides everything, but thick ropes snaking through the passages between hills and mountains. A few curl inside the cave, crawl across the black floor. Ruby lies down amid the icy tendrils and sleeps. She dreams of Marianne.

In her dream, it is late spring. In the middle of a small meadow of flowers on a hillside a child sits. Behind her are the thick firs of the mountains. Marianne stands motionless where the trail ends at the meadow's edge. She is transfixed, watching the naked child. The child is Ruby. In her hand is a flower. She watches Marianne with curiosity and a strangely adult expression. In the dream, Ruby knows that behind her in the shadows of the trees are the Old Ones.

Ruby wakes, shaking. She is not cold, or, at least, she doesn't feel cold, though throughout her body is a fine tremor. She is confused. Why is she a child in the meadow? Why is she naked and the Old Ones present? Has she confused images of the blue child with her own childhood in Marianne's care? And, for the first time, Ruby lets herself wonder about her mother – the eldest of Marianne's daughters, the one who was never mentioned.

But the pull of the blue child intrudes into Ruby's questions. She wants – more than she can remember ever wanting anything – to follow where the Old Ones have taken her. Is there some way, other than the ledge, that Ruby can find to get from the cave back to the saddle? Ruby returns to the inner cave and lifts the lamp. There is little oil left, the wick is almost finished, but maybe there is enough to see which direction the doorways across the cave lead. The one on the south is closest to the trail, the most likely of the doorways to end there. Holding the lamp aloft and leaning into the dark tunnel, Ruby can see the sharp incline of its descent deep into the mountain. Not where Ruby wants to go. Discouraged, Ruby explores the next, but the small light of the lamp doesn't reach far enough to tell Ruby what she needs to know. There is not enough oil left for exploring. What is the purpose of these tunnels anyway? Surely the Old Ones don't live here.

If Ruby has any hope of returning to the trail, the ledge is the only means. Back in the outer cave, Ruby contemplates the ledge. Allows herself to ponder the impossible. Could she make it? The thought of the curving bulge where the ledge narrows brings drops of sweat to her forehead and upper lip. Her breath grows shallow and quick. She will probably fall, perhaps even jump, never see the blue child again, but she is going to try.

Allowing no more time for terror to build, she drops to the stone floor, and already gasping, crawls out onto the broad porch and moves onto the narrow ledge. Her head is down; eyes focused on the exact place where cliff's face and ledge meet. She refuses to look towards the long drop. Ruby places one knee, then a reluctant hand. And the next. Sweat runs over her ribs and belly, drips from her face onto the snow-blotched surface.

Ruby makes it to the cliff's protrusion where the ledge narrows. Unwilling to look up, she sees it at the upper edge of her vision, and wishes she could not. There, where the ledge is most narrow, the fog stretches a long arm. Though Ruby knows it doesn't, the fog creates the appearance that the path ends. Ruby doesn't allow herself to stop. One knee, the next; one hand.

But, half-way around the bulge, Ruby begins to hallucinate. She cannot see the ledge, the direction of its bend, where to place her hands. Instead, she is back inside the dream with Marianne. She is not watching as before, but *is* the child. She watches Marianne's cautious approach, one eye on the Old Ones in the trees; knows Marianne is wondering if she will be ripped apart. The child has never seen this woman before, but knows she is leaving the mountain with her. She is sad.

In a burst of light, Ruby is back on the ledge, gasping, dizzy, her forward movement halted. Marianne had kept a secret. It is that Ruby is not Marianne's granddaughter. There was no older daughter – Ruby's mother – who disappeared, or died so tragically Marianne could not speak of it. When Marianne saw the child in the meadow, it was for the first time. Purposefully, the Old Ones brought the child to the place where

Marianne gathered plants. They gave Ruby to Marianne. Much as they are giving the blue child to Ruby.

The flood of information stops. How she came to be with the Old Ones on the morning Marianne found her is not revealed. Ruby doesn't know who she is. Nor, really, even what. She does understand why Marianne and her grandfather told her not to spend the night on the mountain. Why they were so concerned that Ruby might not be able to find her way back to them. They feared Ruby would disappear in much the same way she'd appeared. The vision, the dream does not make Ruby feel closer to the Old Ones. Not grateful for their long-ago help. Instead, she feels alone, separate from Marianne, separate even from her grandfather.

Ruby moves a cautious hand forward, feels for stone hidden by the fog. Rubbing against the cliff with her shoulder she can be sure she is not about to reach into nothing. It seems like she has been here for years. The blue child, the blue child, the blue child. For the first time since leaving the cave, Ruby thinks she might make it.

And she does. When the saddle is in the periphery of her vision, she hugs the cliff. Before, she'd been terrified to look at it. Perhaps, she still would be, but to feel it against her shoulder is all the security Ruby has left. Its cold, black surface, solid and sure. She will rely on it until she feels the dirt under her hands.

When she touches the earth, the small stones, she keepings crawling until she reaches the trees. Only then can she believe she's actually succeeded. There she drops, rests her face against the earth and sobs – heaving, wracking, choking sobs – something she has seldom done before. She made it. But, in a curve of stone, she lost Marianne and her grandfather. Both are connections she never thought could break. They are the backbone of Ruby's identity.

Ruby scoots across the dirt saddle to the trees on the southern side. Facing west, she leans her back against the firmness of gray trunk. The same view as from the cave but the height of the cliff does not disturb her, its long drop. No vertigo this time.

Dirt, smeared with tears, cakes her face. Her hair hangs in gray tangles, sticks to her wet face. It broke free from the bun when the Old Ones took her to the cave. She's made no effort to fix it since. She is very thin and very cold. She is like fog. Or a snow filled cloud.

Ruby stirs. Yes, the clouds are moving in. Snow-filled, their blue bellies hang low. If she is going to track the child, she should begin. Pushing against the tree, she rises to her feet, staggers to stand, looks toward the trail. There, half hidden among the bushes, the old woman squats on her haunches. She also looks west, waits for Ruby to regroup. Would the old woman have saved her if she'd fallen? Ruby thinks she wouldn't have. Does the old woman know that Ruby has recovered some of her early memories? Probably. Perhaps it was her intention – this slow unraveling.

The old woman shifts her eyes to meet Ruby's. Ruby has a wisp of memory hovering in the shadows of her mind – she has been on the ledge, in the cave, before. Ruby knows it is there, but doesn't reach for it. She doesn't know who she is, why she was with the Old Ones as a small child, why she lost her memories of then and them.

But there are some things she does know. Marianne was afraid Ruby would forget her family if she spent the night in the mountains. Or remembered her relationship had been first with the Old Ones. Ruby's fear helped. It kept Ruby away from everything that might trigger the old memories.

Eye to eye with the old woman, Ruby is suddenly back in the meadow, remembering more. Marianne walks slowly toward the child, picks her up, gently swings her onto her hip. Silently, step by careful step, she backs out of the meadow.

When she arrived home, Marianne took the child directly to the living room where her father sat warming his old bones beside the stove. Marianne handed him the little girl, told him in detail what had happened, asked if he thought the child was lost, was protected by the Old Ones until someone found her. He shook his head; told Marianne an old legend about spirit children in the mountains. "We don't know what they are."

Then, he spoke to Ruby, "Your name is Ruby," he said. With that, a veil fell. Ruby forgot everything that came before.

Ruby shakes her head to clear the memories. None of this matters now. The old woman and Ruby continue to take each other's measure. Any remnants of trust disappeared when the Old Ones left her in the cave. She is not sure she even believes they intend her to raise the blue child. Though they haven't lied so far, they have certainly been ruthless, perhaps even cruel. Ruby, who can't remember being angry, is angry now. She will not give up the blue child.

The old woman probes gently at Ruby's mind. With all the effort she can muster, Ruby resists, knows it will not be enough, but nevertheless, she tries. The Old One withdraws. Ruby edges toward the trail – the only direction they could have gone with the child. But before she has taken two steps, the young one comes from where he was hidden behind two trees. In the curve of one big arm, is curled, the limp, unconscious child.

Her eyes are closed, her skin still blue and around her body is a paler aura. Ruby moves nearer to see if she is still breathing. To Ruby's relief, she is – no change since leaving the cave. Now that they are outside, Ruby can see the child's robe better. Wool, finely woven. Mountain goat? It appears white, but in the blue aura, it could be blue or gray.

Ruby touches the little girl's arm. She is as cold as the stone on which she lay in the cave. Colder than Ruby. The young one shifts the child and offers her to Ruby. Unused to holding a small child, Ruby's arms are awkward. In them the young one places the child's surprisingly solid weight. Ruby is entranced. She studies each detail – fingers curved into palms, soft curls of black hair. For the first time in two days, Ruby takes a deep satisfying breath. In the presence of the blue child, she is content.

Breaking into her absorption, the old woman steps forward. The unconscious child is, after all, not out of danger. If the Old Ones are to be believed, she is also pursued. If they are to travel quickly, Ruby cannot carry her. Reluctantly Ruby permits the old woman to take the child. They turn toward the trail.

Ruby takes a last look at the saddle, the ledge, the black cliff. That she is alive and leaving is a miracle. But, the foundation of her identity did not survive. It was left in the cave, fell from the ledge. She is a mystery to herself, almost as great a mystery as the Old Ones and the star child.

The western clouds thicken. Ruby follows the Old Ones. There is no choice. If Ruby and the child are to get off the mountain, it will be with their help.

Chapter Six

The peculiarities of quantum physics are not limited to small particle dimensions. If you live in the spirit, trust your dreams, believe what you see and what you hear, the ordinary life of cause and effect – the one offered by Isaac Newton – will change. You will change.

Knee deep in the swift water, Agnes hesitates. Something is wrong. Something other than the danger of the water and the dam. Should she go back to the truck and wait for dawn? But as long as she is already undressed and in the water, Agnes decides to explore the dam – not to actually do anything until she knows what nags at her attention. Only explore to learn how firmly the trees are wedged and if the blockage can be moved. To help her body adapt, she plunges under the frigid water, comes up again.

Using the bank as a guide, she walks close to shore. The silky current outlines the shape of her legs and pulls steadily. Agnes stays as close to the bank as she dares in order to resist the deeper water's strength, but far enough to avoid the thick debris in the shallower water – roots, small limbs, uprooted vines - where it is easy to put a foot wrong, twist an ankle and fall. As she gets near the dam, the water becomes much deeper. In a mere two steps Agnes goes from waist deep to swift water over her head.

With the sudden plunge, Agnes loses her balance. Only one foot, toes digging into the mud, keeps her from being swept away. The other is captive to the current's hold. Frantic for air, she dares not spring up to the surface to fill her lungs. If she loses the grip of her toes, she'll be lost. Instead, she reaches toward the tree hoping it is closer than she thinks. Her hand is answered by the prickle of needles, needles that belong to a thick limb of a big tree, a limb too substantial to be scooped into the current. Patiently, methodically, hand over hand, lungs protesting, feeling her way along its length, Agnes pulls her weight toward the tree and her head above water. Gasping for breath she wedges herself between trunk and limb and rests.

The rough bark scrapes the tender skin under her arms.

The owl chitters again, its voice loud above the sound of the water. Draped over the limb, Agnes listens. Her situation is perilous. The water is deeper and its pull much stronger than she'd expected. Yet, she is so close to the middle of the dam that she hates to turn back. If she could get a little closer, she might be able to use the strength of her legs to dislodge the smaller limbs on top. If she could shove them loose, the pool could drain and let her cross. She abandons her intention to only explore.

She feels along the tree with her legs and feet, finds other limbs like the one she clings to. Eyes closed to protect them, ignoring the sting of needles slapping against her face, she moves from one branch to the next toward the dam's middle. By staying on the shore side of each, the current's strength helps stabilize her – defense against being swept away. If that happened she will be lodged against the logs and drown. Or sent over the top and broken on the rocks below.

As she approaches the waterfall, the current grows more swift and the limbs Agnes clings to grow smaller. Sometimes they are buried under the tree by the pull of water. Agnes holds firmly to each and hugs her body to the tree's length to ease the strain. Her feet become hands, feeling ahead for weak places in the dam – the small branch that might be the key to breaking apart the whole thing.

She is almost at the center, but the branch she holds is short and not very thick. She dare not move further down the tree to one even less able to hold her weight. Instead, she loosens the grip of elbows looped over branch, hangs by her hands and lets her body drift with the current closer to the center, all attention gathered in her exploring toes. There it was – the cut end of a tree three or four inches across. If she can only…

But suddenly, like a flock of roused birds, her focus scatters. A cracking branch, sound more felt than heard, runs through her body. The limb her hands are wrapped around, under the strain of both her weight and the pull of the current, is breaking. Face barely above water, the current's pull so strong her body is horizontal to the surface, Agnes considers her options. For a moment, she can't think of any.

Agnes moves her hands along the cracking branch to its thickest point near the trunk. Using all her strength she pulls against the current hoping not to break the branch. Slowly she gets far enough above the limb to get her strong shoulders into the action. Another crack. Agnes reaches for the limb above, gets one hand around it.

Agnes is strong but she can't use this arduous means all the way back to the safety of shallow water. Instead, she swivels her body atop the tree hoping it reaches all the way to shore, digs in her heels, and climbs. Because the trunk is under water, at first this tactic means her head is beneath the water, too. Blood pounds in her ears. In its rhythm she can hear the beat of a drum. Her grandfather's.

At the end of each effort, Agnes surfaces for breath, fills her lungs and ducks beneath. Twenty feet later she is close enough to shore that she no longer needs to dive.

Even though the water beside the tree is now shallow and Agnes could walk to shore, she does not. Instead, she continues to crawl; she doesn't want to return to the treacherous water. Near the bank, she finds the tangle of its roots and knows she is safe. Agnes slides to the ground, makes her way through broken blackberry vines and the litter of small branches to the truck.

Every inch of skin is scraped by bark, raked in long bloody cuts by thorns. The spent muscles of her strong arms shake. Agnes sits in the rain propped against the tire, head bent, considering what happened.

It isn't like her to do what she had. Take risks, depend on her strength – yes. But, her last decision, the one to suspend from such a small branch and hang by her hands - that was foolhardy. And more, she had not waited to first see what was troubling her spirit. Not like her. So,why? Fear for Grace? Maybe.

Agnes climbs inside the truck, collects the thermos of hot

tea, a bag of dried berries and jerky. She is reluctant to put on her clothes because her skin is so raw, but nevertheless she does. Thick socks, boots, coat – everything to help build her body's heat. Outside, she sits on the pickup's bumper, sips hot liquid, chews the berries to send quick fuel to her body. The pool, wider than before, isn't going anywhere. Neither is Agnes. But she isn't going to turn around either, not until she knows what troubles her. Something she can't quite get ahold of – not the bigger problem of Grace – but something just out of reach.

Above, something catches Agnes' eye. A dark shape flies from a tree above the pool, past the dam, disappears in the dark. The silence of flight, the size, the hour tells Agnes it is the owl she heard earlier. It is headed toward the beach. Agnes does what she should have done to begin with and gives the bird her attention. She will follow it.

She collects the flashlight, shines it toward the forest crowding the creek. The rain falls so hard it reflects most of the light, but Agnes finds what she sought – a trail used by animals and fishermen. Agnes gulps the last of the tea, stuffs jerky into her pocket.

Once under the shelter of trees, it is easier to see. The path is narrow. Pools form between big roots. Mud clings to Agnes' boots. The path twists around the bulk of big trees, around the alcoves of the flooded creek. Agnes doesn't know how far the owl went, but if she doesn't find it beforehand, she will go as far as the beach and wait.

That is what she does. At the edge of the trees Agnes sits in the dark on a driftwood log. There is no wind, but the ocean is loud with an incoming tide pounding against the rocks on the beach. Treacherous in its beauty, it carries logs washed down from the forests, lifts them high on the crest of a wave and then hides them again underwater. Not a place to wade or swim.

Not a place for a child to sit all night with her mother dead in the crashed car nearby. Some people say that Agnes' mother was drunk that night, but Agnes knows she wasn't. Agnes mother was driving too fast for wet roads and tight curves, but she wasn't drunk. Marianne said it was treachery and that she was lucky Agnes lived.

Agnes can see the whitecaps breaking far from shore, thundering in, unraveling on the beach. Agnes' mother would never have put the child in the car if she was drunk, and, besides, she didn't drink all that often. They lived an hour off the reservation, a small house at the edge of town. Agnes' mother worked in a day care, but they spent each weekend with Marianne – arriving on Friday night and returning on Sunday afternoon. No one ever learned why her mother was rushing home in the middle of the week. But with the use of the words "bad work," Marianne had hinted that someone or something had destroyed her daughter on purpose.

These memories lead to others. One untangles itself from the rest. One early evening her grandfather had called Agnes and Grace to join him outside. He'd built a fire, put on green branches to make it smoke. Because of campfires, wood stoves and forest fires animals are not disturbed by the smell of smoke. He lifted the girls, held each there in the smoke, fanned their coats. Pulled their hats tight around their heads to keep them warm, insisted on gloves. By this Agnes knew they'd be outside late into the night.

To her surprise they didn't head to the pickup for a trek into the mountains. Instead they headed south by foot from the house into a wild, uninhabited stretch of forest reaching many miles along the coast and into the coastal hills. There had been no logging there, at least not in hundreds of years. The trees were massive. In some areas, the berries were abundant – a favorite place of bears and birds. Nearest the salt water brackish pools formed – not quite fresh water and not entirely salt.

He led them over a familiar path and then further. When dusk had almost turned to night, he stopped at a pool of fresh water fed by a spring, the only fresh water among its brackish neighbors. Trees grew thick, but thirty feet from one end of the pool was a particularly spectacular cedar. Its roots stretched into the water of the pool infusing it with red-brown color, the same color as its inner bark. It stretched high above and had a broad circumference of bushy limbs. Her grandfather pushed the limbs aside and led the girls under. Once inside the outer limbs, space opened up. There was room to sit.

He chose a place for them where the three could see the pool between the cedar's fronds. He whispered for them to sit, added they would be there many hours and were not to make a single sound – not so much as gasp, sneeze or to scratch an itch. The girls were well acquainted with such expectations – at ceremonies, when old people told stories, or sometimes at night when Marianne and her husband grew still and quiet. The girls instinctively knew at these times to be still as well – as if something important might be disturbed. So, with their grandfather sitting behind them, they found comfortable positions and settled in.

First to arrive at the pool was a deer with a shy spotted fawn in tow. The doe drank, lifted her head frequently to look around, flinched with each sound, ready to flee. The fawn, even more skittish than its mother, was hesitant to drink at all. Finally, she dipped her head to the water. When finished, they moved around the far side of the pool toward the beach and disappeared in the trees. Other than these two, for a long time only small animals came – raccoon, possum – and a few birds late for a last drink before dawn.

Night is never quiet. Nocturnal creatures are noisy. Even deer are only silent when they are still. The only exception is when a predator is near. This is the reason total silence at night raises hackles on the neck of anything that might be prey. Agnes was barely breathing. She waited for something to break the tension. But it only increased when at last something did appear – a very big cougar.

Agnes wasn't sure when it came. She didn't see it move from trees to water, only saw it suddenly there. In a slow regal way it looked around the pool, sniffed the tracks of doe and fawn. And then it drank for a very long time. When finished, it surveyed the pool once more, its big head swiveling. Then it suddenly stopped. Tension lifted its shoulders and ran along its back. Once and then once again, the long tail switched.

Agnes was absolutely motionless, mesmerized by the eyes of the cat trying to see what it knew was there. She knew how it felt to be a rabbit or a fawn, to be food. Oddly, she wasn't terrified or even afraid. What she felt was more fundamental, deeper. The relationship between herself as prey and the cat as predator united them in something more whole than either. If the cat attacked, she would taste her blood in its mouth; she was sure of it. Only her grandfather's training kept her from falling into the hypnosis of sacrifice, kept her from agreeing to be the cat's next meal, the answer to its hunger.

The cat shifted its attention and turned away as if there was nothing of interest hidden by the cedar. Its muscles relaxed, and with slow sensuous steps, it followed the path of doe and fawn around the pool. Agnes understood that the fawn would serve in her stead.

Beside her she was again aware of Grace and her grandfather, but for a few minutes it had seemed that Agnes and the cat were the only life anywhere. She felt her grandfather's pat on her shoulder. She'd done the right thing – she'd remembered to keep something of herself separate, something in reserve. Without that, she would be either prey or predator. There was no other choice.

Hours passed. Her eyes adjusted to the night and she could see most of what came and went. She kept herself alert, or at least awake, by carefully examining one area around the pool – systematically right to left – and then another, letting the periphery pick up detail, resisting the forward focus that only works in daylight.

Agnes didn't know how late it was, but knew it must be midnight or later. She'd just completed one careful scan, begun another, when an apparition grabbed her attention. It was directly opposite across the pool sitting on a bare branch. It was at least four feet tall but without arms or legs. Bewildered, Agnes tried to determine what it was. A small change in Grace's breath said she was doing the same. The creature bent its head sideways, first one way and then the other; looking in the direction of the cedar, it stooped forward as if for a better view. When it spread its five or six feet wingspan and clicked its beak, Agnes knew it to be a bird – a huge bird, the kind that stole fawns. Or, perhaps it was a spirit bird.

The bird seemed too big in the reach of its wings for the small area of the pool. Nevertheless, it swooped from the tree, flew around the circular shape of the opening and returned to the branch. Seconds later, it took off again and landed where the cat had stood, looked directly at Agnes and Grace, cocked its head. There was something human about it, at the same time that it was so alien it made Agnes' skin crawl. When it took off again it disappeared between two trees, but for half an hour the girls could hear its chitters, its long haunting hoots before silence fell again.

Without moving, Agnes sought the comforting presence of her grandfather. He wasn't there. For the first time since he'd brought her to the forest, Agnes was frightened – really frightened. Had something happened to him? As long as he was present, Agnes was safe. He wouldn't take them into danger he couldn't protect them from.

Agnes realized she was about to break a rule. She was about to move or whisper. Then, beside the pool, she saw him. He walked toward the cedar, parted its fronds and sat down. "Now we talk," he said. He told them not to mind the cat or the deer. "The lesson," he said, "is the owl. Always listen to the owl, to what it has to say." He told them to listen even when they were grown, even when he was dead.

On the beach, Agnes sits in the rain and remembers. She can't believe she'd forgotten what her grandfather taught about the owl. The owl at the cabin before she left, its chitter before she entered the pool above the dam – clear signals that should have made her stop and reconsider. Not like her. She always remembers. She always listens. Except this time she had not. Agnes decides to move back under the trees out of the hard rain, to be still until she understands what had nagged for attention – what the owl wants her to know.

She rises from the wet log, turns away from the surf,

heads to the trees. She's barely left the sand, when she sees it. The owl sits not fifteen feet away. It is big. Big enough to injure – claws, beak – if not kill. Agnes isn't afraid. Instead she begins to cry, tears mixing with salt spray and rain. She sinks to her knees, slips sideways and sits. He'd come. Grandfather had come. She isn't alone. Doesn't have to be confused any longer.

Agnes props her back against a bank of moss and decaying wood, becomes as still as she'd been as a child under the cedar. She watches the owl and she listens. She remembers again the night beside the pool with Grace. Remembers what else her grandfather said. He'd told them that Ruby would inherit his drum, his gear and his song. They, the younger girls, would have the property. He added that they were spirit sisters, not only cousins, that they were two parts of one whole. That each must come when the other called.

And then the owl is gone. But he'd brought what Agnes needs. She closes her eyes and listens. What is niggling like off-note music? Something doesn't quite fit. Agnes' mind returns to Grace and their trip home from the Pow Wow last summer.

After they had left the old longhouse, Grace drove south, a longer and indirect route back to Agnes' home. She took back roads, first through dry-land wheat fields and then onto the mesas. At the edge of one, a dusty road became a series of switchbacks down the steep side. No guardrail. The canyon was so narrow it seemed to Agnes she could almost touch the rimrock on the far side, but it was deep. So deep that she could see the backs of hawks hunting far below, wings motionless, floating the updrafts between canyon walls.

When she looked from the passenger window she didn't see the edge of the road; it wasn't wide enough, seemed as if the van was held aloft on an invisible track. She had no idea what happened when two vehicles met though twice she saw wrecked cars in the sagebrush below. Across on a long slope was a collapsed barn, the angle so nearly vertical, Agnes wondered why it didn't slide into the canyon. Perhaps it was held in place by the wish of some long ago farmer.

At the bottom of the canyon was a green river. In places

red stone formed vertical banks and forced the river from its broad bed into sudden deep rapids. Projecting over the tumultuous water were small platforms with rough scaffolding braced against the rocky shelf. These were as empty as the roads, but when the salmon ran, they would be crowded with Indian fishermen, with vans outfitted like the one Grace drove – bed, a place to cook. Night and day, as long as the fish ran upstream to spawn, the men stood on the planks extending over the channel – often only a single firmly-fixed board – and fished.

They were strong shouldered men made so by the weight of the long heavy poles they used, nets fixed at the end. Hour after hour a man would hold the pole motionless, almost vertical, in the rushing water alert for the extra weight of a fish in the net, then scoop it against the powerful current to the surface before it could leap free. Hard work, but the canyon was filled with laughter, the sounds of joy arising from the enduring relationship between the people and the fish – a relationship become religion, made into story, given place in the stars and in the names of the children. One story says the salmon were brought by a beautiful maiden. If so, this was a trysting place where the men met her beside the river.

Grace had left the river and taken another gravel road into the foothills. By noon, and after many unmarked turns, they'd arrived at the Sundance grounds – a sacred place for the Sundance people to practice the central feature of their religion. It was mostly used by people living in the northwest as a closer option than traveling to the Dakotas. Neither Grace nor Agnes followed the Sundance way, but Grace was known everywhere and there was a good chance her name would be known here as well.

Grace parked the van under the trees and waited. There seemed to be no one around, but Grace knew otherwise. One of the Sundance people was always present. They were the ones who protected the place from casual campers, hunters, the curious.

A man, with a rifle held loosely at his side, came through

the trees from the left. He wore jeans and a long-sleeved, gray cotton shirt, boots. No welcoming smile greeted them, not even for the lovely Grace. "Where are you headed?" he asked gruffly, implying their destination should be somewhere else. Grace didn't meet his eyes. She looked toward the dance grounds, invisible behind a screen of trees.

"We want to pray," she said, and introduced herself. He paused. Minutes passed. Then he grunted consent and motioned them forward with his rifle. Grace nodded her thanks and drove inside, parked close to the open field. The slamming truck doors were loud in the afternoon silence.

Grace led Agnes to the arbor. It was made of bare poles cut from sapling trees. During the dance, brush would be laid overhead to protect the families of the dancers from the sun. Of course, the central tree wasn't there since it is erected anew each year just before the dance. The tree established sacred ground, designated the center of the universe, the entrance by the people to the holy.

Grace sat in the dirt, leaned against one of the poles. Agnes hesitated, stood at the arbor's edge. Across the already dry meadow two men came from the woods, one with a rifle, the other with the bulk of a pistol on his hip. Agnes slipped her hand into a pocket, felt for her knife. Grace had her pistol in the bag always slung across her shoulder. It wasn't likely these men would harm them in a place like this, but the women were careful. Not that a knife and a small pistol would answer three men and two rifles, but sometimes just the signal that a fight was at hand is enough.

Behind them a shrill whistle pierced the afternoon. Evidently it was the "all's well" signal when a vehicle arrived and wasn't heard to leave, a message from gatekeeper to his companions. The men crossing the meadow turned back to the woods.

Agnes joined Grace under the arbor. It was like stepping from one world to another. What she felt in the outer arbor was nothing compared to what gathered in the inner circle. Grace remembered the first time she'd seen a Sundance tree, the shock of its beauty.   But even here in the outer circle, light vibrated. Shapes almost formed then dissipated in the moment before they became visible. More than the effect on the eyes, however, was the presence of something unnamable.   It felt like a powerful electrical field, one with a thousand eyes – strict and demanding, but also compassionate.

Grace began.   "This is the only place I could think of where we could talk and not be heard." Agnes knew Grace meant "not heard by unwelcome spirits." Evidently, Grace was worried that something was following her, a spirit she didn't trust.   She was using the power of the dance grounds as a shield.

"When I told you the elders wanted me to relay what they said, I didn't tell you everything." Agnes reviewed what Grace had told her - that a medicine power had been hidden when Europeans invaded. It was placed beyond reach because it was too powerful to be used in the presence of hate and rage. The genocide of the people would arouse those feelings. Those are feelings easily understandable in victims but so much power fueled by rage would initiate an avalanche of destruction.

The cave where the medicine was hidden was in the southwest, but the elders here have always known about it – perhaps elders everywhere know – knowledge passed from one generation to another. Earlier, because she hadn't wanted to say too much, Grace said only that something looked for it. Now she told the whole and awful truth – the enemy seeking the medicine had found it, had even managed to release a portion of its power from the spells that bound it. The elders in the southwest sent word to the elders in the northwest asking for help. In fact, the elders told Grace, they had already seen it arrive - a red streak of fire crossing the sky.

"It has a purpose," Grace continued. But, the elders said, that powerful as it is, the medicine is only one part of a bigger, more destructive effort.   One to make people forget, turn against one another, create chaos. Grace finished by adding that the elders also said that help had been sent. From where and what kind, they didn't seem to know, or at least they didn't say.

Only that it was overdue.   And the elders were emphatic –
Grace must tell her sister.

At the gate on the top of a flat rock, Grace placed a can of
coffee, a sack of loose tobacco with cigarette papers, and a bag
of jerky. Though the women saw no one, they knew the men
watched, and would gather the gifts before they could be
scattered by jays and chipmunks. After what Grace said, Agnes
was reluctant to leave the security of such carefully tended
power.

By the time they reached the Columbia River, they
watched for the transition from the desert on the eastern side of
the Cascades to the lush ferns, moss and waterfalls of the west.
It was always magical. Even when you tried to catch the exact
moment of change, it was always a surprise. Somewhere in the
blink of an eye, it had already happened.

The river was beautiful, but it was difficult to not see
what was missing - the layers of roaring waterfalls stretched
wide across the old riverbed that were now hidden by the dam.
The big fishing platforms that made those on the river they'd
seen earlier in the day seem like toys. The descendants of the
old tribes still lived in small communities between the canyon
walls that held the river. They still fished, but from boats. The
grief of the people who had watched the waterfalls die was still
a pall over the river. There are those who say that under the
river, the waterfalls wait for the people. Agnes looked away.
Grace became silent.

Grace knew Agnes had no tolerance for cities, so she
avoided them and drove across a long bridge to the other side.
They were tired but didn't stop until they reached the coast.
The fog was a light blanket of mist.   Grace rolled down the
windows of the van to better hear the comforting sound of the
ocean's breakers, to breathe the cool, moist air so different from
where their day began.

At one beach, unlike the others, she stopped. The shore
is a bed of small stones resting inside the curve of a short cliff.
As the tide comes in, the rattle of stone against stone is
deafening in a delightful way. Grace and Agnes followed the

trail between dunes, climbed midway down the cliff and sat to let the stones do their work. Cleansed, the clutter and clamor of the mind and emotions fell away. What was left was as clean as the water, the wind or the stones themselves. It was what Grace and Agnes needed. Grace had done as she was asked. Agnes had listened. They were as prepared as they could be. Fear, anxiety, worry – none of these would help. Better to be clean and wait.

Grace stayed several days at Agnes' cabin. They gathered clams and cooked them in pots over an open fire on the beach. They sat late and watched the stars and the coals of the fire. On the third day, Grace loaded the van and left for a conference. When she was gone Agnes put the kayak in the water, paddled along the north coast until missing Grace was lost in tired muscles. Until the alert, curious faces of the seals following her made her smile.

It is not that Agnes forgot what Grace told her; not that she didn't take seriously the elders' message. It is instead that she did not connect the medicine's evil to tonight's events. The niggling sense that something was wrong, her uneasiness, was lost in the over-riding fear that Grace was in immediate, catastrophic danger. She'd lumped the two together so hadn't listened to the warning at the back of her mind. But her grandfather's appearance made her look at everything again. Is there a way if she brought all of this together, it would make sense?

Agnes can see that she's been unlike herself since the call, been off-center, made bad decisions. It is to be expected given that Grace had been so frightened. But, even so, Agnes is usually reliable in a crisis. But then it isn't like Grace to panic either. So what is happening? Then Agnes recalls that Grace told her one of the evil effects of the medicine is to cause confusion, to take up residence in the mind and lead one astray.

When the pieces fall together, Agnes prods carefully over each to make sure. It is so simple. In the phone call, Grace asked Agnes to bring their grandfather's drum. But Agnes doesn't have grandfather's drum. Ruby does. Was Grace sending a covert signal, one Agnes would certainly recognize? If so, what did Grace want Agnes to do? Arrive with reinforcements? Call the tribal cops?

Or was the caller someone other than Grace? In ways the voice sounded like Grace but the reason Agnes had been so distressed was that in important ways it hadn't sounded like Grace at all. Had someone who didn't know who the drum belonged to slipped up?

Then, in a leap of intuition, the last piece falls into place. A pattern emerges that holds all the parts. A pattern with the familiar upside down, inside out quality that spiritual truth so often has. It is not Grace who Agnes is supposed to follow, it is the drum. She is going in the wrong direction. She should be headed for Ruby's cabin. The trickery of evil had somehow managed to imitate Grace's voice to lure Agnes in the wrong direction, but something else had intruded to leave a clue. It was this clue, this inconsistency, that had nagged and wouldn't let go. She hadn't let the whole message seep into awareness; she'd listened through the grip of fear.

Agnes waits to see if there is more, but there isn't. Before she leaves, she walks to the shore, takes off her clothes and steps into the waves. Avoiding the deeper scrapes on her skin she scrubs her body with the sand and rinses. She wants to be clean of the last of the confusion, the panic and terror. She knows what to do, though she doesn't know why.

Agnes dresses, walks back through the forest to the pickup. A gusty wind begins to blow. Rain falls in sheets first from one direction and then another. In the lights of the truck, the wind and rain form small whirlwinds. The pool is much wider now. No one will be going north until the rain stops and the pool has time to drain. She opens a jar of salmon and eats with her fingers, drinks the salty oil from the bottom. A long night lies ahead.

Agnes retraces a portion of her route; stops to get gas at a station lit by a single low watt bulb. The man inside takes her money without speaking, leaves it to her to pump the correct number of gallons. From his bloodshot eyes, Agnes can't decide if he is drunk, or on the downhill-side headed toward hangover. Driving away, she sees him lift the bottle, his head tilt. Perhaps, he is at that most miserable state of being both.

Agnes drives slowly and carefully. There is no hurry now. She doesn't know where Grace is, or Ruby for that matter. She can't allow herself to think about them. The further south she goes the stronger the storm becomes. In more than one small ravine the road is covered with mud and water. The water isn't too deep yet but in several places it will be before the night is over.

Agnes considers the road ahead. There are places it often slips or is blocked by mud when storms blow in, isolating the coast from the rest of the state until bulldozers and crews open them again. In fact, as saturated as the ground is, it might already have happened. Agnes decides to take a long detour using the logging roads through the foothills to avoid those areas. There were several possible routes, ones that also avoid the higher elevations where the rain will be heavy snow.

No one who doesn't know the logging roads would be able to find a way through the confusing maze particularly in a storm. A wide, solid road that seems well traveled might suddenly reach a dead end where log trucks load trees and turn around for the return trip to the mills. Some become nothing but grass tracks that end in a meadow of stumps. Others turn a curve to an exposed side of an eroded hill with little place to turn around. Weather like tonight's can cost the life of anyone who doesn't know the way.

Four hours later Agnes comes to a blacktop road that leads back to the highway. The lack of traffic on the main road from the coast says she made the right decision. Before she takes the road north, the last leg to Ruby's cabin, Agnes makes one more stop for gas and coffee.

Two hours later, she pulls into Ruby's yard. Exhausted, she eyes the dark cabin for signs that Ruby is at home. Her car is gone, but with Ruby you never could be sure of anything. Finally, Agnes gets out, closes the truck door quietly, though if Ruby is inside, the truck will have wakened her; she could be watching Agnes even now.

Agnes opens the cabin door. No Ruby. On a nearby shelf Ruby always keeps lamp and matches. Agnes strikes one, lights the lamp, lets the light fill the room. Nothing. It is cold and there is no scent of recent fire. Lamp in hand, Agnes walks through the cabin to Ruby's bedroom. There on the wall is the drum. This is where she is supposed to be. She will wait for Ruby.

The ring of the phone breaks the silence. Agnes walks back across the cabin to the kitchen, picks up the receiver. "Yes," she says. Over the crackle of a poor connection, a voice answers, "Thank God, you are there!" It is Grace.

Chapter Seven

Unravel. Let go the spiny structure so carefully erected. See what remains – the song of stones, the language of water, the voice in the trees. Let these be the sacred text of your resurrection.

The strange group walks down the trail to the gap between the stones. Ruby stops at the first creek. She hasn't drank or eaten since the day before and very little then. She washes the sweat and grime from her face, looks around surprised to find it is late afternoon. How long was she on the ledge? How long asleep on the floor of the cave? Snow begins to fall and has the feel that it is settling in. Ruby is glad she doesn't have to find the trail alone. Everything will look very different under several feet of snow.

When it is dusk the young one leads her to a cedar tree and puts the pounded cedar beneath where it is dry. When she is under its shelter, the old woman hands Ruby the child. Ruby wraps the small bundle in her arms and falls into deep sleep. She doesn't dream about the woman on the mountain. No weeping. No rumbles. No visitors.

When Ruby wakes for a moment it seems she is back in the cave. Overnight deep snow slid from the limbs above to make a low wall. Where she lies under the tree is room-like, sheltered, almost warm. Breakfast – a long hank of venison rests on a stone.

But the child is gone, taken while Ruby slept. A wide break in the fresh snow shows where the Old Ones entered, and left. Venison in hand, Ruby scrambles from under the tree, shoves the cedar boughs aside looking for the child. But there she is in the arms of the old woman. It is obvious from the old woman's rumbling that she is impatient to begin the day. With their bulk the creatures break a trail through the deep snow. Even though it is still falling heavily enough to cover their tracks, the Old Ones are vigilant and watch the back-trail with as much care as before.

This seems curious to Ruby. No one could have followed

them from the cave except a spirit. The old woman said that something was trying to destroy the child, that something had followed her. Is it so close then that the Old Ones need to guard the immediate perimeter? If Ruby could see through the snow, would she see some of their company guarding on all sides? Is the child in more danger now that she is outside the cave?

Ruby concludes that the enemy must be close and powerful. The anxiety of the Old Ones is confirmation enough. Ruby moves closer to the old woman, to the child. She will fight to the last breath to protect her, but the old woman had said her job was to raise the child. Not to die for her. As long as they are on the mountain, Ruby will leave the work of protection to the Old Ones. What other choice does she have?

Ruby feels that she has walked in the same place all afternoon, stepping in her own tracks over and over. Such is the effect of the snow, the whiteout of its falling, the thick monochrome over rock and trees. The only variation is the pale blue shadows cast by the humped shapes.

Ruby and the Old Ones travel in the snow for three days. Each night she tucks the child inside the cedar bed so the Old Ones cannot take her without Ruby waking. When the young one comes each morning to bring her breakfast, he finds her awake and ready to travel. Except for the snow, each day is much like the trip into the mountains – interminable. And, that the largest of the Old Ones walk in a tight group sheltering the child in the center. And one other thing – on the way into the mountains Ruby was still Marianne's granddaughter; she still had sisters.

On the third day they reach the creek with the flat stones, the one near the bridge where the man had stood. Ice has formed on the stones and Ruby crosses with care. The handrails of the bridge are barely visible under six inches of perfectly piled snow. Ice rimes the creek, snow scallops the edges. The water is a deep blue gray and looks backlit from the reflection off the snow. Though the bridge is visible through the falling snow and the whole scene appears unmarked by animals or people, Ruby wonders if there are footprints on the bridge.

There is no sign of the man, but perhaps he has been here.

Startling herself, Ruby hums to the old woman. When did her casual communication with the Old Ones begin? She doesn't know if this is the first time, or if she has been doing it for days. No matter, the old woman stops. Ruby slogs her way to the bridge, stands at the near end to see if there are recent prints under the fresh snow. There is nothing. Nevertheless Ruby walks further onto the bridge where she thinks the man stood, looks toward the Old Ones waiting – exactly where she was the day he watched her.

The Old Ones are ghosts almost hidden now by the increasing storm. She isn't sure why standing where he stood moves her, but it does – something about his isolation and the persistence with which he followed her. Though she can't see far, she looks toward the wilderness on the other side of the bridge. There are tracks at the end. They aren't human. She looks closer. Wolf? No, Coyote. What is a lone Coyote doing this far in the mountains in a worsening storm?

The old woman hums. She is right, they need to try to get on the other side of the mountain while they still can. Ruby turns back. The group takes the uphill trail above the ravine, but Ruby is no longer afraid of heights. The secret hidden behind the fear has been revealed and no longer has a purpose. Though she is not equally reassured about her other fear – she is still not sure she will ever spend the night in the mountains again. That is, if she survives this ordeal.

But Ruby doesn't have to worry about the vertigo of the edge. The snow falls so heavy there is no way to differentiate trail from ravine. Without the guiding bulk of the Old One ahead and the one behind she might step off the edge by accident even though she is no longer tempted.

The uphill climb takes forever. By the time they are at the top, night is closing in. Still they walk. They have to. With the snow so deep around the base of the trees there is no shelter. Ruby is walking blind and grateful to hold onto the arm of the young one. Again and again she wills herself to take one more step. She holds the image of the child in her mind, the knowledge that when they arrive at tonight's destination, she will hold her.   And then from nowhere comes another image – an old man sitting beside a fire in an adobe room. Exhaustion? Vision? Ruby doesn't think she has the strength for one more vision.

Late in the night, the group arrives at the cabin where Ruby slept so many nights ago.   It seems a lifetime since she was here; it was someone else, not Ruby.

Somewhat protected by the trees, the snow is less deep. The old woman leads to the cabin and Ruby follows, finds the steps only because she knows where they are. Ruby staggers to the door on uncooperative legs and numb feet.   She puts her shoulder to the door and pushes it open.

The old woman waits beside the steps. Ruby doesn't spend much time wondering why the Old Ones don't help at times like this when she is exhausted or times when she is in danger. She doesn't waste much energy on the question – there are no answers from the Old Ones about so many things. They are just the way they are. And she doesn't waste time on that thought, either – the way they are, what they are.

Ruby staggers back to take the child from the old woman.   The Old One hands her over and, on wobbly legs, Ruby hobbles inside. In the dark she feels her way to the bunk and lays the child down. She works her way around the cabin, locates the candle and strikes a match.   With its light, she examines the child – breathing, still unconscious.

Tears of relief and exhaustion fill Ruby's eyes. But Ruby has no time for emotion. She makes her way once more across the tiny cabin that now seems like a broad, difficult expanse. Ruby needs fire for her saturated clothes. She digs deep into the wood on the porch to reach dry pieces. From one of the branches, she peels thin splinters to start the fire. Once it catches Ruby waits patiently until it can support bigger chunks.

Ruby removes boots, socks, pants – puts her boots on top of the counter and hangs the rest of her clothes around the cabin. They won't dry by morning – a scant few hours away – but they won't be dripping either. Ruby pinches out the light, wraps in blankets, climbs onto the bunk, curls around the child. Every time she hugs the child against her heart, her belly, she is surprised at how right it feels – the comfort, the visceral satisfaction. Ruby seldom smiles, but as she goes to sleep, her lips lift in what a careful observer might call a smile. As she descends into exhausted unconsciousness, Ruby and the child are breathing in tandem. Despite the child's unconscious state and Ruby's wretched exhaustion, their breath is a single rhythm.

Ruby wakes late the next morning. She can see the glow of coals around the edge of the firebox of the stove. Otherwise the room is filled with white winter light coming through the window. Ruby slides off the bed to see what today's agenda holds, but when she tries to stand, her body won't quite unkink. The most she can achieve is a hunched shuffle. Her muscles are stiff and her joints unyielding. Age, arthritis and effort have finally taken their toll. She won't be going anywhere soon. Heat will help. She wraps a blanket around her waist and shuffles to the door for wood to stoke the fire.

Outside the old woman sits on the porch. She doesn't turn to stare at Ruby, which is a welcome change and her pose has none of yesterday's urgency. Just as well. Ruby grumbles – she is keeping the child in the cabin until she can walk again, until she knows that where ever the child is taken she can go, too. Ruby trusts nothing. The language of the Old Ones doesn't lend itself to separating information from feeling. So be it. Let them know how she feels. Trust is based in expectations fulfilled, but every time Ruby has adjusted her understanding of the Old Ones, she has been wrong. She lays a plan; she intends to know more about the Old Ones.

On top of the woodpile is meat. Beside it something is wrapped in a thin bark packet. Ruby puts the meat and bark in a fold of blanket, struggles to tuck two pieces of wood under her arm, goes inside, closes the door. She stokes the fire to a brighter blaze. For days she has been cold, supported and sustained by it, but now she needs bone-deep heat to unwind the tension in overstrained and exhausted muscles.

In the fire's warmth, Ruby's wet clothes begin to dry, water evaporates and steam fills the room. Ruby opens the bark package. *Devil's Club.* Help is not always from the light. Ruby pulls one of the pans from the stove, makes one more trip to the porch, this time to scoop snow for tea. She pulls the root apart into slivers so the tea will be strong, sets it at the edge of the stove to simmer. In the small space the smell of Devil's Club is strong – wet earth and spice, a funk that is more animal than plant. The simmering tea adds its moisture to what has become a medicinal sweat lodge. Ruby sips the hot tea.

In the afternoon she ventures to the porch, sits on the steps to take stock of the Old Ones. One leans against a tree, watches from near the water. The Old Ones are filled with contradictions. They intentionally triggered Ruby's memory of the day Marianne took her from the mountain, the realization that Marianne was not her grandmother. But, why? Ruby sits quietly, waits for the confusion to settle, a pattern to emerge. It doesn't. All she knows is that the Old Ones have layers and layers of secrets. Many more layers than they have so far revealed – not the least of which is, "What is a star child?" Who is her enemy? For that matter, who are the Old Ones? And how did Ruby's odd but stable life become caught in such a strange story?

By dusk Ruby can stand almost straight again. The pain in her hip has eased, her legs steady enough to be trusted. At dusk, she curls around the child again and seeks healing sleep. She dreams – the old man in the adobe house again. He reaches toward Ruby. She can't hear his voice, but can see the shape of her name on his lips.

When Ruby wakes it is still dark. The medicine has done its work – Ruby can move freely again. She dresses, and silently, eases the door open, sneaks just outside it, sits and props her back to the wall. In her arms is the child. Ruby wants to watch the morning come; she wants to watch the Old Ones before they are aware of her – if that is possible. If she watches carefully, maybe she will learn something about what they are, what they intend. Maybe more about the blue child as well.

Ruby certainly doesn't intend to set off a firestorm.

The snow has stopped falling. Ruby knows from the wet smell of the air that it will not be for long. Everything in the clearing is still. Ruby closes her eyes and calls her grandfather's song. She hears the drum, the way his voice quavered the last few years of his life; she sees his old hands tying the cedar bracelet around her wrist, feels his hand wrapped around hers. Ruby is pulling on the place where medicine lives – where reason shifts and one can know anything. Marianne might not have been her grandmother but Ruby trusts what she taught. However Ruby came to live with Marianne, their love was real. The medicine was real, too.

Day is moving closer, the last long moment of night before the shift towards light, the time when the spirit sends its last dream. Ruby can feel it and opens her eyes. She is a still point, focused, waiting. She may no longer know who she is, or where she came from, but she concentrates everything she can reach into the moment. There are those who find her power formidable, but Ruby only hopes that what she has, what she knows, is enough.

Ruby watches. Shapes begin to separate – trees take their tall forms, bushes stand under them, reeds in the pool point toward the sky. The darker color of the pool separates from the blue snow. Something is moving in the trees. It is not the Old Ones, doesn't have their bulk. Blue shimmer, crystal glints. Moving. Coming. And now tiny blue sparks, a cloud of them. Ruby doesn't try to understand. She is past that.

Night retreats and dawn takes the lead. At first the tiny sparks continue to hang dispersed in the darker area under the trees but then move closer to the clearing's edge. Ruby's heart beats faster, but she is very still. When the lights emerge from the trees into the open, they separate and coalesce into several tall columns, white and cloud-like, contrasting with the blue light of early dawn. To miss nothing, Ruby focuses on the one closest. It becomes more concentrated and then a hive of activity – agitated sparks, swirling silver threads. Before Ruby can grasp what is happening she sees the face of the old woman.

Fear grips Ruby; she jumps to her feet clutching the child. Who are the Old Ones? What trickery have they used? The old woman transforms into her familiar shape, her eyes on Ruby. Ruby holds the blue child tightly. For an instant she considers hiding in the cabin, but it is a dead end. The Old Ones would tear it apart. She decides to race to the trail. At the end of the porch she slides off into deep snow. Because of the weight of the child, she lands awkwardly, loses her balance and falls.

Covered with snow, Ruby looks frantically around. Several Old Ones stand between her and the trail blocking escape. Ruby looks desperately for another route, quickly looks inside her heart to see if there is medicine she can use. Nothing. Ruby stumbles to her feet, backs towards the forest. Her heart pounds, her breath heaves in dry gasps. She wanted to see and now she has. It is much worse than she feared.

The old woman roars, "No!" Sound rips the air. Trees shudder; piles of snow are shaken to the ground. Ruby recalls the reputation of the Old Ones for violence, stories of limbs ripped from living bodies, blood thick on the forest floor. No expressive faces. No ancient wisdom.

The old woman stops in mid-step, grows silent and switches to a soft, buzzing hum. That is when it finally penetrates – the little girl's body is still and limp, her arms dangle lifelessly, her head is a dead-weight against Ruby's chest. Ruby dares a glance down. To her horror, the child has stopped breathing.

She forgets the Old Ones, forgets the urgency to escape, and drops to her knees, feels frantically for a pulse. There is none. The child's blue light is fading. She is dying. Despair and grief fill Ruby's spirit. She keens a sharp cry that cuts like a knife through the cold morning. It contrasts sharply with the soft hum of the Old Ones that rises and falls like the waves on the ocean, or an unceasing night wind. It laps at Ruby's consciousness, then in one single tsunami, it overwhelms her. The old woman is inside Ruby's mind.

Ruby is disintegrating, scattering, like she did at the ledge, the elements that make her as dispersed as one star from another. She is far above the earth, somewhere in a black place between constellations. It is very cold. Ruby feels the force of the Old One's song beneath her, the trembling effort of their voices holding her. Then she is floating, weightless, a column of light much like the Old Ones were this morning. Beside her is another. It is the child.

From the center of four stars, a woman approaches. She isn't singing like the Old Ones. It is as if she *is* sound, a repeating configuration of several notes or tones, or perhaps the essence of a single song. Ruby struggles to stay conscious in order to see what the woman is doing to the child's body.

The woman sweeps an arm in an arc and a room appears. It is a bubble of slightly milky substance that little distorts the view of stars and planets. In the middle of the room is a high raised bed similar to the one in the cave except that it is made of the same material as the milky walls. On it is the lifeless child.

Moving quickly, the woman extends a long white arm through a wall, creates a rent, glides through. Ruby is jerked forward, pulled in the woman's wake, leaving the child behind. Ruby tries to protest, tries to turn back, but cannot; the power of the woman's gravitational pull is too strong. They pass stars, planets, giant asteroids that make patterns traced over eons, each meticulously careful of its neighbors. Constellations – wolves, bear, a spiraling tree, a maze.

Traveling at dizzying speed, Ruby is distracted by the variety and majesty of it all. She is captured by one constellation in particular – a dark woman in whirling skirts and draped shawls of turquoise and blue, flashing under-garments of hot pink and red. A dancer in the ecstasy of dance. Pulled by the dancer's piercing beauty, Ruby revels in the fast beat of her feet to the music, the swirl of the blue and turquoise skirts. Ruby, who has never danced in her life, wants to feel this joy, wants to join the dance that is greater than the dancer. She wants… But the woman escorting her seems to have a firm grip and Ruby is pulled away. She is swept in the woman's wake again; Ruby turns her head, watches the dancer as long as she can.

Before her, a long tunnel snakes through the sky. Or perhaps it *is* a snake. Though she looks, Ruby cannot determine if there is a head or a tail. She and the woman enter through a wide opening at one end, so if it is a snake, Ruby is now in its belly. Inside, it broadens into a cavernous room with a silvery, shimmering floor. Across its expanse is a wide, high-backed luminous chair that takes up one whole wall. The chair seems alive. In its interior, threads of light twist and turn; bright blue and white flashes explode.   On it sits a tall, very thin black woman.   Ruby hears the delighted squeal and laugher of children behind her. When she looks, they aren't there, but their voices bring a smile.

Weeping inconsolably, the woman Ruby followed drops in a single fluid movement to a heap on the floor. Over her heart a cobalt flame pulses. When she brushes away her tears, sapphires roll across the floor. The voices of the children stop and only the woman's weeping fills the silence. Ruby moves closer and kneels beside her.

For a moment, the black woman is very still, her brow furrowed, expression severe. Then she reaches into the chair and pulls free a long, spinning fragment of blue flame. It is of such intense blue, it is almost blinding. She bends forward and throws it to the sobbing woman. As the cobalt woman catches it, bolts of red lightning cut through the air from the back of the room and the ceiling; the maniacal laughter of the black woman, joined by the children, fills the cavern, rebounds off the silver floor. On her throne the woman grows immense, thrusts her finger, now as long as a staff, towards the entrance. The cobalt woman grabs Ruby's hand and races for the collapsing door. The walls whip back and forth, a snake in frenzy.

Outside, Ruby is dragged behind the cobalt woman again. Leaving is not as smooth and graceful as the arrival – waves of invisible turbulence cause them to skid off course in first one direction and then another. Each time, the cobalt woman rights their path towards the bubble Ruby can see in the distance, the one holding the child. Just as it seems the waves are subsiding, one, more massive than the others, rolls across the constellations, jolts the dark rivers between. Lights blink on, others disappear.

Ruby is tumbling and cannot see the cobalt woman, doesn't feel the gravity of her pull. In fact, she is sucked in the opposite direction, hurtling backward toward the snake and the laughing children. Her shape distorts, elongates – rope-like, snake-like. And then a miracle – as Ruby passes her, the dancing woman flicks her turquoise skirts, gives Ruby a mischievous, sensuous smile and the tumult recedes. Like an over-stretched rubber band, Ruby snaps back into familiar shape. The cobalt woman is beside her, and, as if nothing had happened, they are off again. Ruby looks back at the swirling woman, but the dancer is once more rapt in the dance, her head thrown back exposing the glitter of diamonds at her throat.

When they arrive at the bubble, the child is just as she was left. The woman reaches through one wall, tears an entrance; she and Ruby enter. The cobalt woman moves quickly, molds the light given to her by the black woman into a ball. With both palms she presses it into the chest of the blue child. From somewhere, Ruby hears, "It might be enough."

And then just as suddenly as she left the earth, Ruby is back in the clearing. She may have been gone for hours or minutes, or only seconds. She has no idea, but her mind seems to be hers again. She is sitting on the porch, the child is breathing again. Though still unconscious, her blue color is vibrant. Ruby holds the child closely and for a moment, gives way to weeping.

When she looks up again, the old woman is different than the figure Ruby has followed so many days – less dense, her shape less certain. Ruby looks around for the other Old Ones. Some are missing. She looks across the clearing, looks at the end of the porch in both directions. One of those missing is the young one.

The old woman catches Ruby's gaze and gently pushes. Why she gently pushes one time and rushes in like an angry bear at others is a mystery. But, the child is alive, evidently with the help of the Old Ones. Yet, what caused her death?

Was it the Old Ones? Or was it Ruby? And who are they?
Whirling sparks of light, or wise ancient animal-like creatures?
It is too much. Ruby needs answers. But she is hesitant – the
last time she sought answers, the child died.

The old woman persists, adds a note of urgency. She is
at the edge of Ruby's mind, not quite entering but not
withdrawing either. With the image of the missing Old Ones
and a low murmur of sadness, Ruby asks a question: "Where
are they?" Or more to the point, where is the young one? Did
he die? The old woman responds. The Old Ones are not
immortal. To save the child, each of them had to expend all the
power they could to lift her and the child. It was not enough.
Three chose to sacrifice themselves. A long haunting moan of
sadness penetrates the old woman's voice.

And finally, the old woman tells Ruby what she wants to
know – the one who feeds you is away collecting medicine.
Tears form in Ruby's eyes. Her emotions make no sense, their
rapid oscillation and contradictions – empathy, terror, paranoia.
She flounders for perspective, a point of view, a place to stand.

Ruby opens her mind. The old woman enters. Images
form in rapid succession, some overlapping, some awash in a
single color, each with its own complex of feelings, all tied to
the music of the old woman's voice. The Old Ones are light
beings moving in and out of form. They assist transitions.
Their nature is not violent. Unless, she adds, someone threatens
the places where their young are raised. Or intrudes – despite
repeated warnings – on their ancient hunting grounds. This
information raises more questions than it answers. If it is meant
to be reassuring, it misses the mark.

In a kaleidoscope of more images, the Old One makes it
clear that these mountains, this forest is a door through which
spirits enter from other dimensions. The Old Ones are the
doorkeepers. When the earth is in crises, help is sent. The Old
Ones receive the help that comes and assist it to enter the world.

With rare exceptions, the Old Ones are never seen by
humans. But accidents happen. When they do, the Old Ones
wipe the memory from the human mind. What the person

remembers is a shadow, or the ripple of a breeze in the trees, a shiver up the spine. When it isn't possible to wipe the memory, it is not a light-being that is remembered. It is an animal, often a brute.

Traveling with Ruby, the Old Ones chose to be seen in this familiar way. Not as brutes, necessarily, but as animals. Slowly, they revealed more and more. Step by step they pulled her into their multi-dimensional world. What they hadn't intended was what happened this morning. It was the powerful link between Ruby and the child that created the disaster – the link plus Ruby's terror.

Ruby's experience can accommodate light-beings, places on the earth that are doors, can even accommodate doorkeepers, but the thought that the Old Ones are creating a series of crises that explode her identity, that pull her into their world, and that they choose their shape to reflect her beliefs – all this adds elements for which she isn't ready. It makes reality too fluid, even for Ruby. How can she know whether she actually traveled the stars with the cobalt woman? How can she know anything for sure?

Ruby looks around. The Old Ones are in their more or less familiar form. There appears to be no intent to hurry back to the trail. Ruby lifts the child and returns to the cabin, re-kindles the fire. She needs to think, but sleeps instead. At one point, between naps, she opens the cabin's journal. There is the picture of wild ginger she drew a week ago, its hidden flower. When she drew it, she had no idea how much really was hidden, and still is. *Wild ginger*, deceptively gentle, finds hidden places in the back reaches of the spirit – best used by women who are sure they want to know.

In the late afternoon, the Old Ones begin to make agitated, impatient sounds. They gather near the trail in their way that says it is time to go. It is an odd time to start, but Ruby joins them. The young one has returned; he hands her two pieces of meat – one lean, the other a hunk of fat. The old woman takes the child from Ruby's arms and the hike begins. It is snowing hard.

The long strides of the Old Ones set a rapid pace. Their soft voices are anxious whispers. Ruby tries to tune into their meaning, but all she understands is that danger is near. Closer than they'd thought. The crisis in the clearing, the resulting delay, though unavoidable, is now creating a second one. Ruby assumes that the child's pursuer has found them. Or is close enough that it might.

Ruby walks fast, at times almost trotting. She stays close to the young one so she won't become separated from the group and lost in a thick curtain of snow. But her mind is elsewhere. Ruby had thought at one point that the woman with the cobalt color might be the spirit of the mountain. After the journey into the sky, however, Ruby is not sure. Maybe the woman is a star person like the child. If that is true, then where does the enemy come from? If it "followed" the child, did it too come from the stars? Why doesn't the cobalt woman destroy the enemy? But these are only questions and speculations. The truth is probably far more strange.

Though still overcast, the clouds lift and the snow stops. The Old Ones plunge from the trail into the trees. In some places the accumulated snow is deep and in others, sheltered by the trees, the ground is almost bare. If the map in Ruby's mind is accurate, they are near the meadows at the edge of the tree-line. Perhaps this is a shortcut to avoid the longer route of the trail's twists and turns; maybe it will take days off the journey. Or perhaps the Old Ones have another cave, a system of caves in which to hide. Ruby suspects this is wishful thinking.

Scattered through the trees are many Old Ones, many more than Ruby has seen before. They are in their animal form, but each is surrounded by a narrow band of light. In complete silence they move through the trees. The young one beside Ruby murmurs. Yes, the enemy has found them. They have tried to avoid a fight, one they might not win, tried to out-distance the enemy above and avoid its allies gathering below. Wading through deep snow, Ruby stumbles over hidden debris. The young one grips her arm, helps her move more quickly. Ruby is grateful for the fat eaten earlier, its sustaining energy.

They are angling uphill across a shoulder of the mountain. Trees thin. Stones, slick and wet, jut from the snow. Some are low enough to trip Ruby; others, scattered in the trees, pile high in miniature replicas of the mountain. Ruby knows they are near the peak, but it is hidden in low clouds. Dusk will be upon them soon. Clouds will make their way down the mountain. Visibility will be gone.

Through the trees is a meadow – flat, snow-covered, and sheltered by a wide ridge above. The Old Ones stop still inside the thick fringe of trees along the southern side of the meadow. To the northwest is a dull red glow, an oval larger than the biggest of the Old Ones. It doesn't quite touch the ground, doesn't have distinct shape. The color lacks strength, almost disappears, forms again. There must be more than this, Ruby conjectures. How could this be an enemy dangerous enough to make the Old Ones afraid?

The group parts and the old woman approaches Ruby. Her one message is – be everything you are. Surely, they don't intend Ruby to fight as well. Surely, there is nothing she can do that they couldn't do better. The old woman hands the blue child to the young one, lays a hand on his shoulder for a brief moment.

Ruby surprises herself with a low murmur to the old woman – affection. As she does so, the red cloud moves in their direction – not much, but several feet closer. It elongates horizontally six or seven feet above the ground, one end pointed towards the group. It waves slowly up and down like a blind snout seeking. The young one lays the tip of a restraining finger over Ruby's lips, makes an almost inaudible soft sibilant sound.

While the Old Ones could not avoid a battle, they have chosen the site, he whispers. When the evil spirit found them, was closing in, they lured it here to an open area where the Old Ones could mass. No, he answers Ruby's silent question, the cobalt woman cannot come. She can help only indirectly. She can send messages, influences, call on allies, but the battle at hand belongs to the Old Ones.

The old woman and nine others step into the snow covered meadow. Twenty feet further on they stop and begin to sing. Blue and white sparks scatter across the meadow. The tiny, beautiful lights hug the ground, vibrating in a band several yards wide. As the Old Ones continue to sing, the shimmering band lengthens to the ridge on the other side. It stretches the full width of the meadow, a wall of blue light. Ruby turns to see if it reaches into the trees below. It does. A barrier? A barrier of music? If this is war, if this is the only weapon... But, then the red enemy doesn't seem very powerful either. Ruby watches to see if it responds.

More Old Ones join those in the open meadow. The song is no greater in volume, but in the center of the band light concentrates, climbs, becomes a wall of color. At this, the oval red cloud withdraws further back under the trees. Even though the response seems timid, its sound is shattering. A high-pitched screech erupts, beats against the ears – fingernails on blackboard, tires skidding on wet pavement, the scream of small prey newly caught – but multiplied, fractals filling space. The sound compresses around Ruby's head like a rubberized hat several sizes too small. She feels as if her skull will crack; she grabs her head with both hands to relieve the unbearable pressure. It doesn't help. She feels hot and nauseous. Ruby cannot look away from the red cloud.

Though the horrible cacophony is undiminished, it releases Ruby. Its screams have another purpose. In the woods to the east – the direction opposite the red cloud – red snakes in the trees race towards the meadow. Unlike the dull color of the red cloud, they are the bright red of fire. Some travel on the ground, but others fly several feet above the forest floor. Snakes, dozens and dozens of them. The enemy's allies have arrived.

The old woman trumpets. Several of the Old Ones remain to hold the barrier of blue light in place. The old woman and the others turn to face the snakes. The trumpets, the drums, the high-pitch of wire in storm – all the sounds Ruby has heard the Old Ones make – are in play. Somehow they do not seem to diminish the awful, continuous scream of the red cloud. From her place in the trees, Ruby wonders if the mountain will collapse under the tumult.

The red snakes hesitate. Some gather at one side of the meadow. When the Old Ones move to respond, a second group of snakes turns to the meadow's other end, the one near Ruby, the young one and the child. A few Old Ones veer to meet them. With the Old Ones engaged at both ends of the meadow, several flying snakes gather in an arrow aimed straight at the center of the blue barrier. For a moment they hover, then, as if released from the bow, they explode into speed. One of the Old Ones maintaining the blue line moves to sing more strength into the middle. Another Old One leaves the group on the far side of the meadow to help. As the arrow of red strikes the barrier, the scream of the red cloud rises. It moves closer. The barrier bends at the arrow's point. Only a thin white rim of light stands between the red snakes and the red cloud. And then it is gone. The red arrow strikes the red cloud.

The discordant scream of the enemy becomes one of ecstatic triumph. The arrow of snakes disappears, integrated into the enemy cloud. Its color brightens and now contains fiery red sparks. Its shape changes. No longer an amorphous cloud, it is now a partial outline with arms and legs, a trunk and head – a suggestion of the monster it will become.

From the mesmerizing scene, the young one rouses Ruby with a shake. The child's blue color is bright, almost as bright as the cobalt woman. The young one has a firm grasp on Ruby's arm, guides her to a large pile of stones. The red creature spots their movement, or perhaps it sees the child's bright color. It shouts encouragement to the snakes and they seem to redouble their efforts. Some feint one direction to distract the Old Ones while others rush toward what seems to be their master.

But the young one, oblivious to the battle in the meadow, is intent on a mission. On the other side of the rocks, erosion has left a half moon at the base, overhung above with a deep shelf of stone. It is a small recess with a broad front open to the meadow; more a shawl of stone than shelter. Pressing on Ruby's shoulders, the young one motions her inside, hands her the child. This doesn't seem like effective shelter to Ruby, but if the Old Ones cannot contain the red enemy, there is nothing anyone can do. Clutching the child, she crawls inside, sits facing the meadow. The young one squats outside and sings. A blue net appears, a spider's web across the cave's entrance with sparks at the intersecting threads. It is similar to the barrier across the meadow, but less dense. His intention however is obvious – he is creating a last defense for the child.

In the meadow the snakes hurl themselves one after another at the blue barrier. Most disappear upon contact. A few, those coordinating in groups, make it through. Every time they do, the red creature's shape gains substance. Its eyes are now fierce fires. Its gestures and screams direct the activity of the snakes.

The snakes mass in response to the gestures of the creature. It is clear from their formation that they intend to break through in one final assault. The Old Ones spread out across the meadow. Half of them turn to feed the barrier with soft song. The old woman leads the others to confront the snakes. She becomes light, spreads in a long bank of white in front of her warriors. To her dismay, Ruby realizes the old woman is about to sacrifice herself just as the three Old Ones did at the cabin.

This is unbearable. It is almost is as bad as when the child died. Ruby wants to scream in protest. If the old woman is lost, the child will be – killed? captured? Unthinkable, but so is the death of the old woman. The young one beside her must feel the same way, but he is unfaltering in the amulet of sound he weaves. Ruby is filled with anguish. She grieves for the child's death yet to come, for the weeping cobalt woman. She grieves for her sisters.

In this turmoil of emotion, Ruby hears the song of her grandfather. Like a swimmer going down for the last time, she grabs its music and begins to sing. Her voice, the song – it is all she has to offer. Even if he was not her grandfather, even if

Marianne was not her grandmother, their love was real. Turned inside out with passion, Ruby sings. To her surprise, her voice is joined by Agnes'. Agnes is drumming on grandfather's drum.

Holding the child tightly, Ruby sings as loud as she can. The old words rise from her belly, fill her chest, her throat – words, rhythms kept living by a stream of voices from one generation to the next. The song is Ruby's answer to the old woman's sacrifice. Ruby will not run. After all, where would she go? She will not cringe – the result will be the same. It is her intention to sing death's path for herself and the child. She will not allow the star child to be taken by evil.

The song's drumbeat fills the little cave. Ruby's voice rises and falls. Her heart picks up the drum; under her fingers, she feels the child's pulse respond. Behind her and to her left, Ruby hears Marianne's voice and her grandfather's join hers. The power of their combined voices builds, breaks through the blue net over the cave's entrance, becomes a third strand in the battle.

She hears other voices and other drums – not the heavier drums of the northwest – not coastal – but high desert drums. Then Ruby sees them – six old men and women sing beside the river under a lean-to. The snow is falling, melting into the water – sky becoming river. The song rises up the canyons, skims along the mesas; in spirals it rises. Old bodies weave back and forth adding movement to song. Repetitious, rhythmic, following the drum, the words of the song. Remembering.

And then another voice, pure and simple in a single high, atonal thread – a gourd rattle in the background. It comes from behind Ruby and to her right. It is the voice of an old man. He is not singing the same song as Ruby, or the group from the desert. She can see him – he is in an old adobe house somewhere in the southwest sitting in a chair before a fireplace..

Then Ruby sees the snake. The old man's medicine is inside the cave. Silver, eyes of pale lavender. Icy. Glacial.

Chapter Eight

What if colonialism and Social Darwinism have it upside down?
What if those who seem to run the world are the ones not yet evolved?
What if their struggle is about the nature of power? If you own the
right song for gambling, you know how to become coyote. If you grind
the right mixture of plants and colored dirt, you can walk through
walls. Either will fill your heart until you cannot think of a single
thing you want that you do not already have. Is this not power?

Grace's apartment is small and tidy. In one room is a
couch, a small kitchen, but most of the space is taken by two
long tables used as desks. On one is a computer with big
double screens, and a phone. A tall-backed chair on rollers is
situated between the tables to make moving from one to the
other easier. Deep shelves line one wall. Labels on the edges
identify the content of the stacked documents. Short, metal file
cabinets sit under the windows. A wingback chair and a lamp,
sit before a gas heater. It is a room for work, more office then
home.

One wall is covered in hanging shawls, some, woven
wool in the Salish style, are long warm robes meant to be
pinned at the chest leaving the arms free for work. They are
beautiful in natural colors ranging from light gray to cream.
Others are colorful Pendleton shawls with geometric patterns in
primary colors; several are silky Pow Wow dance shawls
beaded and with bangles hanging from the hem; there is even
one of woven cedar and beside it a round matching hat. They
hang from elaborately carved cedar dowels so prized by
northwest weavers because they hold the heavy wool of their
creations without misshaping them. One, in the center has
pride of place, is silky and light, and has a long fringe of narrow
ribbons. Embroidered across the back and reaching over each
shoulder are the pastel flowers of wild rose – medicine flowers
with their green leaves – a wild bouquet.

There is another room, a bedroom with a single bed, a
nightstand. In the closet, clothes are separated by category –

two business suits with slacks, several long dresses, two skirts with matching blouses, and three jackets. Several shelves on one side hold cold-weather clothing, pajamas, underwear, four pair of shoes. Centered on one shelf is a colorful satchel with an old Pendleton design worn bare of its nap in places. Atop it, folded in red cloth is a long straight prayer feather. In the bathroom are no cosmetics, no perfume, but there is a hair dryer, a brush and face cream made of bear fat and herbs.

The location is downtown Portland, Oregon – the old part near the river. It is the area of the city where the homeless can be found; every race – black, brown, white – each with its established areas. These are streets claimed by drunks, addicts, prostitutes and some who are none of these. They are there because shelter is too expensive, because jobs are too hard to find and hold, because they are too ashamed to go home. Some have come to accept the desperation of their economic margin, the predictability of early death. Others, over time, have come to love street life, to embrace its freedom and companionship, its alliances and rules. Many of the residents pity the people rushing to and from work focused on a new couch, a bigger car; people they see as caught in cycles of exploitation. Others, a few, treat the street in the same way they would a forest or beach – a place to hunt, to fish – but the prey are people with jobs. And sometimes, the prey is one another.

This part of town is a way station, a place at the margin between life and death – powerful in its way. Ghosts live here, the ghosts of medicine men and women who have come to help. Spirits, sent by prayers, scout the street. Prayers that originate from the reservations scattered throughout the northwest – the beaches, the mountains, the plains; from the longhouses, the sweat lodges, churches. Prayers that hover over the streets looking for their targets. It is a crowded place, crowded with people and ghosts and spirits. The Indians who claim the corner where an old hotel of apartments stands will tell you they know when death is near – the dead are no longer wispy and colorless but look just like people – as substantial as the watchful cop, people staring from passing cars.

Medicine lives on the street – a staggering man or woman desperate for the next drink, might also know the old stories that keep the world alive, the songs for travel, how to call the elk, sing the salmon home – everything but how to change what they've become. And when it goes too far, a compassionate spirit, maybe one from the bloodline, will come to take them home.

Sometimes a miracle happens. A medicine ghost bends over someone in an alley, someone drunk for a year, someone too near death, too crazy to survive. A choice is given and a last chance taken. A man hitchhikes home, and stays there. A woman goes to detox and leaves the drugs behind. Maybe she becomes one of the throng of urban Indians who create the next best thing to ancestral places – drum circles, feasts, Pow Wows, a sweat lodge hidden in the trees on a hillside overlooking a sea of city lights.

The hotel is old, musty. The apartment where Grace lives is on the second story at the front of the building. With her window open, she can hear the Indians muttering, laughing; she can hear the fights and the songs. She would not live anywhere else in the city. Not in a nice house above the town, not in one with a gardened yard, and certainly not a gated community secure behind its walls. Though she visits the house her grandmother left to her and Agnes, though she stays on the reservation for extended periods, this nest above the street is the nexus of her work.

Next to Indian people on the street, here at the edge of their hodge-podge nation, Grace is reminded of why she speaks at conferences about fishing and hunting rights, the preservation of sacred sites, the protection of land and water, the defense of treaties. She is passionate, articulate, and in demand across the country for issues urgent in Indian Country. There are others like her. They meet in small groups to develop strategic positions, strategies that skirt the edge of many fires – federal trends in legislation, corporate intention, old-fashioned racism, the competition of tribes for resources. These are those who alert the people, who educate tribal leaders, who muster exhausted tribes for the next battle.

Grace fears that if she does not live here, if she retreats to comfort, she might grow lazy, or, worse, slide down the easy path of corruption and collusion. What Grace will not tell you is that her fight is backed with medicine taught by her grandmother and grandfather. Within its power, she is safe from the death threats that are the companion of her work, from bad medicine.

But medicine is not the reason Grace's apartment will never be robbed. When she is on the street she is teased in a rough Indian way, but she is safer there than anywhere. No one will ask for money, or make a clumsy pass. In gratitude, Grace makes sure she is here one day during Christmas week to bring a box of smoked salmon, or sandwiches of elk roast, huckleberry jam. The street smells of winter's filth – urine, vomit, stale beer and cheap wine – are strong, but the delighted welcome to traditional food makes the unpleasantness recede. At least for a few hours everyone remembers who they are.

Tonight Grace opens the door to an apartment stale from her absence of two straight weeks. She'd flown from a conference in upper New York to one in Montana on the Crow reservation. She is tired, anxious to turn on the gas heat and warm the cold, damp room, take a hot shower, and, most of all, sleep. Travel, public speaking, advocacy are exhausting and Grace is ready for a break, time to recharge. Unpacking could come later so she leaves the suitcase beside the door, plops her satchel on a desk top and ignores the blinking light of the phone. It would be someone who wants to schedule an event, or wants her help, or to vent about a court decision. If she answers tonight, her mind will begin to spin, and at the moment she is already overloaded. She wants no claim from anyone until she's rested. Besides, if it is really important, they'd have called on her cell phone.

She strikes a match, turns on the gas heater. With a whoosh it lights, the orange and blue fire counterpoint to the cold rain outside – rain so thick it is almost sleet. Getting out of the taxi, Grace saw the people huddled in doorways, the occasional dark face lit by the glow of a cigarette. Sympathy is of no use. With a tired wave, she'd unlocked the street door leading to the stairs and her rooms, and closed it firmly behind her. In a few minutes she will be warm and the people on the street still cold. There is nothing to be fixed about this; but it is nevertheless a familiar ache.

The blinking phone seems to insistently track Grace's path around the room, and she just as determinedly ignores it. She is hungry. She'd rejected the food on the plane to wait for the treat of canned venison. In the kitchen, she pulls a jar from the shelf, mixes it with elderberry jam and pepper. The bread is stale, the crackers damp. Sitting before the fire, she eats the mixture from a bowl. It is worth the wait – satisfying to the spirit as well as the body. Finishing, Grace leans back in the chair exhausted and sleepy, tempted to crawl into bed without the promised hot shower.

While she still has the will and energy, she rises to shower; the phone's red light catches her attention again. Its size grows, becomes a beacon instead of a small plastic-covered light. Grace is tempted to listen to the message just so she can stop the intrusion, but she knows herself too well to succumb to the temptation. Better to take care of her needs first – she'd learned from experience. Pace, priorities keep her focused, effective and healthy. Balance keeps joy an equal partner to responsibility.

So, Grace doesn't listen to the message on the phone. In her bedroom, she strips, leaves her clothes in a pile on the floor. With tired anticipation, she closes the bathroom door and turns the handle of the faucet to hot in order to fill the small room with steam, to make it hot enough to relax the tight muscles of her neck and shoulders. When the heat in the bathroom is barely tolerable, she adjusts the temperature and moves under the shower's powerful spray. For several minutes she does nothing but let the water finish the work begun by the steam; it soaks her long, heavy hair into wide fans across her breasts and down her back. Turning she lets it beat the tension from between her shoulders, raises her arms overhead in long side-to-side stretches. By the time she reaches for soap, she'd reclaimed her body from sustained effort, conflict, from bright blinking lights and airport terminals. When drowsiness becomes irresistible, she turns the water off and wraps herself in a red towel, another around her hair. Towel-drying her hair is short work before she climbs between the sheets and turns out the lamp. Almost instantly she is asleep. Grace sleeps deeply so she does not wake when the phone rings again. She does not even wake when a fight breaks out on the street below.

The next morning Grace wakes to a room filled with the white light of reflected snow. Just as she predicted the night before, rain has turned to ice. She snuggles deeper under blankets planning a slow beginning to the wide-open space of a day with no obligation, no schedule or deadline. Maybe she'd go down the street for coffee, maybe buy the people below her windows a warming round as well. Or maybe not, though she'd have to leave her apartment sometime during the day to buy food. Not much however, because in three days she is due at a conference in California.

The conference is about the sticky subject of cultural rights, ways to protect spiritual and ceremonial teaching and activities from commercialization. Unlike religions that proselytize or missionize, most Indian paths are not open to explanation, written instruction, or to access by the curious. The teachings are complex, operate on multiple levels, and are deeply woven into daily life. Though comparisons with dominant culture religion might be made, there are few actual translatable equivalents. Many Indian people believe that teaching the principles of a spiritual path in organized presentation depletes its strength, uproots it from the connection with the mysterious, with power. But there are complicating questions. Among them is what to do about people who are spiritually starved and are committed to the work of being taught.

Grace can't imagine this kind of poverty because she was raised in the rich territory of her grandmother's home. She was taught about things spiritual inseparable from the right way to live. These thoughts lead Grace to her sisters, Agnes and Ruby. They are not her sisters; Grace knows this. They are actually cousins, each born to a different one of Marianne's daughters. But they were raised together in Marianne's household, and brought up to think of themselves as sisters; however, Ruby is so much older that the relationship with her is different than the one with Agnes. Grace and Agnes were linked from the moment Marianne put Agnes' quivering body in bed with Grace, after the awful wreck that killed Agnes' mother. Wrapped in Grace's arms, snuggled against her plump warmth, Agnes' horror seemed to subside – the fixed unblinking stare, the panting shallow breath. Grace remembered Marianne standing in the shadows of the girl's bedroom door, watching them and crooning – not quite song, not quite words.

Grace can almost see Marianne now in her own bedroom doorway, can almost hear her voice. The memory is so strong that for a moment Marianne seems really to be there. Suddenly, Grace sits upright, the blanket ignored as it falls away from her shoulders, all drowsiness gone. Her senses are fully awake; she is as sure as she is of her own name, that Marianne has wakened her. Something is wrong. Through the open door, Grace can see the blinking light of the phone. Without bothering to grab the warmth of her robe, Grace runs to the desk where the phone sits, punches the button and listens, braces for bad news. She will not have to wonder which message is the one Marianne wants her to hear. She will feel it in her body. She will know.

When she worked her way past the requests she expected the night before to the one she knows Marianne wants her to hear, it is not from Agnes, not about Ruby. The first of the three messages came several days ago while she was still in Montana. The last was during the previous night while Grace slept. The message is from an old woman, one of the groups of elders living on the high desert who told Grace about the medicine in the southwest that someone is trying to release. It isn't the old woman's voice however. The message was delivered by her daughter, Peg, who said exactly the same thing each time. "About the things we spoke of in the spring – there is a problem. Mama says you have to go to New Mexico right away. Call me." New Mexico?

By this time, Grace is freezing - her backside on the cold chair, her feet on the icy floor. Still, she doesn't wait to dress before she returns Peg's call. The phone on the other line doesn't complete one full ring before it is picked up. No one says anything. The caller is expected to identify themselves first. "Peg, this is Grace." Peg, in relief, makes a long sigh of Grace's name.

And then Peg goes straight to the purpose of the call - no pleasantries, no courtesy, no gossip. Peg's manner leaves no doubt - this is an emergency. "Mama says you have to leave for New Mexico the minute you get this message. Today. There is someone there you have to go see. I have the directions of how to get there once you land in Albuquerque. It is the problem she talked to you about last spring." One of the byproducts of a close relationship to spiritual elders is that this kind of demand - though rarely made - is expected to be followed.

Grace is silent, her mind sputters protests she doesn't utter: in three days, she is due in California; a last minute plane ticket will be expensive; and she doesn't want to go to New Mexico in winter. It is not that Grace is one of those people who doesn't know how to refuse, but Marianne's appearance that morning signaled the arrival of a message with spiritual importance. Compounded by the unusually direct insistence of Peg's mom - an elder of impeccable reputation. There can be no doubt about what Grace is supposed to do.

Peg's mom ties her request to the message given to Grace last spring, the one she was told to tell her sister. With Peg waiting patiently, both women silent, Grace tries to recall the details. Someone or something is seeking to release an old power that elders in the southwest hid generations ago. The elders who hid it also placed strong medicine around it so that no one could find its location. In each generation of elders, there were watchers placed to make sure that it stayed safely tucked away. Whatever is seeking to free it must have raised the fears of these knowledgeable old people - not an easy thing to do. Why the elders on the high desert told Grace about this, much less why they'd stressed that she tell her sister, Grace doesn't know.

"OK, tell me where to go and what to do."

Peg's answer is immediate and has the tone of someone quoting exact instructions. "When you get to Albuquerque, rent a car that can travel over snow and rough ground." If she hears Grace's answering sigh, Peg ignores it and gives Grace precise directions. Grace is to travel west until she enters the tall mesas; she is to turn left on the next road after a sign reading "Casino, five miles ahead." After that the route involves several other turns; Grace takes careful notes. Her memory is good, but she doesn't want to risk becoming lost in the winter-empty back reaches of the mesas where it is so easy to become confused.

"Go now," Peg adds, apology softening her tone, reminding Grace that she is only the messenger. "Take a suitcase" was her way of telling Grace how long she'd be away. Another sigh from Grace – there is no way the trip will be short enough to allow her to make the conference in California. "And tell your sister. Make sure you tell her." Grace is not too surprised that Peg doesn't tell her who she is meeting in New Mexico, only where to go. She might be meeting a crowd or only a single person. There is also the possibility that she will meet no one and that the entire purpose is simply to bring a certain medicine to a specific place.

When Grace hangs up, she calls Agnes immediately, but there is no answer. Agnes could be anywhere and for any length of time – though given the snow, it probably will be hours, instead of days, before she returns. Grace gives up, opens her computer to check airline availability. There is a direct flight at noon. Though it is fully booked, Grace knows that in this weather there will probably be empty seats. She plans to be at the airport early, to be first in line for one of them.

She dresses quickly, then rubs a tiny bit of the treasured last batch of medicine Marianne had mixed for her so long ago; medicine Marianne told her to wear when she was among strangers. Grace wipes the residue through her hair, braids it and winds the braids atop her head. Though Grace often wears it long, an airport security officer taught her never to do so when traveling – he'd insisted on running his fingers through it, ostensibly to check for contraband. His fingers in her hair and on the back of her skull left Grace filled with disgust and simmering rage. It isn't an experience she intends to repeat.

Grace begins to pack. First she plucks a prayer shawl from the wall, covers it with a length of black cotton separating it from the rest of her clothes. Next, every stitch she owns for cold, outdoor weather – boots, fleece, wool, waterproof jacket – goes into the suitcase. It will be icy on the mesas if the wind blows and bitterly cold in the canyons. On impulse, Grace pulls an old necklace from the red satchel in the closet, slips it over her head, tucks it inside her sweater. With her suitcase ready, Grace calls Agnes again. No answer.

Next, Grace does what she dreads; she calls her contact in California to terminate her portion of the presentations. It leaves a hole in the conference agenda and the planners will have to respond to disappointed people who attended because of the array of speakers, or just because Grace was going to be there. Fortunately, her contact is a friend and even though Grace is vague about the nature of the emergency, the friend quickly moves the conversation to ideas about the rearrangement of the schedule.

If Grace takes a cab to the airport rather than the bus, there is time enough for breakfast and coffee. So, she leaves her cell phone to charge, the packed suitcase beside the door, and descends the stairs to the snow-covered city. It is early enough in the day to still be beautiful, the air fresh and clean. Later, as the temperature climbs, it will be a gray, sloshy mess. Grace is determined to enjoy the last free moments before traveling again. Coffee, hot thick and dark, is her first priority. And a fluffy pastry.

With her spirits mended from the disappointment of another long trip without the break she'd longed for, Grace walks the four blocks to her favorite coffee shop, stands in a line made short by the weather. There, she buys an enormous cup

of black coffee, sprinkles nutmeg on top, and chooses a pastry
with almonds, dusted with powdered sugar. Grace walks
slowly back toward home enjoying the empty streets, savoring
the contrast between the warm, sweet taste of almonds and the
hot bitterness of the coffee. Snow on the trees is just beginning
to slip toward the ground; the sidewalks just beginning the
change from pristine to muddy tracks. The snow won't last
long, not on the coastal side of the Cascade Range, not so close
to the river. There are no Indians on the corner; they will be in
bad-weather shelters or stretching breakfast, offered by the
public kitchens where they sometimes eat, as long as possible.

Except for one young man who sits slumped in a
doorway a half-block from Grace's entry. He is unconscious,
his chin resting on his chest. Grace bends to see if he is
breathing, catches the characteristic acidic smell of meth – no
doubt mixed or followed by something else to bring such deep
unconsciousness. His breath is shallow but regular, so Grace
moves on. It is time to leave the morning's last few minutes of
stolen leisure, call a cab, and start the day's long journey.

Grace takes no more than three steps past the
unconscious man when she hears a few notes of a coastal song,
a drum. In mid step, she freezes. Few have ever heard the song
– it belongs to her family – and no one sings it now except the
three sisters – Ruby, Agnes and Grace. She closes her eyes to
better focus, pick up all the muttered notes. Yes, it is her
grandfather's song – no doubt about it – and the muted timbre
of his unmistakable drum.

With every cell, Grace listens. She doesn't turn back to
the man in the doorway – he will either be there or not. It
doesn't matter if he is spirit or a man used by spirits. First,
Marianne was in the bedroom doorway early this morning and
now grandfather is sending a message on the street. But what is
the message? Grace thought she'd done what Marianne wanted
when she returned Peg's call and agreed to go to Albuquerque.
There must be something more. Slowly climbing the stairs to
her rooms, Grace tries to let the answer come. Ruby is the one
who has the drum, and grandfather's ritual gear. Agnes and

Ruby have the right to sing the song, but only Ruby "owns" the medicine of it; only Ruby can decide its inheritance.

Back in her room, Grace calls a cab and waits outside on the curb for its arrival. She hasn't seen Ruby for months, and of course Ruby never calls and seldom answers the phone. If Agnes and Grace did not invite themselves to visit her at the cabin, Grace suspects they'd never see her. Not that she doesn't love them; she is clearly moved when they arrive, and, oddly, always has food prepared and tea simmering on the stove. This is just how Ruby is.

Then Grace, following her intuition with action, pulls the cell phone from her pocket, and dials Ruby's number. She doesn't expect an answer, but nevertheless, she calls. "Yes," the answer comes almost immediately, but it is Agnes. Grace glances at the number on her screen to make sure she'd chosen correctly and not accidently re-dialed Agnes.

"Thank God you are there," Grace answers. Tears thicken her throat and fill her eyes. Agnes is silent. "Agnes, it is you, isn't it?" With a long breath, Agnes answers, "Yes, it is me. Something strange is happening, Grace. I think you are in danger. Or maybe it's Ruby. Someone called and pretended they were you. They tricked me and sent me in the wrong direction. I heard grandfather's drum and knew I was supposed to come here. But Ruby is gone." For Agnes, this is almost a speech.

Climbing into the cab with the phone braced between ear and shoulder, Grace answers, "I heard grandfather's song just a few minutes ago and I saw Marianne this morning. But Peg called too. Her mother says I need to go to New Mexico, somewhere out in the mesas. I'm on my way to the airport now. She made a special point that I was to tell you where I am going and why. As if I knew. It has something to do with the old medicine someone is trying to use, the medicine I told you about this summer."

Agnes doesn't say anything. She is silent so long the cab is halfway to the airport. Grace stays silent, too, giving Ages time to digest, to think. "Do you want me to come?"   At another time, the idea of Agnes trying to negotiate security in an airport would make Grace laugh. The results might make national news. Agnes' offer is a measure of her fear for Grace, her loyalty and love; not realistic, though there would be no better help if airports were not involved. Then Agnes adds, "But Grace, I think I am supposed to be here."

"Wait for me there. When I leave New Mexico, I'll come straight to Ruby's. But, Agnes, keep grandfather's drum close. Sing for me; sing for Ruby – wherever she is. I'll call you when I can." Two hours later, Grace nabs a seat on a plane with a direct route to Albuquerque.

It is just as well that Grace has too much travel experience to be easily dismayed by bad weather. The plane dips, shudders and alternately drops for much too long before righting itself with a sudden jolt. The pilot apologizes, tries to get above the worst of it, and can't. The stewardesses are solicitous of their white-knuckled customers, offering reassurance and warm drinks. Somewhere high over Nevada or Utah, Grace wraps herself in a scanty airline blanket and goes to sleep.

Albuquerque is winter beautiful. Unlike the northwest the snow is dry, the air colder. When the airplane lands, the weather is between storms and it is no longer snowing. The air is very still, the sky clear – but low on the horizon dark clouds gather, bringing the next storm.

At the third car-rental counter Grace finds a vehicle able to handle the unplowed back country indicated by the rough directions in her pocket, the ones given her by Peg. Grace wants something with four-wheel drive and a chassis high enough above the ground to not bottom-out on the first rough patch of road. Evidently, everyone else arriving in Albuquerque has the same idea, because there are few such vehicles left. However, it also seems that everyone else wants one that not only has four-wheel capacity but is also as substantial as possible – big and broad enough to protect them in a crash. That leaves available exactly what Grace wants – one that is smaller – perfect for the old roads Grace suspects she'll be traveling. Finally, Grace crawls inside a very cold SUV and begins driving toward the highway leading due west and away from the city – straight into the approaching storm.

The oncoming multi-trailer semis on Highway 40 are traveling fast. They are trying to gain as many miles as possible ahead of what appears from the clouds to be a storm of blizzard potential. Trucks going west are fewer, the truck-stops thick with truckers who've decided to ride out the storm in warmth and security – hot showers, decent food, generators. Grace turns the radio on and finds a local station. It confirms her fear – no music, just excited instructions about how to prepare for the coming storm.

Grace shakes her head and chuckles at her plight – everyone else is rushing to safety and she is doing the opposite. They are seeking shelter and she is heading alone into the mesas. At least she's made rudimentary preparations. Before she left the city she bought bottles of water, a sack of nuts, sandwiches and hunks of cheese from a dwindling supply in a crowded grocery store. In one of the last strip malls at the edge of town, she stopped again, this time at a hardware store. Moving quickly she collected the biggest flashlight she could find, a shovel, gas can, flares, matches, cedar kindling and a bundle of firewood. She parked her basket at the back of a long line of people with similar purchases. A dark skin man – one with the physical traits so characteristic of some of the tribes in the southwest – big chest, slender hips – was ahead of her. He studied the pile in her basket, saw its evident signal that she intended to be on the road. Abruptly, he left the line and returned a moment later with a foil blanket, dropped it in her basket, and went to the back of the line – all without saying a word. Good idea, Grace had thought.

The last preparation she'd made was to fill the can with gas. Not that she will need all these things. She intends to drive carefully, and arrive where she is going before the worst part of the storm, but it is already late in the afternoon and the instructions in her pocket are keyed to visual landmarks. It is possible she'll be unable to find her way in the dark and have to spend the night in the car. It crosses Grace's mind to stay in a motel and start tomorrow, but if the roads are closed by the state patrol, she'll be stuck.

Not far from Albuquerque, the first of the beautiful mesas begins and they soon take over the landscape. Their newly-washed reds and yellows shine at the edges of new snow blankets. The lower rock protrusions and rimrock covered with snow scatter into the shapes of fantastic animals in repose. Grace rolls down the window to see if she can detect a delicious whiff of wet sagebrush.

Soon she passes the familiar and ancient names of villages, pueblos. Even with the approaching storm, Grace is exhilarated by the beauty of the enduring land and the old names. It is reassuring that somehow the people might also survive the scouring erosion of government policy dedicated to their destruction. Grace remembers standing on one of the tall round mesas, small in its circumference. No electricity; the houses miniature, the streets narrow. The graveyard there has a wall on the outer edge of the mesa above a vertical cliff that drops all the way to the canyon floor. The wall is punctuated with large round holes to provide access for the spirits of the stolen children to find their way home at death. Grace and her hosts stood silent for a long time, remembering the children, remembering the long pain of the people.

This area is a powerful place, its spiritual essence carried by a long line of holy people. Carried by people who know the necessary ceremonies, the medicine, the stories, and who know the terrible results if they fail. Not just the loss of the people, but the devastating chaos that would lash an impoverished world. The keepers of the mesas are not the only ones who protect the earth; others in caves and on mountain tops, in the deserts of other continents, do their part. But the medicine of the mesas carries so much power that if the old people here were overthrown, the other keepers might be also, and all be lost.

Grace thinks about the little she knows. There are many powers on the earth with their source in distant constellations.

Before the arrival of Europeans, the elders in the southwest used these to communicate: to learn, align their lives along the highest axis possible, become pure, travel the heavens. The axis accessed for these purposes changed from time to time, and medicine shifted with it. Elders met to watch for the signs, to discuss what they meant, to make the right adjustments. One of the greatest sacrifices the desert people made was to put some of these powers away when Europeans came. In the presence of rage and hate the powers might be wrongly used. The teaching says that if they were used with hate the world might die.

Grace knows these things, but had assumed that the old people could always keep the world safe from the worst possibilities. Last spring, however, when she went to the high desert of Oregon as she does every year, the elders there stressed this new danger. Something, someone, perhaps a group, is trying to find the spirits hidden in the southwest. The effort is so sustained and concentrated that the elders in the mesas asked for help. In fact one of the secret places – a cave high in a mountain above the mesas – had been breached.

The first flakes of snow begin to fall. It is almost dusk, and the blue front of the blizzard just ahead will bring night early. Grace almost misses the sign Peg told her to watch for, "Casino 5 miles ahead." She expected something bright and glossy, but the sign is so old it leans on twisted posts, its letters faded. Two miles later a dirt road covered with light snow turns left just as the directions describe. Though the road is a single track with no sign, Grace turns. After all, the directions didn't say the first decent road.

Dusk descends as Grace drives over the tumbled ridge. Ahead she sees the road snake across the desert floor skirting shallow arroyos and piled slabs of overlapping stone. It is lost to sight in the deep canyons on the other side of the expanse. It will be dark by the time she gets there, and snowing hard.

As it happens, night falls and the snowfall picks up long before she reaches the mesas. The snow does not fall straight down as wetter snow might, but it whirls and dances like dust. In the dark and the snow all Grace can do is keep her eyes fixed on the track immediately ahead – a track defined in some places only by the absence of plants. Making it more difficult, the headlights caught by the glittering snow reflect their light back into Grace's eyes. It is going to be a long night.

Grace almost misses a curve in the road because the sparse brush beside it disappears in a bulge of sandstone. She over-corrects to discover that the road has become slippery – not with ice, but a skim of mud that will later become a frozen crust. Now doubly careful, she sits so far forward her chin almost rests on top of the steering wheel, her pace a crawl across the desert pan. The mesas are invisible and the only way Grace knows when she has neared the end of the valley is the increasing size of the stones beside the road – and some on the road – stones fallen from the top of the rimrock above.

In rough spots Grace angles the car between several stones choosing the route least likely to scrape the car's axles. Ahead is a deep gouge in the road beside a long loaf-shaped stone. The stone seems to offer solid support so Grace steers the left wheel onto it with the right on the small rise in the middle of the road. Suddenly, with a solid bang to the under-carriage, the wheel slips. Exactly what Grace is trying to avoid. She brakes lest the stone rip the car's vital functions or bend an axle. The left wheel has slid into the crevice between the big stone and the higher roadbed. The result is a sharply tilted vehicle, not at risk for rolling over, but the car's weight on the left wheel will allow little traction on the right. Grace considers her options. Actually there is only one – she has somehow to drive the car free without disabling it. Walking back to the highway is not a possibility. Sitting in the car in a blizzard that might last for days isn't a possibility either.

Grace digs her coat from the suitcase and wrestles herself inside its red shield. She grabs the flashlight. For a moment she sits with her hand over the medicine she wears, thinking about Marianne, the elder of the high desert who'd sent her, about Agnes and her grandfather's drum. She hopes Agnes is praying; she knows Peg and her mother will be. She knows she is surrounded by helping spirits. She also knows that with spiritual trouble afoot there might be other things summoned as well – powers that want to interrupt her journey. Or worse.

The tilt of the car wedged against the stone permits the door to only partially open. Grace squeezes through and steps directly onto the muddy stone. Even with the waffled soles of her boots and the traction they offer, she slips. She grabs the car door and manages to stay upright, but before she regains her balance, she drops the flashlight. It is now under the car, its light half buried in mud. Hanging onto the car's frame, Grace reaches into the crevice. She can feel the shape of the flashlight but can't get her fingers around it. It is dangerous to put her body between the car and the stone – the car might slip again and she'd be crushed. But Grace has to have light. She turns her face sideways, presses her cheek into the mud, and shoves her shoulder beneath the car. Her cold, muddy fingers find it, wrap around its shape. By the time Grace has retrieved the flashlight, and is on her feet again, she is thoroughly muddy, cold and wet.

She flashes the beam of light over the treacherous round stone and sees the wide scrape where the tire slid. Snow falls thickly; Grace can barely see the road ahead even though the headlights are still on. Around the puddle of light they offer, night is a black curtain.

Grace makes her way to the front of the car, kneels in the snow and shines the beam of her flashlight underneath. Though neither stone nor roadbed actually touch the undercarriage, the wheel is indeed caught in the deep depression at the rock's base. Fortunately the erosion in which the wheel rests is a long cut instead of a single, deep hole. It is deepest near the car and grows shallower at the road's edge where it finally disappears in white-shrouded sagebrush. Grace pauses, bends over the nearest plant and brushes the snow away; she squeezes its gray-green leaves between gloved fingers and inhales the precious scent.

Memories of sweat lodges and Sun Dances fill her. Grace can almost hear the drums and the high notes of the songs. But even more, the essence of the plant brings reassurance and strength. Grace takes off her gloves, unbraids her hair, and shakes it free. She breaks a stem from the plant, crushes the leaves and combs the scent through her hair with her fingers. The plant will help carry her through the night. It will help her find the right road.

Grace pulls the hood of her jacket over her hair and makes her way to the back of the car. She stoops to check underneath, this time to make sure no portion rests on a stone she wasn't been able to see from the front. In one place there is only a few inches clearance, but it appears that if she drives forward following the ditch and then pulls sharply back into the road where it grows shallow, nothing will be damaged.

Once more Grace walks to the car's front, but this time she goes further down the road to see what is ahead so that she doesn't make it out of one hole only to land in another. Certainly the little road is rock-strewn but nothing too difficult if she is careful.

Back in the car, Grace puts the car in gear, angles the steering wheel, and pushes the gas pedal. The left wheels catch immediately. Near the edge of the road, with a sudden lurch, the car breaks free. There she stops the car for a moment, pushes the button to lower the window to acknowledge the spirits. She is certainly not the first Indian woman to travel across the desert in need of help, nor will she be the last.

Even though it is now snowing in earnest and Grace can see barely a few feet ahead, she drives without more trouble. She begins to relax; hopes the worst is over, when the road suddenly disappears. Startled, Grace brakes too sharply and the car begins to slide. Forcing herself to tap the brake lightly and not over-steer, Grace brings the car to a stop, headlights inches from a pile of boulders. Grace hopes this doesn't mean she's reached the end of the road. From her pocket, Grace pulls the directions given by Peg, turns up the interior lights to study what she'd written.

"At the first mesa, veer left." Grace puts on her coat again, gets out of the car, the mud-caked flashlight in hand. Sure enough, a track goes to the left. Grace can tell it roughs its

way over and between rocks. Grass bent under the snow's
weight fills the center of the road, proof that it is even less
traveled than the road Grace is on. Grace checks in the other
direction. Yes, the main road curves there. If it hadn't been for
such poor visibility, she might have followed the curve and
missed the track going left. On the other hand, if she'd been
able to see, she'd have known there was a mesa ahead. She
hesitates. What is she supposed to do? Follow the road or take
the track?

Grace finally laughs at herself. The directions are clear –
veer left. Her hesitation arose from the desire to follow the
better road – such as it is. But there is another question – should
she continue in the dark or wait for morning? Though curling
up in the car is tempting, by morning the snow will be very
deep and the road's treachery even better hidden. Grace backs
the car, faces the road but still hesitates. She needs to think. A
hunk of cheese and a bottle of water later, Grace has a plan.
She'll walk ahead on the road, see what is there, then drive the
portion she's checked – leap frog in this fashion until she has a
sense of the dangers. It will be slow travel, but better than
getting stuck again.

An hour later the track seems to have gotten around the
worst of the fallen rimrock and Grace abandons checking every
inch before risking the car. But when the wind picks up,
blowing steadily down the canyon, Grace hesitates again. If
visibility was bad before, now it is almost impossible. Leap-frog
once again? Wait until morning?

Out of the car again, this time with a wool cap under her
jacket's hood, she tries to decide. The wind is a freezing river
streaming between the mesas. By morning it might shift, or it
could become a howling blizzard.

Grace stands in the middle of the road trying to decide.
She is fearful of traveling blind, and fearful of waiting until
dawn. Hunkered inside her coat, she is a center-point of
sensation – the sound of wind, the biting cold, the blinding
snow – when another, more subtle, finally penetrates her
awareness. It is a faint smell of smoke. Grace sniffs again and

her face opens in a wide smile. Smoke. People. How far away she doesn't know but she is going to find the source. And she is going to find it tonight.

Grace drives. When the road forks, she turns left again as her directions instruct. An hour later she arrives on a talus hill against a canyon wall. More importantly, it is yard to a small cabin. Yellow light from a lamp fills a window. Grace pulls her suitcase over the seat of the car and gets out. She slogs through the snow to the door and knocks.

And then waits. From inside she hears shuffling noises. When at last the door opens an old man is revealed – short and thin, dressed in blue jeans, a beaded denim vest, and a necklace of the biggest bear claws Grace has ever seen. He doesn't say anything, and doesn't open the door wide enough for her to enter.

"Grandfather, I have come," Grace says. "From the northwest." No excuses that she didn't get the message until today, that she's been busy. He nods, pulls the door open wider and steps aside. Grace enters a space even smaller than it had seemed from outside. On one end is a cook-stove, red coals visible. A wooden table is cluttered with small containers, two chairs near one end. Boxes are nailed to a far wall to provide storage. At the opposite end of the cabin is a fire in a stone fireplace, two cushioned chairs, and in the corner a narrow bed. There is nothing else except stacked boxes under the window and the lamp she'd seen from the car. Except, that is, for the rich smell of venison stew.

The man stands in the center of the room, watching Grace. From her pocket she brings tobacco and a packet of cigarette papers. She holds it in her palm so he can see what it is, turns her hand, offers it. Still he doesn't move. Then Grace understands. She reaches inside her shirt to pull the necklace given her by her grandfather. It is a single bear claw set in silver – not nearly as big as the old man's, but lovely. He nods, and extends his hand to receive the gift of tobacco. Transaction over, credentials verified.

He points to a place near the door and Grace places her

suitcase there. With another gesture he directs her to a chair by the table and shuffles to the stove. On top is a black iron pot. He removes the lid and ladles its contents into a white bowl, fills a cup with something from an enameled pot, and places both on the table in front of Grace. She tests the tea – sage with something oily, tar-like. Not delicious, but Grace upends its medicine. The bowl is only half-full, an amount dictated by spiritual work ahead, not satiation before rest. With the last bite barely in Grace's belly, the old man rises, moves the stew to the edge of the stove. From the pot of tea, he fills another cup and sets it in front of Grace. She drinks.

At the side of the room the old man opens several of the bigger boxes, takes small bags from inside, opens them and places the contents on the flat surface of another box. Grace knows not to stare but she can't help but notice that the little bags are dark with age and that from one the old man pulls a tiny stone figure. When he is satisfied, he points to one of the chairs in front of the fire. Grace opens her suitcase and pulls her prayer shawl from its wrapping, drapes its bright shimmer over her shoulders. She sits and the old man settles beside her.

"Charley," he says pointing to his chest. His voice is low, rusty, guttural. "Grace," she mimics and also names the elder in the northwest, Peg's grandmother, who sent her. Next Grace recites the names in Marianne's family. She recites the generations until the old man nods. Grace doesn't think he knows her family; he's probably never left the southwest. But, then again, maybe he has. From what Peg's mom told Grace about the problem of the elders in the southwest, there has to be some means of communication – other than phones as none of them seems to ever use one. Maybe it is by messenger like her visit here.

Charley leans back in his chair, reclines his head against its tall back and closes his eyes. Grace does the same, but with eyes open. Staring at the bright fire, she settles in for a long night of ceremony. The old man begins to sing, his voice barely audible. On the wide arm of the chair, the fingers of one hand tap the beat of the song. Over and over, the same words, the same cadence, hypnotic. Grace straightens in her chair; she is tired but cannot allow herself to fall asleep. The lamp flickers and then its light dies. Ashes at the edge of the fire whirl in miniature eddies. The song's volume grows, its pitch climbs; it is like wind squeezed between stones.

This continues for what seems like hours. The color of the fire changes from orange to blue, pieces of wood crumble into charcoal. Still the old man sings, but his voice has grown deep, stronger and more intense – almost as if someone younger sings. Grace is not surprised when she begins to hallucinate – the tea, the song, exhaustion. The images are confused. She sees a mountain and hears a woman crying. And then nothing.

When Grace wakes it is late in the day. She can't guess how she got on the floor and wrapped in blankets. She must have slept for twelve hours or more. Maybe it was the result of the tea, but even the confident and daring Grace has never felt so safe, secure, or more certain of her place in the world. She stretches her arms high over her head and each toe to its farthest reach. Flat on her back she lies in the sensuous pleasure of a satisfied spirit, a rested body.

The light through the window shines white. The blizzard has settled in and snow falls heavily. Grace rolls to her stomach and cranes her neck. Charley isn't there. She half rises to see if he is on the bed but it is empty, the blankets stretched neatly and tucked under the mattress. She rises to look out the window. The snow is so deep the rental car is a white mound; nothing is visible – not the aerial, the side mirrors – nothing. Grace shakes free of the blankets and pads across the room to the stove hopeful the pot is filled with coffee. It isn't. Instead it simmers with the same tea she drank last night.

She climbs into boots, wraps inside her coat, and opens the door. She can see where Charley has cleared a little porch-like area. Grace steps into the pristine snow not surprised to find it tops her boots. Nevertheless, she heads to the car, wrenches the frozen door open and digs in the back seat to find the sack of nuts. They aren't much breakfast, but are a much better choice than a frozen sandwich or frozen cheese.

Through the snow she can see enough to know she was right the night before – the house is on a hill flattened at the top, its back against a cliff. Charley's tracks lead in that direction, but Grace turns the other way. She wants to know the layout of the land around the cabin. Not far behind the car she finds large slabs of rock that overlap in geometric shapes, beautiful but treacherous. She follows the jumbled perimeter until she reaches a steep drop – another view blocked by weather. Grace traces the edge to the cliff, or as near as she can come, given the tumble of giant stones. Charley's cabin is a protected, hidden island – the cliff behind, the up-thrust of stone, a steep-sided hill. The only way to approach is via the track Grace used. She brushes the snow from a rock, sits to finish the nuts. She wonders if Charley has a back-door escape on the cliff side.

Grace debates walking further, skirting the cliff to arrive back at the cabin from the far side but the light has begun to fail. She hasn't been gone that long, but perhaps she slept later than she thought. Or walked further. At any rate, her prints are almost invisible, filled by the deepening snow and hidden by the early gloom. By the time she finds the cabin again, Charley is a waiting silhouette in the doorway. Inside the fire burns low, the only light. Charley points Grace to the table again. Except for the nuts, she hasn't eaten, but the remaining soup isn't offered – only a cup of warm tea, followed by a second. Just as last night, Grace is directed to the chair next to Charley in front of the fireplace. "Tonight, you must sing." Grace has no idea what he means but drapes her shoulders once more in the shawl.

Charley sings the same soft song as the night before, exactly as generations before him, but tonight he also has a rattle. There is no need to try to understand what Charley means, only to let the music of his song do its work. And it does – first the fire fades away, becomes a gray scene of falling snow, a confusion of dim figures. Grace gasps when she sees Ruby's face – though with an expression Grace has never seen, twisted with fear and rage.

"Sing, Grace!" Charley yells, but Grace doesn't hear. She

can hear only Ruby singing – singing their grandfather's song. And then Marianne's voice rises to twine with Ruby's, and like the essence of love itself, her grandfather joins. But their voices are not the soft familiar ones of childhood; instead they are fierce and loud. The old healing song has been transformed – it is a warrior's song.

The images in the cold fireplace shift and Grace sees war. She sees giant creatures, pale light beings, red snaky shapes. Grace knows the red creatures are trying to destroy Ruby and are very close to succeeding. Afraid though she is, Ruby is preparing to die.

"No, not Ruby," Grace screams; her voice fills the small cabin. It is clear from Ruby's expression that she is willing – no, she is determined – to die if necessary. Necessary for what, Grace can't see, but she knows her grandparents are trying to save Ruby. The old man squats beside Grace, but his reality is nothing compared to what is happening in the vision.

"Sing, Grace," he yells again. "Sing." But Grace is too horrified to hear. It isn't until her grandfather turns toward her that Grace understands. And then, like all things Grace does, she fills her lungs and sings with passion, with ferocity. The cups on the table vibrate as does the glass in the window. The cabin walls tremble. Memories spill across her mind, memories that are not hers, but are the stored history of the people – the people loving their own. Grace, like Ruby, is willing to give everything she has, including her life. She bleeds into the song.

Then to Grace's surprise another song joins hers, but it is not the same one she sings. It climbs on the back of her song and rides, travels the hundreds of miles from desert to mountainside where Ruby fights. As it rides, travels the path of Grace's singing, it takes form. Not the shape of the old man. Not a shape Grace has ever seen. Its lavender eyes glitter.

Chapter Nine

The river's spirit is different from the water that flows. The spirit of the fog wrapped around the mountain is neither fog nor mountain. Who I am, says the teaching, is not me.

The snow has stopped; the clouds lifted enough to reveal the mountain. Those in the meadow do not see a cobalt flame in the recess between two outcrops. They are too busy, the battle too intense.

The red creature screams direction, the fiery snakes mass for attack. The white cloud that is the old woman stretches to reinforce the blue barrier between the Old Ones and the child's red enemy. The evil creature appears stronger, fat with red radiance now in the unmistakable shape of a reptile with a long snout.

The first of the snakes attacks the white cloud. A loud snap penetrates the chaos of other sounds; the snake is charred to ash. But they persist, snake after snake concentrated at a single point in order to break through. The old woman in her light form wavers, thins. Several of the Old Ones line up behind her to strengthen her effort. Joining her sacrifice, a few place themselves in front. It is noble last effort but destined to fail. Ruby, half-crazed with distress by the unfolding drama, sings louder, harder – as if somehow singing will make the old woman's death easier to bear. The fierce voices of Marianne and Ruby's grandfather ring against stone; the voices of the elders from the high desert set the meadow atremble. It is not enough, but nevertheless they give it their all.

And then another voice, pure and simple in a single high, atonal thread – a gourd rattle in the background. It comes from behind Ruby and from her right. It is the voice of an old man. He is not singing the same song as Ruby, or the group from the desert. She can see him – he is in an old adobe house somewhere in the southwest sitting in a chair before a fireplace. Much to Ruby's surprise, Grace is beside him. She is weeping.

The old man's voice twists in the air, becomes a snake at

Ruby's feet.   It is long and fat; its scales silvery, eyes pale lavender – icy, glacial – a color at the edge of the visible spectrum.   Ruby doesn't fear it.   Perhaps the reason is Grace's presence beside the old man.   Ruby continues to sing, to watch the action in the meadow.   The snake glides up her arm; she feels its dry powdery weight.   It hesitates at Ruby's throat, rises further, lightly presses its heavy head against the lobe of Ruby's ear.   Its tongue flickers in caress.

Help has come, a particular spirit chosen by the medicine people of the southwest, help held and nourished by a single old man.   He has been searching for Ruby, and with the aid of her grandfather's song, he has found her.   The essential link was Grace.   The old man could not come until she'd arrived at the adobe house, nor send his spirit until she sang.

In the meadow, the silver snake moves quickly, twists between the strands of the protecting net the young one holds in place.   It slithers between the legs of the nearest Old One, one of those warring beside the white cloud.   First to notice is a red snake at the head of a phalanx pointed at the weakened center of the Old Ones' defense.   It changes direction, heads toward the new arrival.   Seeing this, another group races to join. Others, seemingly eager, even gleeful, speed in the other direction toward the white barrier, throw themselves into its light.   Are they frantic to kill the old woman while they still can? Or do they believe the silver spirit has come to help them? They ignore the increasingly hysterical shouts of the reptile at the edge of the trees.

The phalanx reaches the silver snake.   With the first touch, their formation breaks; they scatter but not into separate, individual snakes.   Instead, each is transformed into a streak of red light racing towards the sky – a storm of comets all headed in a single direction – the southwest.

But this doesn't stop those remaining in the meadow from challenging the new arrival.   They throw themselves in seeming frenzy against it.   The reptile is screaming direction, gesturing wildly, but the snakes no longer hear or see.   They are confused, even self-destructive.   When the silver spirit touches the white cloud, a shiver runs through the length of it.   It coalesces; the old woman takes shape, yet her body is not quite solid. Around her is the familiar narrow band of light. Only the damaged blue barrier remains between the frenzied red snakes and the red creature.

The Old Ones move aside, allow the silver apparition open access to the wavering blue barrier. At its first touch there is an explosion of phosphorescent light. The snakes recoil. The voice of the old man rises in volume, drops in pitch – a low rumble reminiscent of thunder. He is calling the red snakes; they join those already in the ruddy sky.

But the red reptile is another matter. He does not lose shape or color.   The power he has accumulated remains. Nevertheless, with the loss of his allies and in the presence of the Old Ones with the support of the silver snake, he is finished for the night. He fades into the trees and no one tries to stop him.

Ruby falls silent. She can no longer hear her grandfather and Marianne. Grace's voice ceases as does the sound of the drum.   The voices of the desert people soften and then she doesn't hear them any longer. The icy lavender eyes of the silver snake fade. It unravels and is gone. The Old Ones stop singing. Holding the child in one arm, Ruby crawls from the cave, keeps crawling until she is sitting beside the old woman. The Old One hums – relative peace. It is over for now. There may be time enough to get Ruby and the child off the mountain.

The meadow is bare of snow and Ruby wonders if the mountain's medicine will ever grow here again. It is night. Cold seeps slowly into Ruby's awareness, but the blue child still breathes and that is all the comfort Ruby needs. The young one bends to help her to her feet, takes the child, tucks Ruby's hand under his arm and leads her south across the meadow.   It has begun to snow again.   The young one enters a break in the trees, perhaps a trail. Ruby cannot think of sleep, doesn't want to stop until she is far from the meadow. The Old Ones seem to understand, or feel the same themselves.   The group walks down the mountain far into the night. Ruby does not stumble even once though the night is very dark. She does not seem to notice that each of the Old Ones, though in their familiar animal form, also has the same narrow band of light as the old woman. She doesn't notice that she does too. In fact, from a distance the group appears to be a glowing presence moving through the forest.

When Ruby is eventually directed under a tree adrenaline has burned away. Underneath the shelter, Ruby wraps the child in the cedar, but doesn't join her. Instead she leans against the cedar's cold bark to let the night's experience settle. Ruby has given up trying to understand. Better to accept the many-faceted nature of the Old Ones, their multiple agendas, to accept their power and their constraints. To not waste the effort of questioning why the reptile is on earth but the cobalt woman cannot come to fight in a battle to save the child. Ruby digs a shallow hole, pulls the child against her.

It is morning. Ruby blinks awake staring over the child's tussled hair directly into the eyes of the young one. He kneels at the edge of the trees' shelter, leans so far forward his face is almost level with Ruby's. Slash of cheekbones, caramel eyes, thick broad lips – he is so familiar. As if she has known him forever. Loved him for longer than she has been on the mountain.

He smiles, hands Ruby meat and several long Skunk Cabbage leaves. *Skunk Cabbage – plant shaman.* Their color is not the bright green of earlier in the year, their medicine has retreated to the roots, but there is still enough to ease the pain in Ruby's hip. She tucks the leaves inside her ragged pants, eats the meat before joining the others. As she chews, Ruby sees the nicks, cuts, scrapes and scars on her hands, but does not notice the glow. She has never noticed that the Old Ones do not leave tracks, and doesn't see that now she doesn't either.

It is just as well that the young one brought the leaves because today Ruby limps. Not as hobbled as the day in the cabin, but stiff and sore nevertheless. But the battle on the mountain bought time and Ruby's halting pace doesn't seem to cause the Old Ones anxiety. On the other hand, they travel in silence – no conversation. No song.

Ruby stops at a creek to drink, sits in the snow to adjust the leaves. Tracks, bird tracks, dance in the snow along the edge of the water. It is only then that the sweet twitters enter awareness. How long has she been so absorbed in crises that she doesn't hear the birds, doesn't respond to the tiny bells of their voices? She washes her hands and face in the frigid water, holds its crystal beauty in her palms, watches the pale drops fall.

When she stands, her pants almost slip from her thin body. She hikes them up, adjusts the leaves again. Ruby will not last much longer in the mountains without respite; she is too old. Listening to the birds, watching the light on the water – she'd be content to finish here, to step from one moment to the next, become another spirit on the mountain, make a home of this soft joy. But, of course, she cannot allow that temptation to take root. The blue child would die. Turning to rejoin the waiting Old Ones, she runs her hand down a hank of pale green *Usnea*. Yes, this winter, though only just begun, has lasted too long, but the plant's promise – there will be food enough if you know where to look – heartens Ruby.

Half an hour later there is movement in the trees far above. Ruby assumes it is one of the Old Ones flanking, providing protection. But the old woman breaks the silence with a murmur and Ruby looks again. It is the man from the meadow, from the bridge – the veteran who has somehow carved out a life for one in the almost uninhabitable wilderness of the Peninsula. His clothes, including cap, are buckskin. A hide with hair attached drapes his shoulders.

But the Old Ones do not chase him away, nor do they seem disturbed. After all, hiding their trail from the red enemy is no longer the goal; the enemy already knows they have collected the star child, knows where they are. There is no danger at the moment because the reptile and his allies must regroup. Ruby pauses to watch the man; he looks toward her and stops, too. Ruby moves on, but she is smiling. She is pleased to see him, pleased that he is still there.

The trail the Old Ones and Ruby travel is a narrow, rough animal trail marked by an occasional tuft of hair – elk, bear – mapped over terrain suitable for thick pads and hooves, four powerful legs. It leads up steep hillsides and plunges down others. Atop one slope where trees are thin the path is clearly coated with the shine of ice. Abruptly the Old Ones leave the trail behind and take off through the forest. Even though Ruby is limping, the pace picks up. The Old Ones, after almost a full day of a somewhat leisurely pace, seem to have a destination.

When dusk turns to gloom, Ruby doesn't notice that she isn't stumbling in the near dark, doesn't notice that she can see where to place her feet. Yes, she does see that the Old Ones still carry a white aura and if asked, she'd tell you this is the reason she doesn't stumble over roots and rocks. When she does it is because she is too tired to lift her feet. That is the reason, when the Old Ones stop atop a short ridge of rock protruding from a hill, when the young one steps down between a break in the stones, Ruby balks. Her legs are trembling and she fears she will tumble headlong if she tries to follow.

The young one reaches for her; Ruby takes his long fingers for support and once more trusts herself to his care. At the base of the ridge an animal has dug a small cave – an animal that no doubt will vacate the area as long as the Old Ones are near. The young one digs the snow away from the entrance. Inside, Ruby's body heat with the help of the cedar soon warms the small space. Blue light from the child makes the rough stone seem more welcoming than it is – the hard floor, the smell of old bones, musk – Ruby's own smell and that of the animals whose home she has invaded.

Dreamless sleep welcomes Ruby. Once she wakes to the crack of a breaking stick, but safe in the protection of the Old Ones she doesn't try to identify the source. Despite the sleep, the next morning Ruby is stiff and sore, the ache in her hip deep and insistent. She is glad the young one doesn't offer meat; she knows she can't eat, won't be able to keep it down. Fevered exhaustion is settling into Ruby's bones, licks its way into the reservoir of her organs.   The young one brings something else instead.   He loops a cedar ribbon over Ruby's head.   From it hangs a woven bag with a wide top under a covering flap. Dried berries, hazelnuts, bear fat – dried, pounded.   Ruby manages a bite or two.   The old woman stands on the rocks above, watching.

Incredibly Ruby lasts for several more days. At night she is barely conscious of the child; she can hardly tell the difference between sleep and her numb state during the day.   By the end of the third morning she is supported on each side by an Old One but still the old woman insists on going further.

This morning, they'd rejoined the hiking trail traveled the first few days of the journey – back when Ruby hoped to be home by noon, or in a few days at most.   But the trail had ended when the group arrived at the meadow where the shale bed had once been, the shale that had nearly ended Ruby's life.   There was the hump of Salal where Ruby had landed when the Old Ones had plucked her to safety.   The path ended at the meadow's edge where one of the Old Ones had destroyed the meadow that day, had sent shale and meadow off the cliff's edge into the ravine below.   More to the point, the Old One had destroyed the path.   Now there is only a broad gash where the mountain's flank had been and no way to reach the trail on the other side. The old woman turns south toward the broad ravine below.

Without hesitation she plunges down the steep slope sending rocks rolling, and small landslides tumbling.   One of the two Old Ones supporting Ruby slides an arm around her shoulders, lifts her and follows the old woman. By the time they are near the bottom the Old One is running so as not to fall, or perhaps she is falling as much as running.   At the bottom, she places Ruby on a rock on the bank of a fast-running creek. Barely conscious, Ruby slumps.

At the bottom of the ravine, the group moves under the trees beside a deep pool.   Above, the creek zigzags down the steep northeastern wall. Small pools dot its path, spill again in a long cascade of water over stone.   The biggest rocks have a white cap of snow but the water washes it from others. The result is something like the spotted horses of the desert - or the camouflage of hunters. At first the rushing water is one sound overwhelming all others; then it separates, becomes background to many small drips and splashes.

The old woman squats beside Ruby, pushes something against Ruby's lips. Ruby opens her eyes, straightens and sniffs. Osha and something else. Beside her the old woman softly hums as Ruby chews the tough roots to pulp, waits for their effect.

Ruby's pulse quickens, strengthens; her mind clears. In front of her bends the old woman gently rubbing her hands over Ruby's sore legs. So close. Ruby studies her. Gray hair raked back from her face reaches her thick shoulders. The hair on her body is short and almost translucent, perhaps the effect of the white shimmer around her. The old woman looks up; the two are eye to eye, dark eyes and those still darker. In the eyes of the old woman is compassionate power, sureness that needs no reference to personal confidence. Something stirs in Ruby. Something important that she can't recall.

But the old woman turn aside, points to the falling water, traces a path with her finger up the side of one cascade, across the outer edge of a pool and on to the next. Ruby is disbelieving! The climb is not so difficult in itself, but in her present state, Ruby doubts she can walk *down* the valley of the ravine never mind climb up the slippery waterfalls. Ruby had assumed they were headed down the valley in order to pick up the trail on the other side of the rock slide and hence to the car park. Ruby wasn't sure how in her present state she would manage driving off the mountain, but she'd assumed that was the plan. But climb?! Ruby is incredulous.

Nevertheless, the old woman extends her hand. Ruby takes it, stands and the old woman leads her to the falling water. The first few steps aren't difficult as there is an angled open channel between large stones. Ruby scoots sideways between them. From there a tumble of small rocks heads upward. The old woman leads, Ruby decides to crawl – cold stone biting into her knees through the almost threadbare pants – rather than try to keep balance and muster strength. If she allowed the smallest space for doubt to open, she'd sprawl on the rocks wet with spray and go to sleep, not wake up again – an impulse she has had so many times during the seeming never-ending journey. But, of course, she doesn't.

The old woman is one step ahead, her eyes on Ruby's every move. They reach a tall, round rock. Ruby stands, braces against it to see the way around. The only possible way leads beneath the waterfall, a narrow place where the water gathers and thunders over a flat stone. Ruby considers. She could continue to crawl but in the water, duck her head against the impact of the falling water. Would it mash her flat and trap her there?

A tap on the shoulder redirects her attention. The old woman points her in the other direction. On the other side of the big stone is a route that can only be seen when standing next to the falls. Between bank and stone is a cleft. Ruby squeezes through and finds a bay, the result of spring melt when the creek is double its present size. The alcove is cluttered with small stones, but is remarkably dry, protected from the snow by trees above. Their roots eroded, they lie almost horizontal, a sort of roof.

But the old woman does not stop. In two steps she is across and climbing another rough area of fallen stone. Ruby, her knees bruised and scraped, moves closer to the bank and clings to roots. Hand over hand Ruby pulls herself upward. Her focus is so much on hands and feet that she is surprised when she arrives at another wall of protruding stone. Leaning against it, she feels her way around and there finds a small tributary to the roaring creek.

The rivulet is narrow and shallow but over time it has cut a deep break. There is no place to walk except in the creek and that is where the old woman stands. Ruby hesitates; the old woman reaches for her. Ruby takes her hand and collapses against her side. The old woman half drags, half carries Ruby around the next bend. There the old woman deposits her beside a small pool – an alcove that is the spring's origin. Bright green ferns hang on the steep sides, moss stretches into the water. Here there is no winter. It is a place heated by the fire within the earth, and, like all springs, it is medicine. But this spring – like several others in the Olympics – belongs to the Old Ones. No one finds it easily. Actually, no one will find it at all.

A white cloud of steam rises from the warm pool – is trapped by the ferns and branches above, collects, joins the melt of snowflakes, drips in long threads back into the pool. Ruby sleeps where the old woman placed her. Slowly her body warms. Muscles relax. Fed by the complex chemistry of the water, her breath deepens.

Evening comes early to this sheltered spot. At dusk the banks fade, the plants above too, leaving only the rising white mist. Ruby watches the mist disappear. Or does it coalesce? In the dark the pool seems to expand, become a broad black place with here and there a glint of light. It is not reflected starlight because the thick snow laden clouds ride low across the mountains. The source is elsewhere.

Ruby isn't sure when she first begins to hear the music. By the time she notices, it is already fully present. The notes are each continuous – no rise and fall, no measured silence between, but like the mountain's voice – a single sustained sound. One is very high, similar to the voice of the mountain but not quite the same. Between it and the lowest note spread all the others.

As Ruby listens, orbs of pastel light appear above the pool's surface, the colors mainly variants of blue and lavender, but a few are dusty pink, others palest green. They float in the air – rise a short distance then slowly drop again. Ruby cannot determine whether they are the source of the sounds, or if each color is paired with a particular note. The music, the bobbing movements enthrall her. Three lavender ones, closely grouped, rise; their notes dominate for a moment before they are joined by one that is the gray-green of dry moss and several the lovely shade of summer sky. Ruby bends to drink.

Though innocent of the world, Ruby is not child-like. To her, life is not benign; she knows it doesn't respond well to people who can't see where trouble and danger lie. While Ruby lives separately from others, her limited interaction with them – and with nature – rests on the knowledge that both are capable of great destruction as well as great beauty – sometimes both in the same event.   At the interface, as Ruby learned from Marianne and her grandfather, is the responsibility of each person to see, to hear and know, to be wise – even sometimes wise enough to surrender.   But at the moment none of this applies. Ruby's attention is rapt. She is indeed child-like. There is no space, no distance between her and the music, the light.

For hours she is mesmerized, watches the spirit lights rise and fall, listens to the variants in the music as they do. Before midnight the lights move closer to Ruby, shrink by half, their color deepens.   Ruby can smell them now – not like flowers, roots, not mineral or stone, but something breathed into the mind.   Medicine. They come no closer, but instead Ruby moves, is lifted to join them, supported inches above the water, surrounded by a column of twisted pastel strands.

Ruby feels her cells realign, the center of gravity change. The orbs shift, become the many-colored cup of an unopened lily, Ruby at the center. Or perhaps the center is the dark cup of a candle's flame. Ruby feels heat behind her eyes, unsure of where she is.

For a startled moment, Ruby wobbles and almost falls into the pool. Now she is not inside a flower, not in the center of the flame, not even in her own body. She is in the deepest interior of the old woman's psyche; looks from the old woman's eyes – sees herself hovering over the water held by the lights – sees Ruby. This is nothing like the images the old woman uses to communicate, and certainly not like the visit of the old woman to Ruby's mind. Ruby is not Ruby. Or at least, at the moment, she is not. But, oddly, she is not disturbed.

The pool, the lights, Ruby – all blink out. In their place is a green meadow. It is the same meadow as the dream, or vision, that Ruby had inside the blue cave, and when she was on the ledge. It is the vision in which Ruby saw herself as a small child sitting among the flowers, saw Marianne's surprise to find her alone on the mountain. Of course, as Marianne quickly saw, the child hadn't been alone – the Old Ones were in the trees beyond. It is that meadow, just as it was before, that Ruby sees again. Everything the same. But not for long.

Images flutter, dissolve; new ones form. Ruby sees the old woman, the young one. With them is a large group of Old Ones in a circle. They are singing a low-pitched song like the moan of wind. At the center of the circle is a woman who is about the age and size of the young one. Slowly the woman turns her face towards Ruby, looks directly at her. Ruby recognizes the dark eyes. They are her own.

Ruby gasps and this time really would have fallen into the water if the old woman had not caught her. She lifts Ruby back to the mossy bank. One at a time, the balls of light pop. The last to go brightens, intensifies, first turquoise followed by a last long moment of cobalt. Then, it is gone leaving the white steam.   Only then does Ruby see the narrow band of light around her hands, around her body.

But Ruby doesn't question what she sees, or the vision. She tilts her head back, closes her eyes. Her face is suffused with unchecked emotion – the vulnerability of bliss – response to something unnamable. Similar to what Ruby feels when she is moved by beauty, captured by the angle of light on water, the chitter of birds, the morning prints of a night creature's passing. But only similar.

Ruby is elevated, concentrated and yet also broadened. The elk breaking a path through the snow, the squirrel asleep in the burrow – all these are held simultaneously – precious, loved – become sublime like the song of the mountains, the answering glitter of the stars. Marianne, her grandfather, her sisters – they have been returned as family, but in a bigger emotional geography. Ruby *knows*, though she couldn't tell you what.

Though Ruby doesn't see it, the light around her body, the aura, expands, covers the surface of the pool, becomes deepest, darkest blue - water and light inseparable. The old woman – so still throughout – finally moves, cups the lighted water in her big hand and washes Ruby's face. Ruby leans into the Old One's palm; gratitude joins bliss in a heady mix. Ruby opens her eyes, bends and drinks again; the liquid blue light drips between her fingers. Ruby remembers the dancer, the constellation in the sky, the fire of her skirts, the diamonds – colors that here by the pool have become water.

Above the banks of the spring, first-light outlines the trees. Though still an exquisite oasis of warmth in winter, the water has returned to its normal appearance. Ruby strips, enters the water and bathes, washes her hair. She doesn't need soap or silt; the heat and chemistry of the pool are enough. When she has finished, the old woman is gone, but Ruby isn't disturbed. She knows the way down the falls, the way back to the blue child.

Ruby works her wet body back into wet clothes. The water has taken the rawness from Ruby's feet. At long last, she takes the carefully hoarded second pair of socks from her coat pocket and puts them on, and then her boots. Like Ruby's other clothes, the boots no longer fit. Ruby's sweater – worn, stained, unraveling in places – hangs in limp folds. The belt is pulled as tight as possible, and clings to the boney niche above Ruby's hip. Her cheeks are scooped hollows, her jawbone a sharp slash. Anyone chancing upon Ruby would assume she was in the final stages of starvation. Perhaps she is, but not in important ways. Ruby's spirit is fed. It is fed by beauty, by confident belonging, by love. She is not surprised at the absence of meat, or even roots – there will be no breakfast, but before leaving, Ruby drinks for the third time from the warm spring.

Compared to the stumbling climb up the cascading creek, Ruby is stronger. She still needs the support of stone and bank to make her way down, even crawls in places, but not with the exhaustion of before, nor the feeling that more is required than she can possibly give. Shaky, she arrives at the bottom, watches the Old Ones materialize from the trees, the young one with the blue child in his arms.

The route the group takes follows the canyon. They reach the high pile of shale and earth deposited by the landslide to find their passage blocked, the rushing water shoved from its banks. The Old Ones find it easier to walk in the creek's new muddy channel than climb the still unstable hill. Though the young one is beside her, Ruby steps in unassisted, finds her balance, and arrives intact on the other side – wet and cold but grateful she can again depend on her body's strength. The ravine wall gives way to an uphill forested slope and this is the direction the old woman leads them.

It is nightfall by the time they successfully detour the destroyed meadow and are back on the trail. It isn't far to the cedar nursery of new trees where Ruby first saw the cobalt woman, heard her cries in the night. This is where the Old Ones stop for the day, but this time Ruby doesn't lie at the center of the circular nursery, doesn't curl up in the depression left by the roots of the mother tree. It is filled with snow; if Ruby slept there it wouldn't be long until she was lying in a bowl of cold water. Instead she is under the shelter of a broad arm of a big cedar at the edge of the nursery. *Cedar*, always there; always willing.

Lying next to the child, covered by the remnants of the cedar bed, Ruby lies awake. The larger trees are scalloped with snow. She watches them fade into night, but just before they disappear altogether, color flickers – a hint of green like the polar lights. First it brushes the length of one tree and then another – a memory of spring dancing from tree to tree as if each is lit by a single taper.

Ruby's tired eyes droop toward sleep. To stay awake, she props on one elbow. There, where the mother tree once stood, is the barely visible outline of the cobalt lady. Ruby might not have seen her at all if not for the bright flame at her breast. It is a relief that the woman is not crying – her tears seem always to mean trouble.

As Ruby watches, the woman's hair grows longer, writhes out from her head in long ropes of turquoise and cobalt light that twist like snakes. Ruby is reminded of the black woman in the constellation of laughing children. Surely she and the cobalt woman are not the same. Color fills the nursery, reflects off the snow. In Ruby's arms the child's color brightens. Ruby feels heat at her own heart and behind her eyes.

But Ruby is tired. She wants to sleep. It's been a long day full of questions Ruby doesn't want to think about. What she doesn't need is more questions, more puzzles. At the moment neither will serve. All effort and strength must be used to get the child home. Ruby lies down and is asleep in an instant. The nursery, like the pool, is sacred ground to the Old Ones. Until dawn it is filled with blue light.

Ruby wakes to bone-chilling fog. It is still snowing lightly. Cold and hunger penetrate so deeply, she doesn't feel them anymore. She is as light as an autumn leaf. Thought is a series of impressions, not all of them her own. Her mind is without boundary. Perhaps it has always been this way. Maybe Ruby has been too enmeshed with spirit to claim a separate self. And now, given that she doesn't know who she is, the question of what is hers and not hers is moot. Ruby no longer fights for identity. She is content to be the snow, next year's spring breeze.

Even though Ruby is almost without human substance since her visit to the pool, she still has strength to continue. In the fog and the snow she can see only a few feet ahead. The path appears before her as she moves – a landscape of snow over green so dark it is almost black. With the child's weight cradled in both arms, each foot lifted high in the deep snow, Ruby makes her way to the main trail.

There she finds the old woman and the young one waiting quietly – no one else, just these two. The old woman silently takes the child and the young one gives Ruby meat that is torn, shredded. To Ruby's surprise it is not the usual raw offering but is dry, stiff jerky. She tucks a piece inside her cheek, lets it soften there, lets its stored medicine seep into her body. The old woman breaks trail through the snow that would otherwise reach well above Ruby's knees. The cold, clean air saturated with fir and cedar, with the ozone of more snow in the making sears the sinuses and throat. But Ruby is now the mountain's child, and the cold has become food.

If the distance into the mountains is the same as that leaving, there is only one night left before they reach the parking lot and Ruby's car. The snow slows them, but Ruby is stronger now and that makes the difference. Ruby remembers that first night between the logs, her fear, the slime of fish on her hands. Was it possible that was only a few days ago? If days were measured in change, it would be lifetimes.

Ruby stops often to drink at sluggish creeks. The jerky needs water's help to tease the benefit from the stringy meat. Elk, Ruby finally decides. At midday the fog dissipates and is replaced by more snow. Ruby stops beside a small creek, clears away the snow, rests her knees against the bank to bend and drink. The water is frozen, but beneath a blur of ice, Ruby can see the slow current. Pockets of air trapped there make bubbles that elongate with the current. There are no tracks of creatures come to drink, no bird song. Only the occasional groan of an overburdened limb, the hiss of slipping snow, the crack of ice becoming colder – all the sounds of deepening winter. Even the Skunk Cabbage would be frozen, its leaves of no medicinal value; Osha retreated beneath earth as hard as stone. The spirits of the plants are still there; Ruby can feel them, but they've retreated to their essence, sleep in roots fattened by sun and rain and now transformed by winter.

With the side of her fist, Ruby punches the ice. Where it breaks she pulls away the shards to expose the liquid below, dips the freezing water to her lips and sucks it from her cupped hands. Its traces an icy path down the center of her body. Ruby's hands are red, speckled with splotches of white – probably frost-bite. Then she recalls the warm spring, the orbs of light. Her body warms, but Ruby doesn't know if it is only memory or if the spirit of that powerful place is with her. At any rate, her hands still shimmer with a corona of light.

Once more on the trail, following the familiar and comforting back of the old woman, Ruby forgets to eat. The young one nudges her, points to the meat in her pocket. The snowfall thickens. Ruby thinks about the parking lot and the car. If they make it that far – and it seems now that they will –

can she drive through the deep snow? Will good tires and a high-centered car be enough? Will the stark reality of blizzard on an already treacherous mountain road do what – so far – the red spirit hasn't done?

Ruby doesn't falter, chews one mouthful of meat after the other, drinks, walks behind the old woman. Usnea hangs in long hanks from under the snow on the limbs of nearby trees. The inner bark of alder is behind a frozen exterior. *Alder*, medicine to use once in a lifetime.

Roots are locked inside the frozen earth. Starvation food draws Ruby's attention. It is her body's message, its assessment of her state, its effort to direct her attention to possible remedies. Cold, light – even love – are sufficient food for only so long before the body gives up and allows spirit to take all. Ruby centers her attention on the path. One more night, one more night...

When darkness comes, the old woman plows on. In the deep night she moves to a frozen creek. Under a spectacular cedar she scrapes the snow away, making an entrance to what is essentially an ice cave. To Ruby's surprise the young one crawls inside first. Ruby follows, reaches for the child, but the old woman doesn't relinquish her. Instead, she also crawls beneath the tree. The young one pushes Ruby to the tree's base, sits beside her. The old woman takes her place on the other side.

While Ruby and the Old Ones have been through so much together and she has learned to care deeply for them, the physical mass of their presence in an enclosed space is still unsettling. The two Old Ones begin to hum in unison, a buzz somewhat like the slide of seeds inside a hide rattle. Ruby feels the vibration of the Old Ones' music move into her chilled organs, send tremors along the nerves, envelop her. The old woman places the blue child in Ruby's arms. In the damp air the child's hair is tight ringlets around her pretty face. Her breath steady, blue light strong, she doesn't seem affected by the cold. Tears brighten Ruby's eyes. Somehow, she has to save this child and that means Ruby has to live.

When morning comes, the cave of snow beneath the tree is filled with a brighter light than the sun's pale offering. Ruby anticipates its coalescence into the mass of the Old Ones. First the young one materializes close to Ruby, his arm pressing against hers. The remaining light gathers and then the old woman is there, too, sitting beside the entrance. On the flat of her palm a white spark glitters. Lifting her hand near her mouth she blows it at Ruby. Ruby doesn't see it travel the space between them, only feels it penetrate – similar to what happened at the pool. The old woman hums. Ruby feels the place inside her chest answer like a tuning fork. The young one murmurs, Ruby's heart vibrates.

As the last day on the mountain begins, the snow stops. No fog either. The sky, still overcast, still hiding the upper mountains, lifts. The snow-laden forest, branches weighted, sap in the roots, is not asleep. Ruby hears the subliminal voice, the conversation between the mountains. She hears the resonance near her heart, no translation required, no effort. Ruby would not put it into words, but if she did, she would say she is the tree, just as she is the mountain and the water. If she were to check – which she won't – she would tell you that she can also hear the voices from the north side of the Peninsula, the ocean, the struggling elk pawing the white blanket from moss and grass. She would also know precisely from where on the mountain the red creature watches her progress. But she is engaged with the questions of the moment. Is she leaving the Old Ones when she leaves the mountains? If so who will help her?

Even in winter's guise Ruby begins to recognize the terrain: a fir growing horizontally from a hillside and halted in mid-fall by roots bound in stone; parallel to the trail a long hump of rotten trunk is home to a line of seedlings; a big boulder split evenly in two by events difficult to imagine. The slope is steep and for the first time in many days Ruby thinks of her staff. After all she has been through without it, Ruby's cold lips twitch – Ruby's version of a smile. What a luxury she will think the staff in future – if there is one.

Above the parking lot, the Old Ones stop. Ruby remembers how it looked when she arrived – the purple bark of the firs – the tint of their gray skin, the black of their green fronds; snowberries floating like tiny spirits on thin sticks; the bristle of red huckleberry stems, the few berries that didn't remotely suggest the bright red of summer, yet were still beautiful. The sponge of dead evergreen needles underfoot, the orange stump of a fallen cedar. Now everything is shadows of gray and pale blue on white. Yet Ruby doesn't want to leave – the watching presence of the mountain; the cleansing cold falling from the glaciers above and rising from the ice-bound earth. But Ruby has to leave for the sake of the child, and also because in the harsh winter conditions of the mountains the Old Ones have kept Ruby alive as long as they can.

The old woman interrupts Ruby's sadness, the melancholy extension of love, the human longing never quite appeased. The Old One's hand is heavy on Ruby's shoulder. Nearby, the young one scrapes snow and ice, packs it down until it resembles a bench. With the old woman on one side of her and the young one standing guard on the trail, the images begin. There is no invasion now, only a complex internal resonance to sound.

In the first image, Ruby sees herself and the child in the car. They are alone – no Old Ones – no help. Once Ruby leaves the sanctuary of the Old Ones she will enter a spiritual chasm between the mountains and the places where people live, one the Old Ones cannot cross. Between here and there, Ruby is on her own. On the other side there are other Old Ones, relatives, and they may help when needed.

While the red reptile cannot touch her in the crossing, he will tempt her to stop by her own choice before she arrives on the other side. If she succumbs, everything is over. The blue child will die. The chasm, the old woman adds, is a place of illusion. Ruby must hang on to what she knows, what she is, and only that. The Old One does not say "who" she is, but "what."

The Old One has finished speaking but no one moves. It

is a hard parting. The old woman's tall bulk shimmers; Ruby, stick-like in comparison, is momentarily eclipsed. The Old Ones rumble, a sound like rolling boulders. From far up the mountain is an answer – it is the mountain herself – her high-pitched song. Or is it the cobalt woman? Nevertheless, the song rolls down the glaciers, gathers its skirts in narrow canyons, rebounds from stone, slips across frozen meadows – stirs the roots of *Osha*, the frozen mud of *Bear Medicine* and *Devil's Club*, the last sweet scent of fading *Ginger* beneath the ice. In their hidden places, medicine pools dance. The bear in her cave, as near to the earth's heart as she can come, dreams. A band of wolves following the herd of elk pause and sing too. The blue child stirs, settles again against the breast of the old woman, sleeps. Silence.

The old woman, the young one and Ruby descend the last slope. In the car-park the young one digs a stout branch from beneath the snow. He is unwilling to touch the metal of Ruby's car but uses the limb to brush the heaped snow from roof, hood and windshield; bangs the ice loose from the frozen lock of the door; clears a few feet of path in front of the tires all the way to the bridge above the waterfall. Ruby digs in the snow behind the wheel to find the keys where she left them but they are frozen in place. Half lying in the snow she kicks them free with the heel of her boot. She is wondering what will happen if it is the snow that stops her, not illusions, but deep snow. Ruby knows not to ask.

Preparations for departure completed, Ruby takes the blue child one last time from the arms of the Old One. They turn, trudge across the lot, climb. At the bench, the young one turns. No wave of goodbye. No music. Ruby looks him fully in the eye. Something stirs, but before it is more, he turns to follow the old woman back into the woods. To the right movement in the rocks above the bridge catches Ruby's eye. There at the rocky cliff's edge above the rushing creek, wrapped in furs, is the man. He stares at Ruby with the same intensity as when he was on the smaller bridge deep in the wilderness. She can only conclude that he has followed her, and for some reason the Old Ones have allowed it. What's more, he is not on the mountainside of the creek but already across the bridge. There are no tracks on the bridge, none in the lot, so Ruby doesn't know how he got where he is.

She turns to the car, fits the key into the lock, moves the key back and forth, gently persuades it to open. With the child in her arms, Ruby awkwardly climbs inside. Rather than place the child on the seat where she might be knocked around as Ruby negotiates the rough patches on the washed-out road, Ruby eyes the stores in the back seat. She pulls the blanket free, puts it on the floor and wraps the child in its warm folds.

Ruby is relieved when the car starts. She lets the engine warm, takes a deep breath and inches forward. She reaches the bridge, crosses it.   And then, in an explosion, everything disappears. No trees, no daylight, and more importantly, no road. Ruby and the child are inside an opaque world in which only they exist.

Chapter Ten

The story you are in has been going on for a hundred years, maybe longer. Now that story is in your care. It carries you, and me, all of us. Don't under-estimate the importance of what you do.

Agnes lit the fire hours ago. Logs sit on a bed of coals. In a small bowl on the table is cedar oil mixed with sage; a wick floats on the scented surface. Other than these there is no light, no lantern. The old shades, tattered at the edges, are drawn against the night. It is snowing hard, no wind, but coming down hard enough to be called blizzard.

Earlier in the afternoon, the last thing Agnes did before pulling the shades, closing the door, was gather her things from the truck – food, blankets, flashlight. This is no quick visit. What it is Agnes doesn't know, only what it isn't. When Grace called, it was clear that Ruby was in trouble and by now maybe Grace as well. Grace had asked her to sing for them, to use grandfather's drum. Agnes is wary; she knows the drum's power and that it belongs only to Ruby. Nevertheless it sits on the chair beside her. She will know when it is time.

Shadows form in the corners of the room, shapes in the flicker of firelight. Spirits have come to visit, to help Agnes do what she must. The small blue light on the oil shrinks to the merest spark. Agnes is remembering her mother, remembering what Marianne said about the wreck in which her mother died. She'd said her daughter's death was caused by "trouble" which was Marianne's short-hand for evil work. Purposeful. Directed. Marianne did not know why her daughter had been rushing home on a weekday night when she did not usually come until the weekend. No one knew what she'd seen or felt that caused her to drive so carelessly. Agnes only knew that Marianne was unsure if her daughter was the target. She seemed to think it might have been Agnes.

Agnes respected everything Marianne taught, but she couldn't credit this one opinion. Agnes knew she didn't have her mother's remarkable spiritual gifts nor could she bear to think her mother died in her stead. There is only one memory intact from that night. It is not the wreck, not sitting afterwards on the cold beach waiting for her mother's voice. It is instead her mother singing grandfather's song. She'd looked over the seat at Agnes and said, "Sing, Agnes. Sing."

Over and over grandfather sang his song to her and Grace, imprinting the drum's beat deep in the spirit. He and Marianne protected the girls, taught them how to protect themselves. They'd also taught them how to differentiate the call of the spirit from false voices; this is one reason Agnes is so exasperated at being tricked earlier.

The walls recede, leaving only Agnes, the fire and the drum. There is a sharp crack against the outside of the house, a thump as if a tree has fallen. For just a moment Agnes sees her beautiful mother sitting at the table, but the table is in Marianne's house long before "trouble" came to them. She is smiling at Agnes. "Sing."

It is time. Agnes sits forward, picks up the drum and starts the beat. The drum is round and big, its voice deep and resonate. As Agnes settles into the steady rhythm, the house itself becomes drum, picks up the slow measured beat, sends it over the salt water, up the creeks and ravines of the mountains. An owl outside stirs, hoots, spreads its wings and flies northeast through the snow.

Agnes sings; she drums, settles into her belly, prepares for a long night. Ruby needs her. She follows the path of the owl, sings her way onto the mountain. From there, she is pulled by the voices of her grandmother and grandfather until she is in the cave with Ruby, filling it with the sound. She sees the red creature, the snakes, but can make little sense of them. The battle is intense, the outcome unpredictable, but when Agnes sees the child, the small bundle in Ruby's arms, she is distracted. Could she be right? Is the child blue?

She is distracted, that is, until she hears Grace's voice. Agnes sings with Grace to save Ruby and then Grace is gone, the battle over. Before the last scene fades she watches Ruby, still carrying the child, leave the meadow following the Old

Ones. The blue flame on the table lengthens, brightens, casting a blue wash over all, even Agnes.

It is over. The house settles. But the owl is on the mountain, and it will not be back soon. Agnes wraps herself in blankets before the fire. Sleep comes easily. Perhaps it is the comforting spirits in the room.

Early the next morning Agnes adds wood to the coals, drinks tea from Ruby's stash. *Swamp tea* grows in bogs mixed with look alike noxious neighbors. But Agnes does not cook breakfast, nor pull food from her stash of dried meat and jars of canned fish. She will not eat again until her sisters arrive. Tea, yes, but no food. She is in the spirit world now; the only food will be food for the spirit.

Every morning for the next several days Agnes goes to the beach at low tide. There a sand spit protrudes. Even though it snows heavily day after day and she can see nothing, Agnes walks its length. She looks first to the northeast and then southwest. Nothing. She clears the snow from the roof, shovels it from around the house, puts chains on the tires of her pickup – just in case – and makes an inventory of Ruby's shelves and bins, baskets and jars. Agnes stacks wood in the wood box beside the fireplace and doubles the size of the one outside the door. Chops more. For long periods she studies the beautiful drawings of plants that cover one wall. Agnes knows they are by Ruby's hand and that each captures a plant at its peak, its essence.

It is during the mindless task of chopping, stacking that Agnes suddenly feels the pit of her stomach give way. She props the axe beside the door and goes inside. Hurriedly she shucks her coat, throws it on the nearest chair, closes the shades. With shaking hands she lights the wick in the bowl of oil, throws sticks of wood on the fire. In less than a minute she is drumming, singing just as intensely as the night Grace joined her. Agnes waits; Grace doesn't come. She dare not think about what that means, but only that she must drum for Ruby. Agnes sings, but even louder – much louder – is the drum, its deep hollow notes like the heartbeat of the mountain. Or the mother to the unborn child.

If you look behind Agnes' chair and have the right gift, you'll see her mother standing there, and also Marianne. They are singing with Agnes, the intensity of their focus is to pull Ruby home. Ruby, the strange child from the mountain, must find her way back to her people, to her family. Marianne is sure that Ruby is wearing the cedar bracelet; it will help her make the crossing, find the way back.

Marianne knows what Ruby is even if Ruby is not sure. It took years to accept the truth. From her place among the ancestors – the generations of family – Marianne is unsure that when Ruby dies she will join them. It grieves Marianne to think this is true, but she knows that her work is only one part in a complex story. And right now, even from the land of the dead, her work continues; right now it is to help Agnes and through her Ruby. Ruby must come back once more from the mountains; she mustn't be lost between dimensions. This intention had always guided the struggle of Marianne, her husband, and while he lived, Marianne's father – to anchor Ruby in their world without denying what she was, what she had to have to live among the people. As much as they loved Ruby, they knew that there would probably come a time when she did not come home again. But that time is not now. Ruby must make this last, most difficult return. What she is bringing is a gift from the stars. Even from her current perspective Marianne does not fully understand why it is so important, she only knows that what Ruby carries will save the people. Knows she brings a child, much as Marianne did on a spring day so many years ago.

When Agnes puts the drum down, the fire is low, the flame in the pool of oil still bright. Sunlight outlines the pulled shades. The usually grounded Agnes feels disoriented. The feeling reminds her of an incident that happened in the desert at the Pow Wow, the one she attended with Grace. One afternoon during a break between events, Agnes climbed into the rimrock. From there she could see the white mountains of the Cascades. Wild horses grazed on a green bank. She watched a hawk skim low to the ground in hot pursuit of a prairie dog.

But what caught Agnes' eye was a collection of rocks or perhaps only one rock carved by wind. It stood at a point where the ridge ended. Behind it was an alcove of sorts, probably the home of rabbits or winter shelter for a bobcat. Agnes was curious. When she came nearer she saw that the only approach was a narrow vein of stone in a long curve from the top. Agnes dropped to a crawl. But halfway to her destination she had second thoughts. The rocks under her hands were not as stable as they'd looked from above. Some were ready to roll from the mesa to join the tumble below. Agnes placed her hand on a stone preparing to reverse direction but it was too late. The stone slipped from its place, grated against its neighbors, and fell. Agnes tumbled with it.

At the moment of falling she seemed to be in several places at once – she was falling, she was still on the narrow ledge and she was on the mesa's top still contemplating the curious formation. Afterwards Agnes was never sure quite what happened. At the time she'd taken it as a warning and returned to the Pow Wow.

But the feeling of last summer is with her now. Is Ruby safe? Or is she still lost? And what about Agnes herself? Is she still beside the flooded dam? Searching for the way through the snow-covered foothills? Agnes rummages on Ruby's shelves. *Violet.* Bring the spirit where the body is, bring it firmly and fully "here." While the tea steeps she raises the shades to sunlight. A break between storms, it won't last long. Outside, cup in hand, Agnes sits on a driftwood log, watches the ducks fish, the seagulls quarrel over the deposits of the tide. Soon now. Grace would be here soon. And possibly Ruby.

***

From a shoulder of the mountain, the cobalt woman watches Ruby. The beautiful blue woman can do nothing else, nothing to help.

The Old Ones, in their light forms, are taking care of neglected work – nourishing their young, singing to the stars, reassuring the restless bear, lulling her back to sleep. Except for one group; among them are the old woman and the young one. They are in a green meadow beneath a rock escarpment. In a circle they sing. Only one sits; a woman, the old woman's hand is on her shoulder. The woman sitting is not old as the Old Ones measure, but she is not so young either. She'd seen the human woman called Ruby beside the hot magical pool, and looked her in the eye. The old woman feels a sad sigh escape from the lips of the sitting woman, the lift of her shoulders. It had been a big sacrifice, but there was no other choice, no other way. The life of the earth was at risk. Dark powers had learned how to call the old medicine from the cave and the sky. They who called it were excited, it made them rabid for more. More. The group of Old Ones sing, the song surprisingly gentle. They are singing about hope, singing for Ruby. They are singing across time.

***

Grace does not even know there is another crisis. In her work even though she is not part of every battle, she at least knows where they are being fought, about what issues, who the players are. Not so now. Grace is in the air again, flying from Albuquerque to Seattle.

Because of air flight schedules, Grace had spent the previous night in a motel near the airport to catch an early morning flight. A long hot bath in the rose-scented bath salts and after a long luxurious sleep, Grace had felt restored, ready for the long flight above the north/south length of the desert and plains and into the mountains of the northwest. When she lands in Seattle, she intends to head for Ruby's cabin, to meet Agnes there. Together they will look for Ruby.

Grace revisits her last day with Charley, remembers the last image of Ruby from the night she and Charley sang – Ruby walking through the dark with enormous creatures, disappearing into the forest surrounded by them just seconds before the vision faded altogether, replaced by a few remaining bright coals in the fireplace. Grace was silent, not sure when she'd finally stopped singing. But Charley sang long into the night.

Finally, his voice dropped to a low, almost inaudible chant – a rumble in the chest – and stopped. Still he sat for a long time, the winter night stretched time as it does sometimes to accommodate human need. He stirred, built the fire again, lifted the pot of soup from the cold stove in the corner to the hearth. When it was warm, he directed Grace toward it. Exhausted, trembling still with the power of the song, she didn't think she could eat, but collected bowl and spoon anyway; dished a scant half-bowl of the warmed meat and roots. To her relief Charley made coffee – no more tea – and when she'd eaten all she could, he poured a cup for her, handed the can of milk. If food was not welcome, coffee surely was. The fire, the pan of soup, the used bowls, the pot of coffee – the clutter spread before the fire made a rough picnic.

When the window lightened with the first hint of day, Charley hobbled to the boxes chanting again, put the things he'd placed there back in their small packets, tucked them in one of the boxes – except for one small root that he folded into his palm. On the table he dipped water into a clean pan, placed most of the root in it, and deposited the pan at the edge of the coals.

"Oh good," Grace thought. "More awful tea." The truth was Grace didn't think she could drink more of the tea she had the night before and also drive, much less cope with traffic, crowds. How would she make the transition from this ethereal state to the hubbub of an airport? She could, of course, but knew she'd feel distant and disembodied and if something other than normal routine happened, something that demanded extra attention or required strategy, her mind might become blank; she would draw suspicion.

But she needn't have worried. Charley had no intention to let her go so soon. Nor did he allow her to sleep. Charley didn't speak much, but he communicated clearly. He gestured toward her coat and Grace almost groaned. The sun was barely up; it was the coldest part of the day and Grace felt feather-light.

She bundled up; Charley donned a thick wool sweater under an oilskin coat. He turned the damper down on the fire and led her outside. Though the sun would not make an appearance today, the snow had stopped falling, the clouds had lifted. Just as she suspected Grace could see clearly the nest where the cabin rested between cliff on one side, heaped flat stones in front, the curved road leading up the hill.

Charley kicked his way through the snow, led her to the cabin's back. He didn't stop at the woodshed, or the lean-to for drying meat and herbs, the white mound that could be sweathouse, peyote church, or for some other ceremonial purpose. For a moment Grace wondered if the tea she'd drunk was mushroom instead of herb, then rejected the question. She'd seen the bits of plant in the liquid.

The mesa wall was tall and straight, dappled red stone and snow. Behind the shed, Charley threaded a path between boulders. Grace was mystified. They were headed to the cliff. As they drew close she saw there was a break that climbed its entire height. A chimney of sorts, broken rock, a steep trail – Charley's back door escape, a strenuous shortcut to the mesa.

Surely not...but, yes, Charley began to climb. Grace sighed and followed, placing her hand and each foot exactly where he did. It was the only way – he'd know which rocks were stable and would bear a person's weight, and those that would tumble an uninvited guest to the cliff's stony base. Maybe in summer, she'd have enjoyed it, but light-headed as she was, cold and hungry, definitely not. But her preferences weren't consulted – not by Peg's mother, not by Charley, so Grace climbed following the agile old man.

The chimney was steep and before long Grace was panting, her legs trembling, arms burning with effort, but Charley didn't pause. A few feet from the top, half-hidden by a boulder was an opening to a wide crack that slanted upward.

As he neared the mesa top, Charley bent over as if to avoid being seen, though who would be there in this weather Grace couldn't think.

At its end, the crevasse was blocked by a long, low hump, but Charley continued to crawl, and disappeared under the pile of stones. Following, Grace entered a small, low-ceiling room, its stone walls barely visible in the dim light. It was frigid, colder than outside, as if the room was a cold-freeze for ice. Grace smelled the ash of old fires and hoped Charley would light one, but he didn't, He scooted across the floor and clattered about with the rocks. Soon he flipped a piece of heavy, gray cloth aside and light streamed inside. A door, an entrance – other than the hole in the floor.

The pearlescent light outside coming from all directions was caused by a high, but solid, cloud cover and the reflection off the snow. A dreamscape, the world as shamans describe it. But then, Grace reasoned, maybe she was in the land of shamans. She was quite sure that was what Charley was, a hereditary shaman, one you might pass in the grocery store with no recognition. Magic. But magic was hard work, its practitioners secret, not the result of only the right words for a few rituals – a life's work handed from one to the next over centuries, a sustained edifice of intention, discipline, humility but without doubt.

And that was what Charley did – he worked – worked to expand the door. In the distance was a mountain. Grace couldn't see its top hidden in the clouds, only the broad base beyond the mesas. It was perfectly aligned to the opening Charley made. Grace, ever one for the facts, looked around the circumference of the room. Yes, she could see several places where canvas was held in place by stones, each a potential door. She wondered what other views could be revealed and what their purpose was.

From his pocket, Charley pulled the sack of tobacco given to him by Grace, and rolled a cigarette. With a long match he lit it and without turning his face from the mountain, handed it to her. Though Grace doesn't smoke, she knew the protocol, so puffed and returned it, waited out the subsequent dizziness and nausea.

From another pocket Charley pulled a sack – paper – and emptied it in the central fire-pit. Herbs. When he lit it, Grace at first smelled sage, but its scent was soon over-shadowed by others – musky like the tea, and another, heavy and sweet. Without a hole in the roof, the room filled with thick smoke. Perhaps it was Charley's intention to smudge her entire body, clean it of accumulated influences, or perhaps impart a resistant aura. If so, he was thorough.

Grace was not surprised when Charley began to chant. While he sang she watched the changing shadows on the distant mountain – the pale ridges, dark canyons. As the light shifted, color deepened on the northern edge. The base – broad and blue when Charley first opened the door, now seemed a bank of fog; the mountain floating above her earthy root. The eastern side shivered, losing shape and then finding it again. The spirit of the mountain was answering Charley's call.

Just as she knew not to check the periphery of her vision to dispel the spirits when they came, Grace knew not to shake her head, blink her eyes. At the center of the wavering mountain was a darker shadow, across it the hint of pale rainbow threads. As Charley chanted, the threads vibrated, changed hue. In the heart of the mountain was medicine, old power. Power that knew the voice of the shaman, remembered from her youth. It was the mountain – she and her sisters – who helped in the making of the first shaman, who taught the songs. Now, together – shaman and mountain – they worked to hold the world together, hold it against shattering evil.

Not that the power held by the mountain was evil. It was neutral, its impact directed by the intention of the one who controlled it. When too much turmoil – rage and fear – was present on the earth it had to be temporarily hidden, removed from human access. Temporary – sometimes thousands of years. During the long expanse clues were left in case the people forgot. Clues in the arrangement of stones, drawings – all to wake the mind of the people again, wake them to what their hearts had not forgotten.   If evil gained too much power, the people might become confused, even the shamans.   But that had not yet happened; old people, the shamans, remembered.

The mountain grew roots again, her heart hidden. Charley's voice whispered a few more lines and stopped. As he and Grace sat, the sky lowered a dark skirt and the first flakes of the next storm began. "Grace, Marianne's granddaughter," Charley began. "Some people have learned what they should not know. They want what is hidden. They have called this old power," he gestured toward the mountain. "These people would feed it their greed and cruelty so they can make the people slaves. We can hold on for a while longer. Not long. But help has been sent. When you find the child, bring her here to me." Grace could make rough sense of what Charley said until his last sentence.

With the door closed again, Charley and Grace squeezed the bulk of their winter clothes through the floor's hole, crawled to the chimney. Difficult as climbing up had been, going down was more so. Grace could not see Charley, where he placed his hands and feet, only where they had crushed the snow. She was careful to test each foothold, the placement of her fingers. When she arrived at the bottom, Charley was already gone.

Inside the cabin, Charley waited with a bowl of soup. Grace ate her fill. Before she left, Charley rubbed her hair with oil. It was scentless and red. He pulled a small bag from inside his shirt; with a boney finger he dug inside, pulled a dark blue stone threaded through with black twine, hung it around Grace's neck. When he motioned to her suitcase, Grace understood it was time to leave and she wanted to cry. She would have been content to stay with Charley, travel with him in summer, sing in winter. Wasn't that possible? Couldn't she work here with him? Wasn't it as important as any conference, as finding Ruby? And the mysterious child.

Charley stood on the other side of the table watching her; his eyes held the long tunnel of time, of epochs, a filament of sustained intention. Like Grace, he had his role. Like Charley, she had hers. Grace picked up the suitcase and closed the door behind her.

It took half an hour to break the ice off the windshield, persuade the car to turn in the deep snow, to slide down the hill to the desert floor. If it wasn't for the depression of the car's tires left by her night journey to find Charley, Grace would be hard put to find the road. Even so, it seemed to her she felt it more than saw it. She took a right off one track onto one only a little more discernible. The wheels slid from one side of the road to the other, and if not for four-wheel drive and wide tires, Grace would not have made it after the first decline.

Even so, Grace got stuck twice. The first time the car slid into a ditch as she rounded a curve. Efforts to rock the car back and forth only ground it deeper into the hold of snow and mud. Reluctantly Grace dug the shovel from the backseat, moved the piled snow from in front of the wheels, broke limbs from nearby brush, rammed them under the tires for traction, and finally freed the car. The second time, Grace must have fallen asleep. When she felt the car slide, she jolted awake, wrenched the wheels too sharply and, thus, insured the car's slide. It was firmly stuck in the snow and sagebrush at the road's edge.

Grace looked over her shoulder to measure the rough distance behind the vehicle and the other side of the road. Maybe. She rocked the vehicle back and forth, then on a back roll gunned the gas pedal. She made it out all right, but the back wheels landed in the ditch behind. Without a second thought, Grace shifted and hit the gas again, forward this time. Everything in the seat beside her slid to the floor in a tangle of food, flashlight, purse. The suitcase in the back slammed against the back of Grace's seat. The undercarriage scraped something solid, but the car was free. She didn't want to think about how the auto rental company would react to the condition of the vehicle – more than one bent fender and mud that would take a chisel and mallet to remove.

By the time Grace made it back to the highway, she'd almost lost the knack of driving without her face plastered to the windshield and her chin on the steering wheel. The highway had been plowed, traffic was light. There was ice and blowing snow, of course, but with such minimal obstacles compared to the desert tracks, Grace over-steered for the first few miles. When she was near town she dug for her phone and couldn't find it in the chaos of clutter inside the car.

Grace took only her suitcase and purse from the car, found the phone but not the charger. She avoided the hassle of returning a nearly wrecked car to the rental company and made arrangements at the motel for it to be collected the next morning.   No doubt she would hear from her insurance company soon. The next morning her flight was one of the few that found an open sliver between storms. So it was that Grace knew nothing of what happened as Ruby left the mountain. Knew nothing of Agnes' struggle. Nothing of the blue child.

But now she is traveling north. She will be in Seattle soon and find her way to Ruby's cabin, to her sisters.

***

White and pale blue cirrus-like clouds stream past the windows of Ruby's car; it is as if the car is in the sky traveling at great speeds. No trees, no snow piled atop bushes. Ruby knew there would be danger; the old woman had been clear, but how is she to drive if she can't see the road? Doing the only thing she can think of, Ruby rolls the car forward. After all, the bridge is directly ahead. She hears the change in the crunch of the tires when she reaches it. Straight across, then the road curves right.

In the mountains this kind of crisis had required an indirect and unimagined solution. If this is one of those, the answer needs to arrive quickly. It does. As the car reaches the far side of the bridge, the road reappears. But the surrounding view? There is none. Instead, the racing clouds stream past. And the back window? Forget it, too. All is black – no trail, no mountain. The contrast between the slow forward roll of the car and the speed of the clouds is disorienting.

The clouds to the side begin to thin and slow. Ruby still cannot see through them, but they aren't as distracting as they were. She focuses on the road ahead thankful she has not driven to the bottom of the cliff that she knows is there even though she cannot see it. Deliberately, she relaxes her shoulders.

And then comes the first vision – a face outside the passenger window, a child's face, blond hair merging with the clouds. Tears stream down her expressionless face. She places a small plump palm against the window in a clear appeal for help.

Ruby's eyes and those of the child lock. Ruby is mesmerized. A second child? Is she part of the medicine? How can Ruby help without stopping. Perhaps if she only slowed, if she opened the window. The car drifts toward the outer edge of the road, the one above the canyon. Ruby has forgotten to steer.

The child's mouth is pursed in a round shape as if to kiss. It is this, the shape of the mouth, that jars Ruby from the child's hold. Horrified she jerks the steering wheel away from the edge, back onto the road. Sweat runs over her ribs, dots her upper lip. That was close. Once caught in that kind of spirit's grip, the outcome was sure.

The blond child was one of the beautiful spirit people but a cruel one, one of those who lure humans to destruction and death. Powerful, they look so different from what they are, their promise always out of reach. They lead people farther and farther into emptiness and a gray death. They are recognizable by the shape of their mouths – pursed as if to blow – and by the deadness behind their lovely eyes – man or woman, a colorful bird, a lonely child. Cold-hearted. Ruby rounds the next curve safely. The child disappears, but just before she does, she giggles.

Ruby hopes the worst is over, but what she sees next sends a flood of adrenalin, horrible dismay. It is Agnes standing in the snow without coat or boots, only a thin gray shawl. On her broad face is a smile – or as near to smiling as Agnes ever comes. Ruby surrenders. She cannot leave Agnes. No matter what the Old Ones said, no matter the consequences. Ruby glances at the blue child on the floor.

Ruby taps the brake, but as she slows, suddenly the car is a pulsing drum. No introductory beats, but the hard ones at the middle of her grandfather's song. Outside, Agnes reaches for the door handle, raises an eyebrow in question, but then her image wavers, stretches, elongates, distorts. The thunder of the drum inside the car is what saves Ruby. She hears Agnes' voice and she is singing, her voice loud and passionate, the old words distinct and clear. It was not Agnes beside the road, but an illusion.

The power in the crossing is strong. It wraps its fingers around love, reshapes it. Ruby decides to concentrate only on the road no matter what, not let her eyes or heart be pulled from the instructions of the Old Ones. The sound of the drum is no longer ear-shattering, but Agnes' steady singing for Ruby.

Accompanied by song Ruby climbs the first of the foothills unsure that she can be both snowplow and car, but finally they are atop. Surely they are near the end of the breach. Wary, Ruby stares ahead, ignores the collection of cobalt sparks at the window above the child though they are tempting; after all they are the color of help. The idea of help pulls at Ruby's mind. Maybe the cobalt woman has come with help from the stars? Still Ruby keeps her eyes on the road, returns her mind to the rhythm of the drum in Agnes' hand.

But the forward motion of the car is halted. Her heart pounding Ruby assumes it is stuck, but where they are – at the top of a hill – makes this unlikely. Yet, there is the sense the car is straining as if pushing against a powerful elastic band.

Ruby pushes the gas pedal hard; the engine races. The car bucks forward in little surges, sinks back again rocking. Ruby is stuck in a place of equilibrium – forward movement and equal resistance. Think, Ruby, she tells herself, how can she increase the car's effort. The drum, the song are still in place but it is not enough. Trapped. Ruby wasn't tricked; she didn't stop by choice, but something holds her in its grip.

Ruby wants to look around, look outside the passenger windows, see what she can behind, but she knows better. She can see only a short distance ahead but now the road is indistinct, murky. Ruby is terrified that it is disappearing again, that the powers that live in this in-between world refuse to let her go.

Then the miracle – an owl, big as an owl in a dream. Its wings are spread wide, wider than the hood of the car; its merciless yellow eyes intent on Ruby's face. It tilts, claws forward as if to grasp its prey. Ruby knows who it is; help has arrived. Not the cobalt woman, but help nevertheless. Ruby pushes the accelerator to the floor. Resistance gives way and propels Ruby into the next emergency.

The car skids downhill and sideways. The ditch on the left between the rocky bluff that Ruby can now see very clearly is directly in the car's path. If they slide into the ditch, there is no way to get out. Ruby isn't sure if they are safely through the crossing or not, but even if they are she doesn't have the stamina to carry the child through the foothills.

No room to steer with the slide, so instead Ruby jerks the wheel and presses the pedal again. It is an unlikely maneuver, particularly in snow, but it works. At the last moment the car moves away from its destiny with the ditch and the bluff. Just in time. The theme for the day.

Ruby can see the road clearly now, can see through the passenger windows as well. Through a break in the clouds the sun shines. A blue-jay lands on a branch loosening a small snowstorm. Ahead two deer cross the road to the stream below. Ruby slows the car. Is this another illusion?

Peace. The deer, the jay seem not to have heard the screams, the out of control car, the drum. Shadows lie in the right place. No compression on the ears. Dare Ruby think she is off the mountain, with only a few foothills between her and home? Ruby passes the place where wild strawberries grow, recalls a group of laughing women collecting them last summer. She crosses a bridge above deep pools favored by trout fishermen. A wide bend in the road follows the creek. Below is a thick bed of Skunk Cabbage, asleep now like the Bear. Tall branches of Devil's Club are scattered along the ice-edged shallows.

Everything seems as it should be. Ruby dares a look at the blue child to see how she has fared through the ordeal. Her eyes are open. She is watching Ruby.

Chapter Eleven

Each plant has her signature. There is a spiritual path in this, one that does not depend on the group. The old people say that plants are so powerful you can spend your lifetime and not learn even one completely. Some plants live strongest in a single family; if you want that plant in its greatest power, you will seek who that is. But it won't be easy, because no one talks about these things.

Agnes is waiting. Ruby will arrive soon. Agnes doesn't know how she knows this, except that it is her impression – a feeling of impending arrival. True, while she drummed she heard the owl in the trees on the northeast side of the cabin – not so unusual in itself – but still she knows. Owls usually make their home near Ruby, or perhaps it is that they follow grandfather's ceremonial gear, his drum, and it is Ruby who is its keeper. Agnes wonders where it will go after the three sisters are gone as none of them have children. Of course, Ruby is too old, Agnes not inclined, perhaps Grace. Agnes' thoughts don't linger there – the gear will take care of itself, find its home.

The tide is low, so Agnes goes to the beach with a shovel. Nourishing clam soup is what she has in mind. The sun breaks through the clouds here and there but a steady breeze off the snow and water keeps a penetrating chill in the air. Half an hour later damp with sweat, Agnes has a dozen clams, enough for what she has in mind. She leaves them in a bucket of water outside the door to let them dispose of most of their sand.

Back inside, she rummages through Ruby's hanging plants, her jars and sacks and decides on *Nettle* tea – dense with minerals to remind the body of its love for the earth, gentle reminder to the kidneys, food for the blood. She adds a pinch of *Yarrow* to strengthen the connection between the other side and earth; places the mix on the back of the stove to simmer. Tea for now; soup if she adds more Nettles and the clams.

Agnes hasn't eaten for several days and won't until Ruby arrives. Agnes knows that wherever Ruby is, she is fasting if you use the broader meaning of the word; Ruby has sacrificed every comfort, stamina, reality as she knows it. All her reserves are gone. Sustained, extreme sacrifice is hazardous; the body does not always find its way home. Sometimes, it steps over the boundary into spirit even when that is not the intention.

Agnes knows Ruby's need because she feels its pull in her own body, the depletion in muscles, the strain on organs. Agnes' feeling is not the result of only her few days of fasting, but is because of the nature of the fast – its dedication to Ruby. She is offering her body and spirit to help Ruby carry a burden that has become too heavy. By this action, the relative youth and strength of Agnes' body becomes available to Ruby. Of course, it also means that if Ruby does not live, Agnes will probably die as well.

So, hollow-bellied, Agnes prepares the break for Ruby's fast, chooses the food that will best ease the body's transition back toward life. Nothing too rich, too heavy. Warm, not hot. Small amounts. Once the body adjusts, she will add the clams and after that open a jar of fat-rich salmon. All in good time, carefully parsed. Agnes lets the fire die back to little more than coals, lets the cabin cool. Ruby will need warmth, but not heat.

Agnes chooses a chair from which she can see through the window to the driveway, and she waits.

***

Ruby decides to trust the peace after the turmoil of the chasm, the place of illusion. After all, the animals are behaving as they should, the plants, the trees. Besides, she is not sure she can drive right now. The blue child is awake and Ruby is blinded by tears. She stops the car in the road beside a waterfall.

Ruby reaches for the child lying so still on the floor, her eyes the only movement. Ruby cups her in the cradle of her arms and lifts, opens the car door and climbs out. Thin as Ruby has become, she feels almost as light as the child, but she staggers to the road's edge, across the snow-covered stones to the pool at the bottom of the falls.

Ruby and the child are leaving the mountains. Before they go Ruby wants this moment with the awakened child, wants a final moment beside the glacial water, the cold stones, the thirsty cedar. She wants the child's first memory of earth to be the mountain.

In her cupped hand, Ruby lifts the water high, watches the light in its falling. From her place in Ruby's arms, the child reaches. She catches a few drops in her blue hand, lets them drip between her fingers into the pool. She turns her expressionless face to Ruby's. When Ruby smiles the child traces its shape with her finger. She seems old enough to stand, but can she? Is there gravity where she comes from?

The child wavers a moment, finds equilibrium and stands. She steps into a shallow eddy, moves her toes in the fine gravel. Ruby doesn't stop her. She has not raised a child, and she doesn't know the many things adults are supposed to prevent. If she'd been asked why she doesn't concern herself with the child's nearly-frozen feet in the almost frozen water, the questioner would have met a look as blank as the child's. Ruby's own love of mountain water is her forgiveness.

Bending, the little girl fills one hand with water and lifts it to her lips, collects more and splashes her face. Squatting in the water, her wool wrap dragging, the child collects an opaque rock, studies it, shows it to Ruby. Ruby's warm smile answers the child's wonder.

It is then that Ruby learns something of how the future will be – she feels the light touch of the child inside her mind, a tiny tentacle, a moth's wing. Ruby's breath is deliberate, evenly measured allowing the prickle of tiny feelers: the watching pause of the child's question, a movement along the network of Ruby's answers. This reminds Ruby that while the child appears to be an ordinary little girl – except for her color – she is probably not human at all.

One end of the child's wrap is pulled into the stream's current, pulled from one shoulder and leaves the child almost nude. Ruby lifts her from the water, collects the soaked robe.

Human or not, in the time-honored manner of a toddler in adult arms, the little girl loops an arm around Ruby's neck. Ruby's heart melts even as she feels the inquiring signature of the plucked network inside her skull. The sensation is not like the invasion of the Old Ones – one separate consciousness entering another. Instead the child sits like a small watchful entity at the back of Ruby's mind, observes, inquires, collects information.

With the car's heater on high to warm their feet, Ruby drives around mud-slides, boulders, over the snowy road. The road that once seemed so treacherous is in worse condition than when Ruby made her way up the mountain, but its challenges barely register. Too much has happened. And now the child – Ruby wonders what the Old Ones meant her to do other than care for her. She knows that the child is a gift to the earth, that she is help the earth needs against a current threat to its people, but how this is to happen Ruby hasn't a clue.

The Olympic Mountains reach the edge of the salt inlets where snow is less likely to accumulate, and never stays long. When the snow becomes mixed with rain, when the rugged road becomes reasonably smooth and Ruby knows she is near home, she pulls to the side of the road again. She is dizzy, leans her head against the steering wheel; the thought of home – inside rooms, cooked food, water from a faucet, fire – brings vertigo almost equal to that of crossing the ledge.

That she is bringing the star child adds its quotient. The child touches Ruby's arm. Ruby turns to face her. Black eyes meet eyes just as black – the night sky between stars, the back of the cave. With so much loss of weight, the lines in Ruby's face are deep and the bones prominent, skin chapped and roughened by cold. Matted hair, torn and threadbare clothing complete the picture. In contrast the child's cheeks are plump, her skin smooth. The dimpled hand on Ruby's arm, for all that she is so small, is comforting.

The child's presence inside Ruby's mind is like a tiny bird. Ruby has the impression of a beckoning gesture, an invitation. As well as anyone can follow an image inside their own mind, Ruby does. The result is that Ruby seems to leave her own psyche for a world of symbolic images which have little meaning or context.

By now Ruby knows a thing or two about confusing states and waits to see the child's intention. Some images disappear, some reshape and then suddenly there is nothing except the cobalt woman. She smiles at Ruby, and for some reason, this is so reassuring that Ruby takes her first deep breath in many hours. The vision clears and Ruby looks once more at the child. But something has shifted. Not only is the child inside Ruby's mind, but Ruby can now sense the child's internal world.

A chill climbs Ruby's back when the child asks when they will see Agnes. Does she know about Ruby's sisters already, or did she learn of them from Ruby's mind? Ruby turns to the road. It won't be long until they are at her cabin, but it might be weeks or months before they see Agnes. When Ruby heard her grandfather's drum in the battle on the mountain she did not suppose for a moment that someone was drumming it in the present, that someone was actually at her house. Ruby drives around the curves, down hollows, past waterfalls. Valleys widen as she nears the main roads along the salt inlet – the road home, though the location of home has become less certain.

Where the road ends at the larger road, Ruby turns south. Because of the recent snow, there is little traffic. The broad inlet is visible between a thin line of trees, the water deep gray, metallic and still. It is alive with ducks in their winter feathers, collected in loose groups they reveal where fish are. Seals dot the water's surface. Ruby rolls the window down, hears the long low cry of a loon hovering over the water; watches a ghost-like seal appear and disappear, there, and then suddenly gone.

The child sits forward in the seat, her eyes fixed on the water. The wrap she has worn since the cave has fallen away from her shoulders to the floorboard. She doesn't seem to notice the cold air from the window, but then neither does Ruby. In rough imitation of the loon, the child's voice makes a low, echoing cry. With her hand atop Ruby's on the steering wheel, she moves in Ruby's mind looking for information. Ruby is beginning to feel like a library, but she drags up the geometric winter pattern of loon, its love of cold places, how deep it dives, how fiercely it loves.

To Ruby's surprise the child responds, makes her own contribution about the loon, an image of the dark places between stars. Not empty space, but space alive with the making of things not yet shaped. Ruby's world, like an unfolding flower, or a slowly expanding galaxy, grows larger: loon as maker, her song a love song for what is becoming.

The child's coming is not so dissimilar. She has come not so much as maker, but as a saving force in crises. Ruby knows this, but isn't sure how one small blue child can hope to prevent what the red snakes, the reptile and the people who have found them, intend. For now, however, everything is enough. The child's joy at the loon's cry, her small cold hand on Ruby's.

With the window down, the spirit of the loon still present, Ruby turns into the long curve of her driveway, but quickly brakes. Agnes' truck is there, but also a car Ruby doesn't recognize. While Agnes' presence is welcome, a stranger is not. Maybe it is not the cabin that should have been her destination. Ruby backs out of the driveway.

***

The plane carrying Grace flies through thick, dark clouds. Even though the pilot has given the warning to prepare for descent, nothing is visible except clouds, but Grace has landed in Seattle so many times she knows what is there. She feels the plane bank around Mount Rainier's bulk, sees in her mind's eye the *straits*, inlets and islands of Puget Sound that usually make landing in Seattle such a visual treat. When the plane finally breaks through the low clouds, the city is so close it is startling, but even so the view is dimmed by thick snow falling.

In these conditions, it won't be easy to join Agnes at

Ruby's cabin. First, Grace has to get across the water to the Peninsula. She debates going south and across the bridge, or catching a ferry with a possible long wait. But before she can take either route, she needs a car. She does not intend to rent one as she does not know what awaits her at Ruby's cabin, and how long it will be before she can return to Seattle. Returning a car in poor condition as she had in New Mexico was one thing, auto theft quite another.

Grace has a plan but doesn't know how long it might take to put in place. She has friends in Seattle and intends to find someone that will loan her a car. No easy task. Who will be willing to loan a car for an indefinite time? But Grace knows she'll succeed. Indian people are amazingly generous and will help each other. She just doesn't know how long it will take.

The first obstacle is that Grace never found the charger for her cell phone. Her only method of communication has to be a pay phone in the airport. When Grace pries her stiff body from the plane's seat she heads straight for the nearest bank of phones. First she calls Thomas, but not very hopefully, as, like Grace, he travels often. Grace calls him because he earns a lawyer's income and she knows he has an extra Subaru. No luck, too much to hope for. It seems to Grace that each part of this journey has to be the long, hard way.

One of Grace's problems is that she does not have the phone numbers of friends in her mental files, but only in the phone she can't access. Tara, a friend who works with street gangs, will always answer even in the middle of the night – if you have her number. Or, Grace reasons, if you can persuade the organization Tara works for that it is an emergency. Grace scrabbles in the bulky phone book, finds a program that sounds right under the umbrella of Seattle Indian Health Board. But Grace has lost track of the days. It is the weekend and the emergency on-call person cannot be persuaded that Grace's need rises to the necessary level.

Exasperated, Grace decides on the old-fashioned approach; she'll knock on doors. And so Grace catches a bus from airport to city center and from there to one of the urban

Indian communities tucked between Seattle's hills. The houses are ramshackle, though with old-fashioned wide porches. A few haven't been partitioned into apartments and it is at one of these that Grace finally arrives. It is almost dark and no lights shine from the windows. Discouraging.

Grace has arrived at a medicine man's home, far different from Charley's cabin, but not so different in important ways. Cain and his family live here. Cain is only one of his names; he has others: one he is given at birth, a nickname used by many in the Indian community around him, a spirit name. But Cain will do for Grace's purpose – she needs a car and while Cain might not have one to offer, he'll know who does.

But he isn't home. Nevertheless, Grace wearily climbs the stairs onto the porch if for no other reason than to be out of the snow, to rest from the burden of her suitcase. Grace presses her face against a large window facing onto the porch so see if there is sign of recent activity. There is none.

What she does see makes her shake her head, not in surprise, but in wonder. In plain sight around the room are the artifacts necessary to Cain's work and the gifts he's been given: painted buffalo skull on a bed of sage, talking-stick beaded in a spiral of figures like those of rock-paintings. There are ancient shields, a beaded saddle bag, hand drums and in the corner draped under a blanket a Pow Wow drum, carved cedar boxes and a painted pot – southwestern design. The latter has pride-of-place on a table in the corner. Not only do these items identify the home of a medicine man, not only are they spiritual wealth, but they are items that can be sold for fantastic sums to collectors; local pawn shops even know their value.

Nevertheless there are no bars on the windows, no alarm system. Grace once asked about the safety of these treasures so visibly displayed. What a loss they would be if stolen. But Cain's daughter had chuckled. "They'd bring them back soon enough! Or someone would recognize who they belonged to, sit with the thief until one of us came to get what was stolen." The implication was that no Indian with good survival instincts would touch them without permission. The items are too powerful. And if they did take them, the thief's relatives would return them for the sake of their family's health and well-being.

Grace is a creature of the world, a little cynical, and she isn't so sure. Markets are flooded with stolen artifacts, even those from graves. A non-Indian might not make the connection between subsequent personal disaster and the acquisition of powerful relics; they might not realize they'd invited an unhappy consciousness into their midst. No matter how strong the spiritual response to theft, the loss to Indian people would be the same, So much stolen. So much lost.

Of all the wealth inside the room It Is the pot, the one with the spiral of black and white abstract shapes, that pulls Grace's eye. It confirms that this is the house where she is supposed to be, the place where she will find help. So, despite the quiet, unlit interior, Grace knocks on the door and waits. Standing there Grace grows uneasy; she feels watched. Puzzled, she looks around the snowy street, checks the windows of nearby houses, but nothing seems amiss. Finally, the light dawns. It is the house itself that is watching, Cain's house. She should have known. The house had been ceremonially awakened. It makes sense that Cain would do so; Indian people often give spiritual names to space, wake it with ceremony, bring it consciousness. The idea of an awakened house is that it will take care of itself, will call what it needs – what the family needs.

The power of the watching house grows stronger, intimidating. She feels as if a large animal crouches above her. This time when Grace knocks on the screen she uses the side of her fist, gives her effort additional punch. The screen bounces on its hinges. Suddenly Grace is inside the house. It is as if her spirit is divided; she is both on the porch and at the foot of stairs leading up, her hand on the worn bannister-post. She hears a faint stirring, the floorboard's response to someone's weight. Shivering, not liking to be inside Cain's house uninvited, Grace grows still, watches the curve of the staircase.

A woman's sleepy face peeks around the edge, long black disordered hair hanging almost to the step below. "Oh

for God's sake" the young woman exclaims. "Not now."
Impatient as her tone is, she shuffles down the stairs. Inside the
flannel gown a tall stout body fills the folds; bare feet protrude
beneath the hem.

As the woman nears the bottom stairs, Grace – to her
relief – is back on the porch. The door opens. The woman
seems grumpy. She doesn't invite Grace to enter nor wait to see
if Grace does. Instead, the woman heads across the room of
artifacts and toward another door. Grace follows the woman's
wide back into a small kitchen, watches as she fills the coffee
pot, sets it on the stove. With that done, the woman crosses to
an old-fashioned fridge, removes bread and meat, puts it on a
plate and then on the table in front of Grace. From a cupboard,
she collects salt, oil in a pint jar and places them next to the
food. Grace silently prays that the oil is not seal or worse.

Into this silent, surreal scene, words finally come, "He'll
be back soon. Wait here." With that the woman shuffles out.
Grace hears her steps on the stairs again. She knows that
"soon" can mean anything from hours to days, so settles her
suddenly ravenous appetite on the simple meal, pours the first
cup of coffee.

It is early in the evening that the middle-aged man who
lives in the house with his family finds her, head on top of her
crossed arms on the table, asleep. Grace doesn't rouse when his
wife washes the coffee pot, or even when she pulls the skillet
from inside the oven. Grace sleeps without tension, as if she has
nothing to fear, nowhere to be but here in this house. The smell
of tobacco finally wakes her to a kitchen filled with activity and
a man sitting at the table beside her. It is not Cain.

He isn't old like Cain, but a man of middle years, broad
shouldered, hair braided. His face has the tired look of
medicine people, who are needed by so many, but also the sure
confidence that only comes by absolute trust in internal
resources. He seems to be a mix of bloodlines – the long bones
of the plains, arched nose but with the broad cheeks of coastal
people. The spirit in the house has shifted with his arrival, its
brooding presence replaced by the man's own. Though he

doesn't look directly at Grace, she feels his probing. He pushes the cigarette package toward her. She nods, taps one free and lights it.

As they smoke to the clatter of a meal's preparation, his eyes come to rest at Grace's throat. She knows it to be a question and pulls Charley's gift from inside her shirt. He doesn't touch it; he doesn't need to. Instead he puts his cigarette out and goes more deeply inside himself. Finally, he asks, "What do you need?" "A car," she answers.

He leaves the room and Grace hears him call up the stairs in a language she doesn't speak. Soon both he and the young woman are back inside the kitchen, the woman now dressed in jeans and flannel shirt. She is younger than Grace thought. "Find Wilbur," the man says.

With that the mood in the kitchen shifts. "I am Elizabeth," the young woman introduces herself. "This is my Uncle Kaleb and my Aunt Beau."

"You are not Elizabeth," Kaleb jokes. "You are Sleeps-All-The-Time."

"I am still growing," Elizabeth answers, to which Beau snorts in response. Laugher replaces tension, Elizabeth leaves through the back door, and Grace hears the firing of a car's engine. Does no one use phones anymore?! To find Wilbur, it is evidently necessary to drive. But Grace and her need have been accepted. The house becomes a place of Indians claiming their own, or perhaps better put as an acknowledgement of a rightful claim.

Kaleb explains Cain's absence. "The old man has gone home." Whether that means he has died, or simply gone back for a visit to the home reservation, Grace is left to guess.

So it is that hours later, the door opens to admit several men: a man introduced as Wilbur, and by the looks of them, his sons. Loud, laughing, teasing, they hug Beau and sniff loudly in the direction of the stove. Beau pushes them aside and says, "Wash." Introductions made, the group devours fried fish, hot fry-bread and jam served by Beau in a seeming endless supply.

"Pickup or Jeep?" Wilbur finally asks Kaleb.

"Jeep." With that, one of Wilbur's sons pulls keys from his pocket and puts them on the table in front of Kaleb. With his fork, Kaleb pushes them to Grace. In the silence that follows is space for Grace to answer unspoken questions – Where? How Long? – but Grace doesn't know so says nothing. The men nod. In its way, her silence is answer enough.

Grace spends the night warm beneath a heavy elk hide, hair still on, her sleep so deep it seems dreamless. Early the next morning she is on the road, a thermos of coffee and a brown sack of venison sandwiches beside her. Traffic is light and Grace wonders if it is a holiday. She takes the bridge to Bremerton, turns south toward Ruby's cabin. When she finally pulls into the yard, she is relieved to see Agnes' truck and disappointed not to see Ruby's car. Never-mind, she has finally arrived.

As Grace climbs from the Jeep, Agnes opens the cabin door. How thin Agnes is surprises Grace. And tense. Grace has not seen such tension, such a haunted look since Agnes was placed in Grace's bed after the car wreck that killed Agnes' mother.

Thin she may be, her face tight with strain, but her smile is warm with relief. For Agnes, Grace always brings the light. Grace slips her arm around Agnes' shoulders in a long embrace. As she enters the cabin she sees the simmering pot on the stove, smells its contents, but Agnes doesn't make an offer. It is then that Grace realizes there is no smell of food, nothing of meals cooked today or even last night. She understands. Agnes is fasting. Ruby must still be in danger. While it was Grace that helped sing Charley to the battle on the mountain, she hadn't seen all that Agnes had.

It is chilly in the cabin and Grace keeps her coat on, sits at the rough table, glad she'd eaten the sandwiches on the way because it does not appear that food will be eaten here anytime soon. Agnes sits in the chair beside her and, after a deep shaky breath, she begins to speak.

"She had a child with her, but not an ordinary child. And she was with the Old Ones," Agnes brings Grace up to date. "I could see them when we sang."

Yes, of course, Grace thinks. The giant creatures she'd seen with Ruby were Old Ones. Grace knows of them but has never seen them. Perhaps Agnes has. She spends so much time in the forest it is possible, but if anyone could have a relationship with them it would be Ruby.

Both sisters are thinking the same thing. Ruby is their sister, but she is also very different. She doesn't talk much, but it is more than that. Ruby is ghost-like, disappears and reappears without notice. She always has been as far as they know: gone when the family woke in the morning, coming home at night, gone again. When they'd asked Marianne where she was, the answer was terse, "In the mountains." They'd stopped asking.

Grace does remember asking another question, though. "Who is Ruby's mother?" Grace knew who hers was, and Agnes', but no name had ever been offered as Ruby's. If Marianne answered, Grace didn't remember it. Instead what Grace remembers is silence, one that filled the house, pushed against the walls and seemed to want to escape along with Grace's words.

"Do you think...," Grace begins, but Agnes cuts her off. "I don't know. But I think she'll be here soon. With the child. We have to help Ruby."

Grace nods. It is a measure of Agnes' anxiety that it has even to be said. Of course, they will help Ruby. No matter what that means, or requires.

"But the Old Ones...," Grace says in awe. "Yes," Agnes answers. "The Old Ones. They were there. Many of them. Fighting something in the trees, something red."

"And the red snakes. They were there, too," Grace adds.

Agnes rises to put another log on the fire and answers, "Yes. Those, too."

"Have you seen anything odd here?" Grace asks.

"No. But when I last drummed, I saw Ruby and the child again. They were alone." Agnes adds, returning to the table. "Tell me what happened in New Mexico."

Grace tries to put the pieces together. "Peg's mom sent me to an old man named Charley. I sang grandfather's song, and while I did, Charley sort of piggy-backed on it with his own song. That was how I came to see Ruby and the red reptile. He said that the people who are trying to use the old power he protects might succeed because they are stronger than he is, even stronger than the combined efforts of the elders. What he also said was that help had been sent from the sky."

"So what does that have to do with us? Or Ruby?" Agnes asks.

"I am not sure. It has something to do with the work of the old people: Peg's mom, Charley. We may never know. Maybe our part is over," Grace answers.

Intruding into the conversation is the sound of a vehicle in the driveway. Probably someone lost, the women think, as the car enters and then begins backing out again. Agnes glances out the window.

"No!" she shouts, startling Grace. Agnes races towards the back door and flings it open, runs up the driveway. "Stop, Ruby!"

Chapter Twelve

Listen to each of the old words in the story, the song. Sometimes the secret the soul seeks is in the wording of a phrase, in the rhythm of its music. Be careful of translations that smooth the edges of the reading, the listening.

Watching Agnes closely, Ruby brakes. While Agnes slogs her way to the car window, Ruby scans the area around the cabin to make sure nothing is out of order. Then she sees Grace standing in the doorway and understands the presence of the strange car. Agnes now stands beside Ruby's car door staring at Ruby's face. Ruby is hardly recognizable – emaciated, skin painted on bone, her eyes unnaturally round and seemingly hot, fixed.

Then Agnes' eyes shift to the child in Ruby's lap: black matted curls, black eyes, blue skin. Yes, the child is blue; not only her skin but she seems to glow with blue light, an aura of sorts.

"Agnes," a voice calls softly across the yard, Grace pulling Agnes from her frozen state. Yes, Agnes thinks, this is no more bizarre than the last few days. Well, it is, but not by much.

Agnes reaches for the car door and opens it. "Welcome home, Ruby," she smiles. "There is tea on the stove."

Ruby doesn't even nod, but slides from the car, the child in her arms, and staggers toward the cabin. Grace is shocked by Ruby's appearance, her stick-like figure, ragged clothes. She puts her arm around Ruby's shoulders as she had with Agnes earlier. She meets the child's intense curious gaze, tries not to react to her blue color, or even to the fact that she is naked in the cold.

Agnes pulls a chair from beneath the table and Ruby silently sits; the child rumbles at the back of her mind looking for names not only as to whom but what. Ruby allows her to find her own answers. The child doesn't seem to be disturbed, only curious. Agnes sets a cup of steaming tea before Ruby, but doesn't say anything. Ruby has that far-away look that Marianne taught the younger sisters to respect.

Finally, Ruby murmurs her thanks and sips, seems to breathe a little deeper as the familiar, earthy liquid slides into her body, begins its work. The silence in the room remains unbroken except for the shifting coals in the fire. Grace is tempted to ask questions, but makes herself wait until Ruby is ready.

But it isn't Ruby who speaks, it is the child. Pronunciation is mushy, but the sisters recognize the attempt at Grace's name. Looking directly at Grace, she repeats it. How can you not smile when a child's first words are your name? Grace does smile, and so does Agnes. Ruby is still too far into the other world, or perhaps too close to death itself. Agnes sees this and pours another cup of tea.

As Agnes goes outside to collect the clams in order to make them into soup with nettles and tiny Ozette potatoes, Grace sits transfixed, she and the child still staring eye-to-eye. The child shifts her gaze, looks intently at Grace's hands, throat, face.

"Blue," the child says. It may be that the child means that she is blue and Grace is not. It may be only that, but it becomes something else. The little girl has just named herself. She is not Tabitha or Marsha. She is Blue.

At this Ruby finally smiles. Grace laughs, points at the child and says, "Welcome, Blue. I am so pleased to meet you."

Agnes is at the stove pouring clams into steaming tea. She chuckles. "We don't have a guest, Grace. We have a niece." So it was. The sisters shift the configuration of family to make room for a blue-colored child from the mountains.

Ruby clears her throat and speaks, "Blue is a star child." Star Child has no previous home in either Grace's or Agnes' understanding, but just as they'd included Blue in the family, they make room for a new idea. More information would no doubt come. Or not.

Agnes spoons clams and broth into a bowl and places one in front of Ruby. Grace, always the most forward of the three sisters, reaches for Blue so that Ruby can eat. It works. Blue raises her arms and Grace lifts her from Ruby's lap. At first Ruby looks startled, but seeing Blue sitting as contentedly in Grace's lap as she had Ruby's, she smiles again, picks up the bowl and drinks the clam and nettle nectar.

Next Agnes places a bowl in front of Grace. Grace scoops a bit of fluid into a spoon, blows it cool and holds it to Blue's lips. At first the child seems affronted, pulls away, looks at Ruby. Ruby, prying a clam from its shell, lifts her eyes and nods at Blue. Still Blue hesitates, and it is then that Grace almost dumps the little girl onto the floor. Blue is inside Grace's mind.

Shocked and not a little frightened, Grace blurts, "Ruby?"

Ruby actually laughs. Or at least her shoulders and torso shake and she is smiling. "She is learning," Ruby says.

"Does she do this all the time?" Grace asks, still disconcerted. Blue is still inside her mind, following the vibration of her thoughts. Grace wants out of her own skin.

"Yes. I think she will," Ruby answers.

From the stove, Agnes is listening. She moves to the table and asks, "What?"

Grace's face is still a picture of dismay. "She is inside my mind."

Agnes looks at Blue. "Blue," she begins, "can you come inside my mind?" But Blue is puzzled.

Agnes looks around, spots a clam in Grace's bowl, picks it up and shows it to Blue. Blue reaches for it and Agnes places it in her strangely colored little palm. Then it is Agnes' turn to look startled, but all the sympathy she gets from Grace is, "Well, at least she is in your head and out of mine." But Grace, like Agnes, accepts this new sensation. It is probably only a small part of the overall dramatic change in their lives that has come to stay with Blue's arrival.

Grace holds the clam soup to Blue's lips again, and this time Blue opens them. She does a tolerable job of swallowing. The three sisters hold their collective breaths and wait for the response. The child blinks several times and opens her mouth for more.   After several sips, Blue seems to get the hang of eating, and reaches for another clam.

Soon Ruby taps the table for the child's attention. When Blue looks up, Ruby shakes her head. "Enough for now." With that Ruby pushes her bowl away, and Blue, imitating her, does the same.

Agnes leaves the room for a few minutes and then returns. She has clean clothes for Ruby and one of Ruby's long sleeved tee shirts for Blue. She lays them on the table as a question. "Thank you," Ruby answers. And with that begins the long process of explaining the idea of bathing to Blue. Ruby's clothes, even her boots, are placed in a sack for later disposal. Blue's shawl, carefully folded, goes inside a cedar box.

From Ruby's stores, salve – yarrow, comfrey – is rubbed on the deeper cuts on Ruby's body. Just in case, a little *Bleeding Heart* is added – antidote to unfriendly power.

Later, all three sisters sit before the fireplace. Still wet, Blue curls in the familiar comfort of Ruby's arms.   Ruby begins, "The Old Ones say she is a star child, that she is sent to help and I am supposed to take care of her. It's something to do with that red reptile, those snakes that were in the fight in the meadow. They are Blue's enemies."

Grace spends the next several minutes bringing Ruby up to date. She tells her about what she learned in the summer from the elders on the desert, about Peg's mother, about Charley. The child never takes her eyes from Grace's face, and, indeed, Grace can feel the strange light touch, so intimate, inside her mind. Might as well get used to it, thinks Grace. Get used, also, to the pale aura of light around Ruby's body that neither sister mentions.

Next Agnes makes her contribution, describes her journey to Ruby's cabin.   The sisters are puzzled by the misleading phone call Agnes had received. It can't have been the red spirit. Could it be that the people seeking the medicine are also actors, other than calling the medicine, in this larger drama? The women can't put together a story that carries all the elements.

Never mind, they seem to agree. Their work is in the moment. And except for Grace, it is not the habit of these women to think much about the world outside the water, the forest, the medicine, family. It isn't relevant. Though soon it will be.

That night Agnes sleeps on the store-room floor, Grace in front of the coals of the fireplace. Blue lies beside her, still but with eyes wide-open. Ruby sits in a chair dozing; she isn't yet ready for a bed, hardly ready for a roof, but she knows she has to learn again to tolerate warmth, cooked food, a few comforts, that is, if she wants to live. Otherwise she will waste away, grow thinner until the next breath does not follow. The cells of her body need to expand, move away from the contraction of survival. Quietly, she rummages in the baskets in the kitchen, finds dried *Bear Medicine, White Earth, Pipsissewa*. From a small jar she adds a tiny pinch of medicine she has rarely needed. She puts a bit of each in the fire.

When Ruby finishes, she sets the cup beside her chair. She dozes and that is probably how it happened.

Ruby wakes with a start, gasping, freezing. The sound of her rasping breath wakes Grace. Both women know immediately that the child is gone. The door is wide-open, the one on the water-side of the cabin.

"Agnes," Grace yells. Agnes comes running. "She's gone!"

Ruby grabs a flashlight from the windowsill. Just outside the door the child's prints are clearly visible in the snow. With Ruby leading, the women, still barefoot, follow the prints toward the water's edge. They don't much need the flashlight. It has stopped snowing and the moon has broken through the clouds.

Without the warming cloud-cover the ground will soon have an icy crust, enough to cut bare feet. The women have the intense focus of someone trying to control impending panic. As they break from beneath the trees, there is nothing ahead but water. The beach in front of Ruby's cabin is one of the widest places on the inlet, and as such it almost resembles the open sea.

Tonight the water is calm, the surface stretched taut with high-tide.

"There," Agnes gasps. It is Agnes' amazing night vision that allows her to spot the tiny blip in the water, to differentiate it from flotsam, to identify the curls that belong to Blue. Agnes splashes in, Grace right behind her. Ruby, groaning, follows. Agnes scoops the child from the water, turns and runs to meet Ruby. Ruby clutches the child almost violently to her chest. The child is limp, and for a moment Ruby thinks her dead, but Blue's eyes are round with surprise. Puzzled, Blue studies Ruby's expression, moves inside her mind. Then, as if to banish Ruby's panicky thoughts, Blue brushes her palm across Ruby's face.

All three women stand waist-deep in icy water, their shoulders draped in long hair. The night-gowns worn by Agnes and Grace float like overgrown jellyfish. If someone had seen the women, they'd have assumed they were dream figures, or a coven, perhaps.

Finally the three realize that Blue is fine. Ruby turns, splashes to the shore and treads back into the cabin, her sisters in tow. Inside, Agnes closes the door and Grace throws several logs on the coals, wraps a blanket around Ruby's shoulders, then lights all the candles. At the stove, Agnes, predictably, puts water on for tea. Nettles again; the root this time. She adds *Columbine* – the spirit decides.

For a while the sisters sit silently before the fire drinking warm tea. Why Blue doesn't choose this moment to investigate their feelings is a mystery, but she doesn't. Ruby puts her cup on the floor, turns Blue's face to hers, and tries to remember the path into Blue's mind. How to do this, Ruby wonders. How to explain, understand.

Blue seems to catch on, and lights a path for Ruby to follow, an inner room of the mind. In it Ruby lets herself feel the terror of waking and finding Blue gone, of seeing the curls only a little above the water's surface. Blue brushes her hand across Ruby's forehead again as if in sympathy. Understanding dawns; Blue is sympathetic but doesn't see the causal connection between her behavior and Ruby's feelings. Ruby almost laughs.

"Can we use words, Blue?" Ruby asks. Blue nods and Ruby feels the child trade places so to speak, Blue moving inside Ruby's mind. "Words," Ruby repeats. She is beginning to sound like the mother of a small child.

"Will you tell us why you went outside?" It seems like a good place to start, but it doesn't achieve what Ruby wants – a modicum of understanding about why the child so dramatically endangered herself.

"Water," Blue answers. Ruby can feel Blue searching through her mind looking for language. "The moon and the water. The outside is beautiful." OK, so nothing sinister; no one tried to lure the child to her death. And she hasn't lived inside a house before – or so Ruby assumes. More, Ruby has to admit that Blue is right – it is nicer outside, particularly if, like Blue seems to be, you are immune to the cold.

"Blue," the more direct Grace interjects, "would you not go outside again without telling one of us?"

"Alright," the little girl is clearly puzzled, but agreeable.

Grace continues, "Blue, do you know that humans can't breathe under water." Grace braces herself for the exploration of mind that she knows will result.   But, instead, Blue laughs as if Grace is being silly. The three women, seeing how ridiculous the question seems to Blue, join. Hard to know what Blue knows and what she doesn't.

The next morning Ruby puts the child in an old pair of rubber boots, takes her by the hand and leads her outside. They walk the beach, Ruby naming birds and shells. Soon they are talking as if they always have. Ruby doesn't notice Blue's intrusion anymore, nor does she identify when she herself moves inside Blue's thoughts. The edges of communication are smoothed out.

Near the house, Ruby bends to examine tracks under her bedroom window. What she sees takes her breath away. For a moment, the child is forgotten. Coyote, and also moccasin. Ruby looks into the thicker trees to the north side of the cabin.

Could it be? Eventually, she remembers the child, looks down. But Blue is looking up at her, a gentle smile on her face. Ruby is momentarily confused. One moment she treats Blue like she is a small child who needs to learn everything, the next moment Blue is laughing at Ruby's assumptions. The child waits for Ruby to understand the bigger story, to remember, and, for a moment, it almost appears that Ruby will.

Later that evening Ruby places a white saucer with meat atop the tracks. She stands, filled with an odd loneliness. In the trees there are shadows. Ruby hums. Someone answers. Ruby takes three quick steps toward the sound, when a grunt stops her. But, they are here. The cousins of the Old Ones on the mountain that the old woman mentioned – they are here. Grateful, Ruby weeps.

When it is dark, it is agreed that Blue will only go to bed if she chooses, but the sisters will take turns staying awake with her. Ruby will take the first watch as she doesn't sleep much more than Blue does anyway. But before the plan can be implemented, before the last cup of tea is finished, the phone rings. Everyone stares at it as if they are all looking from another galaxy. So far, since the phone call to Agnes, calls have brought more trouble than anything else.

Agnes picks up the phone, answers, and silently hands it to Grace. While Grace talks, Blue joins her, places her hand on Grace's arm, her eyes on the phone.

"Yes, she is here," Grace says, looking down at the child. "Now?" Grace asks, her voice a little louder than it needs to be, but whatever the person on the other end of the line might be answering, the child is already nodding.

"OK, we'll leave tomorrow." She hangs up, turns to her sisters and says, "We'll need to go through Seattle so I can return the car." Agnes gathers bags from the storage room and begins to pack food, package tea, a few pans, even kindling, blankets. Grace hasn't said, but everyone knows where they are going. Not pleased, but they know. Ruby goes to her bedroom, bags a few clothes. Most importantly she takes the drum off the wall.   Hesitates, then also picks up the cedar box holding grandfather's gear. She doesn't know when she'll be back.

With Ruby's car packed, Grace calls Kaleb and leaves a message that she'll be returning the borrowed car the next day. She does. No one is home and she leaves it unlocked, the keys under the seat.

As the women leave town, they stop so Agnes can go inside a store to buy children's clothing. Blue can't go out into the world naked or only in an adult's shirt. She also buys a cap with a long bill, shirts with long sleeves, items that will hide the child's strange blue color. Agnes wonders briefly if the narrow rime of light that hovers over the child's skin will shine through cloth. One thing at a time.

The little group, three sisters and a blue child, head for the high desert; they've been beckoned by Peg's mom.

***

Fortunately Ruby's car has all-weather tires because the pass over the Cascades is icy, the road narrowed by deep piles of snow at the edges. It is snowing again. The trip is long, but Blue seems to enjoy it. Once she discovers how to roll down the windows, the ride is frosty.

When they descend into the high desert the air changes. The scent of sagebrush and juniper has everyone rolling down windows. The scent is delicious, intoxicating. As the clouds are blocked by the mountains the snow isn't as deep and the washed rimrock, the blue-gray canyons, are beautiful. By the time the group slides down the switchbacks to a little house facing south and tucked into the folds of a tall rock face, they are ready to stretch their legs. Ruby and Agnes haven't been here before, so the tall carved posts along the river catch their attention.

To Ruby, Blue looks odd in store-bought clothes, but the child seems not to mind. Sometimes she seems like a wise ancient, and at others, like now, she is an exuberant child. She leaves the car, ignores the house, heads to a sloped, snowy bank and begins to slide down its icy length. Unfortunately the bank ends in a small bluff at the edge of the river. Ruby watches, but leaves Blue alone.

Peg is at the door laughing at the child, calling everyone inside. The house has a big window looking onto the river and the canyon wall on the other side. Like the location of the house, the place across the river is protected, and a herd of deer have taken shelter there. Some nibble sagebrush, others lie on the stones absorbing the day's heat stored there. You could say the scene is peaceful if it had not been for the power around the homestead. It isn't only the spirit posts, but the presence of something else, something as long and wide as the canyon itself. It is the kind of place, Grace thinks, that if you happened upon it by accident would have you backing up again.

Clara is Peg's mom. She sits in a rocker beside the window half turned to its view. She watches events along the river, the deer on the other side, sees when the eagle catches the prairie dog, how early the owl comes in the evening. She reads nature in the old way, knows the timing of things. Her white hair is tied at the back of her neck.

Blue walks directly across the room to the old woman, leans against her legs, joins her in watching the grazing deer. Finally, Clara turns toward Blue, studies her face, looks at her palms, and begins to weep – the quiet sobs that come when the faintest wisp of hope is fulfilled. Blue puts her hand on Clara's arm in comfort. The blue aura around the child intensifies, expands. For a moment Ruby is sure that she sees a turquoise spark – not cobalt, but turquoise – at the little girl's heart. Perhaps she imagined it.

Clara looks up at Peg and the sisters clustered across the room; though her sobs have subsided, tears continue to stream down her face. "It is her," she says. Verdict rendered.

The warmth of the scene, the quiet joy Ruby feels is shattered when Clara adds, "She must be taken to Charley immediately." Though Ruby says nothing, her heart revolts. The Old Ones told her she was to raise Blue, and she isn't going to give her up. But it looks like that fight, if indeed there is to be one, is with Charley, not Clara.

For the most part of two days, Blue and Clara sit at the window. They seldom speak. Sometimes Blue goes outside to ride down the slick hill above the river again. She seems to enjoy curving away from the edge at the last moment. Ruby might have thought this the stunt of a daredevil, but the graceful movement of the child so reminds Ruby of the elegance of the cobalt woman, of the dancer in the constellations. It is, Ruby reasons, the nearest the child can come, earthbound as she is, to the freedom of the stars.

The first night at Clara's, Ruby wakes from a dream. She'd slept on one of the couches in the living room, the one with the window in front of which Clara usually sits during the day. Clara is now asleep on a narrow bed against one wall. Blue for once seems asleep, curled in a chair, but with Blue the matter of sleep is always uncertain.

Ruby rises, collects a glass of water from the kitchen, slips on a pair of boots near the door, and goes outside. She needs to think about the dream. That it was a traveling dream is certain. She'd been in another country, stood hidden behind a curtain, listened to people she doesn't know or understand. Symbols were carved into the walls of the room where the group met. Only one of them caught Ruby's attention – a reptile the color of the creature on the mountain.

Standing on the bank of the dark river, Ruby waits for the moon to rise above the canyon wall. She waits until the coyote's call rises above the soft murmur of the water. She waits for Marianne's voice. "Ruby, let the light work on the water. Pray. Drink the water, and wait." While it is a ceremony usually reserved for sunrise, the moon serves best if the purpose is to see into dark places.

So, Ruby waits. In the dream, she'd heard the people talking. Most of what they said she couldn't understand until they mentioned the names of her sisters. Until they talked about the snakes. One of the group, a man with a broad chest and light skin, said that Grace and Agnes had to be stopped. The bloodline, the drum, he said, had to be destroyed. The sisters mustn't be allowed to reach the old man with his snake medicine. Suddenly, the man tensed, whirled, his expression disbelieving; his attention riveted on the curtain where Ruby hid. He was out of his chair, his finger swinging toward Ruby. With a jolt, Ruby woke up, barely escaping she knew not what.

Or had she escaped? A shadow separates from one of the outbuildings, trots down-river. Coyote, again. It stops near a stand of willows, looks back at Ruby. Ruby isn't sure she needs the extra warning. What she needs is extra help. When she finally goes back into the house, she finds Blue sitting in Clara's chair. Still and silent, the child stares into the dark beyond the window. Above the river a snowy owl glides.

On the final day, Clara calls Ruby, Grace and Agnes to her side. With her gaze fixed across the river she takes a deep breath and begins. "You do not need to know everything, but there are some things you should know. There is an old spirit road between the southwest and the north. The road is one of the reasons you must go to Charley. If Charley wants you to know more about this, he'll tell you himself."

The old woman sinks more deeply into her chair, takes a sip from the cup sitting on the sill. "The ones who want that old power, they aren't governments. They are people more powerful than countries. We are told they are Europeans, though I imagine they are everywhere. They have power, but it is not enough. Nothing is enough for them, so they look at us now. They learned we are not dead. We were content to let them think we are, but then they saw us and knew."

Snow began to block from view the scene across the river and even the river itself. If they are to make it safely off the desert, they must leave soon. The old woman continues, "We have things they want, but they will not use the power in the way our people once did. It is why the medicine was put away, so they couldn't use it. And to be honest, so that we couldn't either. These people are only a few, but powerful. Their desire is simple. It is to own the earth, to own its people. They want the power in Charley's mountain; they want that sky power."

Clara's voice is tired, barely a whisper now. "Those people must not get our sky power. We worked hard for a long time to call the child, and now she has come. Go. Take her to Charley. He knows what to do." With that Clara seems to droop. Peg crosses the room, her forehead furrowed with worry, and props pillows behind her mother's back.

But Clara isn't finished. Still whispering she says, "You three were always part of the medicine. Marianne knew. They only need to kill one of you." Clara's eyes flicker to Agnes. "Or, if not that, to trick you."

When the three sisters and Blue quietly leave the room, Peg still squats beside her mother, eyes fixed on the falling snow. The journey up the switchbacks is somewhat like Blue's slide on the icy snow above the river. No one in the near future will be leaving this valley where Peg and Clara live. Treacherous as the road is, as much as the women in the car wish to gain the top, the winds they meet once they are on the mesa, give them pause. Snow whirls, reminding Ruby of the snow storm on the mountain. There she had the help of the Old One. Now she has her sisters.

Grace drives near the road's edge so she can see through the passenger window what she can't see straight ahead. At this rate it will take all day to get to the relative shelter of the hills. The spirals of wind and snow make Grace dizzy but when the wind dies for a few minutes, it is still more disorienting as her eyes try to adjust to the change. Grace is thankful no one else is on the road, though at the speed she is traveling a wreck will hardly deserve the word.

By the time the car's inhabitants reach the protective hills leading from the open mesa, everyone – except Blue – is exhausted. Blue sits in the back seat in the strange, quiet way she has at times, as if she is contemplating scenes far away, or listening to distant voices. At those times gravity seems more dense around her and the sisters are loath to interrupt her silence. It is a courtesy similar to that of not interrupting someone speaking. Or someone praying.

The intention is to drive straight through, alternating drivers between Agnes and Grace, to drive south across the western side of California, then turn east and thus avoid the more unpredictable high passes of Utah, Wyoming. But east of Mount Shasta the roads grow so bad that the state patrol closes them for a while. The little group pulls into a rest-stop where Agnes and Grace take the opportunity to sleep.

But Ruby doesn't. The snow has stopped falling so she and Blue leave the car, crunch through the deep snow into the trees. Ruby misses the cedar trees under which she slept so many times, their scent, the protection. With Blue's hand in hers, they don't go far – they don't need to because it is not far to the area's nearest kin to cedar – juniper. Juniper grow more slowly than cedar, aren't as tall, and, frankly, not as comforting. A little wilder. *Juniper* – be careful what you call.

Ruby has just stretched her arm to part the limbs of a particularly big specimen when she freezes. Shadows, big shadows, more than a few, stand among the trees. Ruby lets her spirit expand, seeking. Yes, they are there, but just as the juniper is different than the cedar, so are these Old Ones from the ones on the Peninsula.

It is Blue who takes the initiative. She hums and receives a rumbling response. Blue pulls on Ruby's hand and together they approach the Old Ones. The creatures pull further and further back into the trees, leading the old woman and the blue child deeper into the juniper forest. They don't stop until they reach a nearly frozen spring that rises from between two stones.

The sounds of their language are different than the ones that Ruby learned in the mountains. It is a different dialect of sorts, but after a few minutes Ruby understands. They tell Ruby that developments have been rapid in the few days since she left her cabin. The group beckoning the red enemy has found them, knows where they are, guessed their route. Traps have been set. So, once the road opens again, the Old Ones say, Ruby is to turn west into Nevada.

With that, the Old Ones pull even further back into the trees. Ruby sees there are other creatures with them, small and thin. One of these is last to disappear. It pauses, looks back over its shoulder, and laughs. Surely these are not the same creatures as the one in the illusion when Ruby crossed the chasm, the illusion of the pleading, blond child. Why would the Old Ones here travel with such treacherous spirits, the ones that had almost killed her and destroyed the child? Unconsciously, Ruby tugs on the cedar bracelet around her wrist.

On the way back to the car, Ruby hears a chorus of coyotes, the eerie voices coming from far out on the desert. She smiles, glad she left food beneath the window at the cabin.

But Ruby hesitates. Dare she trust direction given by any creature who accompanies these small, treacherous spirits? Should she turn east into what is surely more treacherous weather, or stay on the road heading south, the route Clara indicated? But Blue is there among the questions, talking in her mind-to-mind way. The little people are complex, she says. They form liaisons for their own purposes. Depending on their needs, or inclinations, they can be deadly, or they can offer help. The key to deciding which they are at the moment is to look at their allies.

Ruby and Blue don't sit in peace beneath the juniper trees. Instead they follow their tracks back to the car. Ruby wakes a bleary-eyed Grace and points to the road. Grace doesn't protest, or even wonder if the road is now open. Ruby would know. So, she starts the car.

They do drive south, but only far enough to catch the next highway open to the east. After that, it is Blue and Ruby who choose the direction, sometimes over almost impassable roads. In this difficult zigzag way, they come to the snow-covered track that turns toward Charley's cabin.

Agnes' eyes are swollen slits from lack of sleep, from staring at snow – falling snow, blowing snow, the reflection of sunshine off glistening snow. What she sees now is more snow but this time on a road never exposed to the blades of a snowplow, a pristine white path through the brush, between the mesas. Grace, no less tired than Agnes, sighs. They sit for a moment in silence contemplating what seems insurmountable.

"Chains," Ruby says. Stunned, Grace and Agnes turn in unison to face Ruby sitting in the back seat beside Blue.

"You mean we have chains?" Grace asks.

"Yes. Under the spare-tire," Ruby answers.

Questions tumble through the minds of the two younger sisters, but they know there are no answers. Besides, Ruby has that spooky look. Her eyes glitter, silvery with reflected light. Agnes and Grace haul their tired bodies from the car, unload everything from the rear, dig the chains loose from the hidden compartment.

***

It isn't that they don't get stuck, don't have to cut brush to provide traction, dig the car loose from frozen ruts, but they do finally arrive at the base of the hill where Charley lives. Grace gets out to assess whether, even with chains, they can make it to the top. Standing there, kicking the snow aside, it finally penetrates. No smell of smoke. Its absence surprises her as much as its presence had when she was trying to find Charley the first time. That is when? A week ago? More?

Spinning from one side of the road to the other, the engine racing so as not to lose traction on the way up, the car finally reaches the top, slides so violently from the floored pedal, it almost slams into Charley's cabin. Moving the car back and forth, Agnes finally gets it turned around and pointed facing the road up the hill. As she turns off the engine, she slumps. She does not much care where they are, or what their purpose is, only that they are finally able to stop. She began this trip only a matter of days ago, but it now seems to have been endless. Her body still carries bruises from trying to loosen the dam when she'd thought she was meant to get to her childhood home, meant to get there to help Grace. Of course, that had been an illusion, and she sincerely hopes that the journey to Charley's cabin is not another one.

Grace stumbles from the car, followed by the better-rested Ruby, and the child, who never seems to need any. There is indeed no smoke coming from the cabin's chimney. However, Grace thinks, he has to be somewhere near. He must have realized they were coming. She sighs. With medicine people you just never know.

Near the front door, Grace finds only old tracks. Agnes would know how long ago they were made, but Grace doesn't ask. She had fully expected to arrive with Charley waiting as he had the first time. She sighs. Expectations. She raced across country like a child wanting to throw all her worries at Charley's feet, have him tell her what to do. She depleted her bank accounts and maxed out her credit cards to get here, not that it matters. What matters is that without Charley she doesn't have a single idea of what to do next.

Ruby doesn't seem disturbed. Head tilted, she is listening to a coyote yipping further up the canyon, smiles, then opens the door of the cabin and enters. She crosses the room to the fireplace and immediately begins to build a fire just as if she was at home. Blue stands near the boxes under the window with her hand on top, a contemplative expression on her face. It is an odd look on such a small child's face but her three "mothers" seem to be adjusting to the anomalies of caring for a "star child." The color of her skin extends further than usual from her body, blurring the edges. She is like a walking wand of blue light.

Grace shrugs. Maybe they know something she does not. Agnes begins making a fire in the cook stove – no doubt for tea. An idea dawns and Grace goes back outside, follows Charley's tracks around the house. Yes, they skirt the lean-to and curve toward the cliff. Standing at its base, looking upward, she thinks she can make out where Charley placed his hands and feet not too long ago. Are they recent? Is it only wishful thinking? If he is up there, he'll smell the smoke. Probably the reason Ruby built the fire in the first place. Exasperated with herself, Grace shakes her head. Wherever he is he will know someone is in his cabin.

Agnes does better than tea. From the stores they brought she makes a rough soup. When they finish eating, Agnes lies down with a blanket in a corner. It isn't long before Grace follows suit in her own niche along the wall. Only Ruby and Blue sit on in the room by the dying fire. Blue and Ruby are "talking" about what is to come, of the changes in Ruby's life, changes in the medicine. Blue tells Ruby that taboos must be broken. She doesn't say which ones or why.

Ruby is remembering how to open her mind to distant voices. She is remembering how to listen to the mountains even when she is not there, to hear the Old Ones singing. As Blue and Ruby sit, Ruby hears the song of the cobalt woman.

Around midnight, as Ruby and Blue knew he would, Charley slips quietly though the door. He doesn't speak, but joins them before the coals, squats on his haunches. He doesn't greet Ruby or stare into Blue's face as Peg's mom had. He doesn't weep, but seems to gather himself, to sink into his medicine, into its long story. It isn't long until he rises, pours the remaining tea into three cups. Tomorrow will be busy, intense. Together they drink. Still no one speaks.

At first light, Agnes wakes, and then Grace. No one talks. The only sound is the folding of blankets, and Grace gathering snow to melt in order to wash the bowls and cups. Finally Charley puts more wood on the fire and motions everyone to join him at the table.

The rustling of his voice begins. "I will talk for a while to say the things that are never spoken. The power that is hidden in the mountain is snake power. Its work depends on what it is fed. In the old times it was used to understand the heavens, to seek the harmony there and to bring it to the way we lived. Our ancestors knew that it could be used to seek other things, used for hate – that kind of power. It is why it was put away when we saw that the people from across the water would come. We didn't trust ourselves not to abandon the blue woman and seek something else. "

A log shifts, breaks apart. Charley pauses, and then begins again, speaking a little more quickly, as if to be done. "That is what some people have been trying to do for a long time. They are the ones who want to make slaves of the rest, who know that the companions in the heavens to the medicines on earth can be shifted. They learned what we have and are working to free it, to change its color. They seek a new master for the old medicine. Once we were strong enough, but these people got stronger and stronger so we sent for help. Blue will help us make the medicine safe again, move it deeper inside the mountain or perhaps even to another one."

Charley pauses again. "Those snakes got loose for a while. They were called by that red monster and went to him. If you had not sung, Grace, when you were here before, I could not have followed your song to find them, to call them back. But I will not be strong enough again. Something else has to happen. In all honesty we do not know if the snakes themselves have a preference about who their master is, what color they are."

Charley falls silent. It is a long speech from a man that believes talk weakens the spirit. He finishes his tea. With a gesture toward Agnes and Grace, he says, "Stay here." At that Ruby and Blue stand to follow Charley outside. Grace almost moans to think that Ruby, at her age, and a small child like Blue are to climb the rock chimney to the mesa with its stone chamber. Of course, Grace did not see what Ruby endured in the mountains with the Old Ones. She does not know Ruby's tensile strength, only sees her limping through the snow.

Climb they do. Charley leads. The niches into which he places hands and feet are not the usual longer reach, but ones more adapted to Blue's size. At the top the three crawl down the trench even though it is nearly filled with snow. It is, in fact, a bit more like swimming than crawling. Coyote calls, again. A little closer than before.

They enter the stone lodge just as Charley and Grace had. The old man places Ruby near the back wall, Blue directly in front of her facing north. He pulls the canvas covering aside and tucks its edges into the rocks above, and then sits beside Blue.

Charley begins to sing. His voice wavers but its power cannot be doubted. The clear air between the mesa and the mountain shivers. The ground between grows dim as if seen through mist. Beside him sits the child, her back straight, eyes focused on the mountain. Its distant broad pale sides blend into the white top so it appears to be floating. Ruby is remembering the stories of the mountains, the relationships between them – who is wife to which, who the child, which moved south across the river, across the desert long ago when it was water instead of sage.

There are many miles between Charley's stone cave-like structure and the mountain, but from where Charley sits with Blue it is a straight, unobstructed visual shot. Not far outside the open door of the lodge where the old man sings, the air twists, takes on color. It is the silver snake, the one with the beautiful lavender eyes. But it has grown longer. Its length lies in three glittering loops across the mesa, its tail coiled. Blue still sits quietly as Charley sings his medicine into form. Ruby's heart leaps to see her powerful rescuer so far from the mountain, to remember its welcome touch at her throat.

In the center of the mountain a dark circle appears, across it a woven cover with broken threads, rewoven patches. Shabby. The hidden core with its rent protection reveals itself, and still Blue is silent. The silver snake leaves the mesa, disappears, reappears surrounding the place where the snake medicine is hidden. It looks back in Charley's direction as if for instruction. Its eyes glitter, pale, then brighten again.

At its weakest place the broken net shakes, vibrates and seems ready to burst open. Still Blue does nothing. Doubt trembles in Charley's heart, his voice. Has he misjudged the timing? She is only a child, yet. Had she needed more maturity? But there had been no choice. It is now or forever too late. Ruby hears the mountain's high voice. It sounds like the mountain on the Peninsula. Or is it the cobalt woman? Ruby has never been quite sure.

In the cabin below, Agnes grows restless. She goes outside to the car, opens the door, digs under the clothes and drags grandfather's drum from its bag. Looking up she is hardly able to see the cliff's edge. It shimmers and wavers like the landscape in summer when a sun dog is present. Only it is not summer. Grace watches Agnes from the open door and with the drum stick Agnes motions upward. Both women watch from beside the car, watch as the cliff disappears.

It is, of course, Grace who wants to climb the cliff to bring back the others, but when Agnes begins to sing, Grace joins her. The drumming seems to be inside an airless vacuum, really only a slurred murmur of old words. Still the wall of rock behind the cabin stabilizes, becomes almost solid again, offers hope that Ruby, Blue and Charley have not become sky-people, have not drifted away from the earth. Maybe the old song makes a ladder of sorts that the three on the mesa can follow to come home again. Maybe the drum and its song have always been just that – the way home.

The silver snake, its lovely eyes mesmerizing, continues to look toward Charley. The old man abandons doubt, prepares to spend himself in the singing of his medicine. His teaching had been to succeed at all cost, no matter what it took, no matter the obstacles. To do otherwise was unthinkable, but if he can't, he'd been told, if he truly cannot, he was to follow the song home. The ancestors would be waiting. They would be sad, but nevertheless, waiting.

What no one but Ruby can see is that the Old Ones, tall columns of light, are on the mountain too, and headed toward one broad shoulder to the northwest. A fire has begun to burn there, or so it appears; a fierce red burning light. It licks through the trees toward the mountain's heart. Ruby doesn't know whether she hears the Old Ones' trumpeting war-cry over the distance, or in her heart. Her work is to stay with the child, but for a moment, all Ruby wants is to be with the Old Ones, to fight.

If the red fire reaches Charley's medicine what will happen? Actually, Ruby has a pretty good idea in terms of the earth, but what will happen to the child? Will she be captured, killed? Ruby scoots closer to Blue's back, then looks again at the silver snake. Can it be? It is coiled at the center of the mountain around a nest of snakes.

The beautiful, silver snake pales, begins to dissolve. In the weakest places, the net across the heart of the mountain unravels. The snakes inside squirm. The mountain shakes.

Charley cannot resist one more glance at the child beside him. Her face is expressionless, distant. A cry from Charley's desperate medicine, piercing like the scream of an eagle, reaches them.

Into this disaster, Blue finally begins to sing. Her voice is the high pure notes you'd expect from a child, or perhaps it is more like the cold breeze from a glacier, or the first snow of the year. The child's color grows stronger.

Ruby scoots still closer to Blue's back. The child's song is eerie. Across the snow-covered expanse of the mesa, elongated curved blue shapes form. They coalesce and for a moment Ruby thinks she sees the cobalt woman.

Blue begins to sing in earnest. The small stone room shakes. The room mirrors the mountain - both seem to separate from the ground beneath, leave the earth. Still singing, Charley turns to look at Blue. What he can see that Ruby cannot is that at Blue's breast in her small cupped hand is a cobalt flame. But with the other hand, she is reaching toward the mountain, reaching toward the nest of snakes.

Charley's doubt is replaced by alarm. This is not what he expected. When he and the elders had asked for help from the sky, from the blue woman, they'd assumed the snake medicine would be put beyond reach; beyond anyone's reach, even Charley's. To do otherwise, to release the snakes, to use their power, is taboo. Blue reaches toward Ruby's mind, and the old woman begins to sing too. The two are singing Blue's song.

When Charley looks back at the mountain, he sees that the curved blue shapes on the mesa have vanished, but the snake – his glittering silver medicine – has changed color. Its lavender eyes deepen and flash with sparks of light like those from the gleam of a jewel. A ruffled fan forms a crown around its head. Beneath it is the now fully revealed nest of snakes.

With a sudden dart of its head, Charley's medicine dips into their midst and withdraws one, squirming and thrashing and of indeterminate color. Appalled, Charley turns toward Blue. What is she? What has he and the other old people called? Have they been tricked? The old woman and the child sing. The Old Ones on the mountain fight. The old man's medicine is no longer under his control. Blue wields it instead.

Charley is no longer singing, but Blue doesn't need his help now. Ruby's old voice is a strong contralto to the child's higher notes. The fire on the mountain still burns. The Old Ones still fight fiercely.

Finally Charley is sure of Blue's intent. "No," Charley yells. "Blue, we cannot. No!" Charley turns back to the mountain, desperately trying to wrest control of his silver snake from Blue, but, of course, he can't. Charley's medicine is entirely under the child's control. A colorless and intact now net surrounds the remaining snakes, now placed deep in the root of the mountain near its magma. All of them, that is, except for the one freed by the silver snake and now dangling from its mouth.

Charley's medicine leaves the mountain, travels back across the mesa, bringing the thrashing smaller snake. Blue stretches out her hand for it and Charley's glittering snake gives it to her. She tucks it inside her shirt, and calm settles across the mountain. Charley's medicine resumes its former size and color, fades from sight.

Blue stops singing, and so does Ruby. The mesa is quiet, the stone room silent. The fire on the mountain still burns but its advance stops. The Old Ones melt back into the forest, humming their own contributing barriers around the entrances to the mountain.

Charley's shoulders slump. Yes, the nest is made safe again, but it doesn't contain all of the old medicine power. A portion of it has been freed. Charley has failed. There is nothing more that he can do.

Toward him Blue stretches her hand. He hesitates, then takes it. Charley has been routed from the sure path he's always walked, and his world is in disarray. Whatever happens next, it will be the child who decides.

Blue scoots across the floor of the stone enclosure to the entrance hole. Ruby and Charley follow. At the descent Charley takes the lead. Grace and Agnes stop singing, silence the drum. Blue's color still glitters. Ruby, less fragile than before, stands a little taller, and easily carries the child's weight. Grace holds her breath; something has happened. Agnes strains to read Ruby's expression.

Once they are all inside, Charley puts wood on the fire, opens one of the boxes under the window and pulls a tiny figure from a bag. He sits for a long time holding it, and finally turns toward Ruby in the other chair, offers it to her. Ruby shakes her head. Charley's work isn't over.

"It was the only way, Charley," Ruby says. But for Charley the long story is finished. The most sacred of the taboos has been broken. The old people had left no hints about this possibility. Or had they. Charley searches his memory for clues.

Blue leans toward Ruby, whispers. Ruby nods, "Charley, you have to show us the north road. Not the one we took to get here, but the hidden spirit road."

Charley sits still for a long time. The secrets about the road are almost as precious as those about the hidden medicine itself. But perhaps this is the way to keep the snake now in Blue's care, and Blue herself, from the enemy. At least for a while.. Perhaps if the medicine travels the old north road... Maybe there in the north the snake's color can be settled once and for all. Maybe all isn't lost. Or, at least, not yet.

The lives of the watchers are in Charley's hands, they and the ones they've taught to replace them when they die. Should he risk them? Should he risk the road itself?

Charley extends his hand again, the one holding the tiny stone figure. "You will need this," he says. There is no certainty left, no guiding tradition, but maybe there is still a possibility for the earth, for its people.

the day it was cut. Ruby is fond of it, feels secure with it in her hand. There is movement again, something very large and on the driver's side of the car.

Ruby's heartbeat is rapid, but she knows it is only fear of the unknown. After all she cannot see what is there, so why be afraid? But she is. To distract herself, she thinks of her favorite place on the mountain. It is a place lower on the mountain's flank where many times Ruby has parked her car at the side of the road and climbed a narrow valley that curls upward following a cold fast creek. There is no trail but by trekking through the forest and following the creek upwards for several miles a small three sided valley opens. On one side is a black cliff, a blue glacier at its top. When she is called by the spirit, as she was this morning, it is always to the same valley that she comes. Or so it has been until today.

The rugged climb to the valley, clambering around and over moss-covered stones, over old-growth giants brought down by winter winds and heavy snow, or sometimes climbing under them where they have landed at an angle against boulders or each other. At one of these places four trees fell together, the first bringing down the next. Their tops are split and broken where they hit an outcrop of gray boulders, each as big as a small house. The roots are only half pulled from the earth so the cedars are alive; their long fronds form a curtain hanging from the slanted roof of their trunks. Always, Ruby climbs inside the cedar shelter to rest – it is the halfway point between road and valley. Each year that passes she rests a little longer. In the shelter she feels like a child, perhaps a child of the mountain itself – safe and magically charmed.

In places it is easier to walk in the swift channel of the creek dodging the reaching thorns that stud the Devil's Club's long branches, careful of the tangled roots of willow, cedar and fir reaching into the water. After two or three minutes in the icy water though, feet and calves grow numb and Ruby looks for an opening in the brush big enough to crawl through, back to the scramble over and under trees. Moving back and forth from creek to mountainside, she reaches the valley and its surround of steep walls. In the open valley there are few trees. Instead it is a carpet of huckleberry, an autumn paradise for bear.

One wall is a slick black cliff, smooth and polished as glass, black bolstering the blue glacier at its top. The water from the glacier's melting creates a waterfall. The water drops in spear-shaped sheets that lose their form near the bottom of the long drop causing the eye to struggle focusing on first one cascading curtain and then another. The effect is dizzying. The roar of the water echoes in the tight space of the valley overwhelming the senses.

At the base of the black wall is a pool, a basin, of near freezing water. On its stony banks and covering its surface is a cold mist, a pale blue cloud. Enveloped by sound and mist is ecstasy. The anchoring senses overwhelmed. Separateness disappears. Ruby becomes the glacier, the water falling, the stone wall, the hidden valley, the bear, the tangled brush.

There beneath the glacier Ruby peels off her wet clothes, slides into the pool. The water is so cold it is acid on her skin. She merges with the wildness of the valley and wants to stay, wants to be something that does not have to leave. Good sense prevails and she shivers her way downstream, clambers back over the fallen trees again, arrives at the parked car. On the way, fingers numb with cold, she gathers plants. The power of medicine plants at this altitude is strong and she takes advantage of this pristine place: Huckleberry leaves, and in the spring, Oregon Grape stems and roots. The mountain watches her, remembers her. At Ruby's age it is tiring, the climb to the valley and back, but more familiar and beloved than her own skin.

You might think that Ruby has always lived here on this side of the Olympic Peninsula, but she hasn't. Twenty years ago – already well into middle age – Ruby bought her home with money she inherited from her grandmother. She couldn't tell you why she bought a house here on the eastern side of the Olympic Peninsula, moved across its entire breadth from where she had lived all of her life, why she chose the relative calm of Puget Sound waters over the pounding waves of the Pacific

Ocean – a sound that was the familiar background since childhood. On the ocean side, she knew the mountains well. Their medicines were mapped in her mind. When she moved she had to create a new map. Inconvenient but Ruby never questioned the rightness of her choice nor wondered at her reasons.

Ruby now lives in a small house in the trees beside a tiny salt inlet, feeding deer and birds. She sits in her rocker by the fire and watches the flames. She watches the changing light on the water, weaves, makes medicine from plants, and she dreams. Most people are not quite comfortable with Ruby. Her silences are long and sometimes her eyes reflect light in a curious way. Comfortable or not, people sometimes come to Ruby's cabin because she makes medicine. That she has it ready when they arrive is one reason they are hesitant to come. She weaves blankets for the family of the newly deceased choosing the colors with care. When word comes, the blanket is already woven.

Ruby is not young anymore, not as nimble as she once was. Over the last three years her strong, round body has thinned in that way of some women in the last decade or so of life. The body seems to concentrate its reserves for the last long push. Yes, she still collects medicines, still climbs to the little valley, and she came prepared this morning, but the down coat, the blanket, water, food may not be enough. But, this is the way she lives, or, as her grandmother said, the way she was made. If she feels it is imperative that she does something as irrational as driving over the roads just traveled, she does – though tonight's experience over those awful roads tops anything she remembers.

Spirits are as real as trees or rocks; Ruby can sometimes see them – shapes, shadows, patterns that form and disappear, the aura of a plant or person. Ruby aligns herself with these forces and has no tolerance for ordinary life – lunch with friends, gossip, parties. Though she has not retreated as far as the veterans, she is nevertheless hermit-like. Eccentric, some say, and it's true. Otherwise she wouldn't be sitting here atop the mountain called by something she can't name. Still, she is afraid. The call of the spirit has pushed her limits before, but not risked her life as this morning's horrendous trip up the destroyed road. Her skin tingles, her breath is shallow. Something is out there – something she has not encountered before. She stares into the dark searching but doesn't really want to see what is there.

The Olympic range suits Ruby's nature. It is a strange place of temperate rain forest spongy with springs, rills, creeks and waterfalls – mountains as much of water as of earth and rock. Almost the entire Olympic Peninsula is wilderness. Within it are hundreds of miles of tall thick forests and deep valleys. Small towns ring the range, but there are none within it. A hiker with a good map, strong physique, adequate supplies and a little luck can begin on the east side of the Olympics and arrive on the Pacific coast without meeting anyone. Within these mountains the trails are for serious hikers with good survival skills.

Ruby can see a little better now. The dark blue light of morning gives way to pale gray: the shapes of big boulders above the waterfall, a thicket near the trail. There is no doubt now. There is indeed movement on the left near the edge of the cliff. In the muted light it is difficult to see what it is for certain, but it appears to be a large shape, and, yes, it is moving. Bigger than a person, taller, more massive. Ruby gasps and shrinks back against the car's seat as if somehow she can make herself disappear. Stunned and filled with dread, she admits to herself that she does know what is there and knowing brings no comfort.

It is one of the "Old People." Ruby has never seen one, but her grandmother, a woman descended from generations of medicine people, talked about their nature and how to behave if she ever did. A friend of Ruby's sister sees them. In fact he seeks them out because he likes their company and they seem to like his. He knows how to avoid their ire. Not Ruby. Their smell – a little stronger and more pungent than bear – stops her in her tracks, sends her in the opposite direction. Until now.

Surely this place is not one of theirs. Surely the creature at the edge of the parking lot is not who called. Ruby scrambles for reassuring possibilities and finds none.

The Old Ones protect their homes – hunting ground, fish creek, forest. They claim these places as their own and don't welcome intruders, particularly in those areas where they keep their young. Maybe this is a place they come only at dawn. Maybe they will go away. Ruby cannot imagine getting out of the car as long as the creature is there, though it could make short work of the car if it chose. They do not like mechanical things. Or things made of metal. Or weapons of any kind. Ruby is stiff with fear, her mind frozen. And yet, Ruby knows. She knows the presence of the Old One is why she is here.

The creature is still there but has stopped moving. Ruby takes a deep breath to steady her nerves. There is no alternative. She will have to get out of the car to see what is wanted of her, why she was called. She stuffs the small sack of nuts in the pocket of her coat. The knife she uses to gather plants is in the same pocket. She removes it and places it on the passenger seat. Leave the knife. Ruby scans pockets, body – giving her psyche time to get used to the idea that she will have to leave the security of the car. The staff, surely...but, no, she will have to leave it. Its shape is too much like a weapon; its medicine too strong not to rouse a response. Saying goodbye, Ruby brushes its smooth length with her work-roughened hand.

Reluctantly, moving slowly, Ruby cracks the door open. In the silence the sound is like a rifle shot. This car has no safety light as Ruby dismantled it before she drove the almost-new car off the lot. A woman, even an old one, should not provide potential attackers a spotlight as she gets out of the car at night. She closes the door gently, stands motionless beside the car, moves only her eyes to see where the Old One is. What she sees sends a cold shudder through her body. The single creature has been joined by others.

Ruby's gaze is lowered. She relies on peripheral vision to watch the group of Old Ones. Behind her, near the trail, is a soft grunt. Her back prickles. Her mouth is dry and palms slick. Slowly she rotates her head, gaze still lowered. Yes, there is also one standing at the foot of the trail. A hum emanates from it, almost subliminal. Looking back to the others, Ruby sees they have moved – are moving slowly toward her forming a semicircle blocking the road. One breaks away and moves toward the back of her car. Their intention is clear – they are herding her away from the car and towards the trail. "I can do this," she tells herself, bends to place the car's key behind the front wheel, moves her reluctant feet towards the Old One by the trail. Behind her is a short staccato of grunts.

By sunrise Ruby could be just another mysterious disappearance in the mountains, an unsolved puzzle, a grief to her family. It is not the time to think of her younger sisters, her dearly loved and magical sisters – Agnes, the one even more withdrawn and eccentric than Ruby, is surely in her home on the estuary; the other, Grace, flamboyant and extroverted, could be anywhere. No, this is not a good time to think about them or the possibility of not seeing them again.

As Ruby approaches the trail, the Old One standing there steps onto the path in one long stride. With the Old Ones herding behind the message is clear – follow. Ruby does and immediately wishes for the staff. The path is steep and stony, damp with morning dew. She looks back towards the solitary car in the parking lot, its seeming safety, and elicits a cacophony of sound. Turning back to the path the grunts quiet though Ruby knows by the shiver of her spine that they are still there blocking any change of direction, the decision to turn and run. Ruby is too old to run or struggle, besides the commitment was made by getting out of the car, but she does wish fervently that she had the staff. It has been many years since she entered a forest without its sturdy, familiar support.

Her grandmother and sister's friend aside, it is surreal – even within Ruby's definitions – following a mythical creature, being followed by others. And going where, how far, never mind why? Ruby half expects to wake in her bed trying to understand this experience as a bizarre dream. Ruby is a dreamer. Her grandfather said she lives at the edge of time. He said this is why she spends so much time in the forests where she could more easily drift into the between places, into the past and sometimes the future.

When Ruby was young the family grew accustomed to her early morning absences. Even in a household of light sleepers, Ruby could be out the door early and very quietly. When she was fifteen, Ruby was gone every morning for over a week, coming in late, hungry, tired and silent. It was after one of these long days that her grandfather sat down beside her at the table while she ate, silently reached for her wrist and tied a cedar bracelet, still damp from the making, around it. "To find your way back home," he said. Ruby knew he meant more than just returning from the trips to the mountains; he meant the bracelet to keep her from staying on the other side of the veil. The bracelet she wears now is not the original, but in its weight on her wrist, she remembers his long fingers like a caress, what he said about remembering the way home.

Still sometimes she doesn't know on which side of the veil she is. She awakens, leaves the bed and even the house only to wake up later, her body never having left the bed at all. Over the years, she has developed clues as to whether she is awake or not: the lights will not turn on if she is still asleep, the car will not start, even if in all other ways everything seems like an ordinary waking state. Sometimes dream travel is simple, its intention clear, like leading a child from a perilous situation. Sometimes she is shown a plant unfamiliar to her and its medicinal use. It is tempting to think this experience with the Old Ones is one of those, but it isn't. Before Ruby left the house, the lights responded when she pushed the switch, the car started with no hesitation. This is not a dream, but Ruby is definitely on the other side of the ordinary.

The trail begins with a series of switchbacks zigzagging up the mountainside. Under this old growth, the light is dim all day. Later, if the day is clear, the sun will break through in small pools between trees; here and there it will brighten a meadow.

The path is narrow, winds around boulders, roots twist across in ridges, rocks protrude. The Old One – for some reason Ruby thinks of her as a woman – is ahead. Her long strides, the turns in the trail, have taken her rounded back and sloping shoulders out of sight. The early light is still gray but trees begin to take their individual form. The floor of the forest between them shows the soft reddish color of last year's fallen branches. Small forest birds make the first sounds of the day. If this was one of Ruby's usual trips to the mountains, she might fall into the moment's beauty. Of course, she would have the assistance of her stick and be climbing much more slowly.

The pace set by the Old One ahead and the crowding grunts of the group behind is fast, not Ruby's idea of the pace of a hiker with a long way to go which is encouraging. Maybe this trip will be short. Maybe Ruby will be back in the car by noon flooded with relief that this strange ordeal is over. Already there are tremors in her legs and she is thirsty. The water bottle, along with the blanket and the knife, is still in the car.

The creatures are thick-bodied, towering, powerful. The pace up this steep ascent may be easy for them but it is too demanding for Ruby, even if the trip is short. Her thirst grows more insistent. Powerless as she is compared to the Old Ones, she has to assert herself. A small creek companions the trail. She steps off the trail and kneels beside the water, waits for the reaction. Behind her, she sees the shapes of the Old Ones in the periphery of her vision. They have stopped; their grunts begin low and rise in volume. The sound is mixed with humming similar to that of the old woman's when she was at the head of the trail. The hums have a smooth cadence like song; the grunts move up and down the scale, each a single note in sequence. Ruby continues to kneel, head bowed, eyes raised just enough to see what the Old Ones are doing. One peels away from the group, moves toward her and stops a few feet away behind a fern. Ruby's racing pulse is loud in her ears. She sees a thick meaty foot with sparse, coarse hair.

Half expecting a blow, she bends to the creek and drinks. The stream is only inches deep. The bottom is covered with brown rocks – dull gold, amber, almost red and almost black – and silt as fine as powder. Strands of moss wave with the repetitive pattern of the current. Roots from nearby trees break through the dirt reaching into the water. In the mud is a single bird track with the clear outline of its tiny claw. At another time, in other circumstances Ruby would spend the day here absorbing the detail, immersed in the spirit of this peaceful place. Or bathe in the mountain silt fed by deep roots that grow straight down to the rocky source.

The Old Ones have stopped grunting and murmuring – or is the sound a hum? There are undertones like a chorus of several instruments. Ruby's chest vibrates as it does when the big drums play. No recording equals the power of living drums and their impact on the body, but these are not drums. Instead, the Old Ones seem to communicate by sounds somewhat like music.

Sucking long draughts of cold water, Ruby listens. Shock recedes. Or at least her pulse slows. The sounds of the Old Ones vary in tone, pitch and cadence. What is odd – even in a moment that is the essence of strange – is that as their humming changes, so do the vibrations in Ruby's chest and her emotions. She is still bending over the water and listening – listening to their voices and the changes in her feelings. Their murmuring coalesces becoming organized into complex notes and overlapping repetition, all of it in what can only be described as a minor key.

Definitely, Ruby's emotions resonate to the creatures' voices, sound transformed into feeling, sound imbedded with emotion. The dominant one is urgency but it is urgency that is more complex than a single word; it has threads connecting to other meanings that Ruby cannot follow. It seems they are "talking" and Ruby "hears" from the center of the chest. Sound that has texture; sound she wouldn't be surprised to see as color or shape. Placing her hand against her heart, she feels vibration. It is intrusive but also intriguing.

Ruby loses track of how long she squats on the banks of the little creek bent over the water – shocked not that the creatures are talking, but that she can somewhat understand. After one last cold drink, she rises, brushes the water from her face, pins straggling hair back into its bun and returns to the path, contemplating. Vibration as communication, not mind to mind via the senses, but body to body, feeling to feeling. And what drives their sense of urgency?

The surreal feeling continues. Animals have language. So do trees. This Ruby knows. What surprises her is that she is somehow within the Old Ones' language, one that is far different than any she has known. Ruby is no stranger to the unusual, but this morning has brought a new dimension.

The group of creatures behind is no longer so close. After all, how would Ruby escape back to the car? And she has accepted – for the moment – that if something is so important that the elusive Old Ones have come out of their hidden places, she will do what she can. Ahead is the soft shape of the woman, the Old One, her body half-turned toward Ruby, large head tilted toward the peak, listening. The hair on her body is long and white.

The Old Ones and Ruby climb for hours stopping at each creek for rest, for Ruby to step behind a bush. But Ruby's intention is not matched by her strength. By late afternoon, on wobbly legs she trips on the root of a cedar tree when trying to kneel beside the water. She lies down on a thick bed of gray moss to restore her shaking legs. Big mistake. Spasms snake along her spine and grip the arthritis in her left hip. Staggering and off-balance she quickly rises – rest will not help. The only way of making it to wherever they are going is to keep moving and hope that it isn't far. The creatures are gathered nearby murmuring amongst themselves in distress.

Hunger comes and goes, comes again. Ruby nibbles the nuts from her pocket. There are bushes and roots, but nothing nutritious enough to be worth the effort to collect it. Cold wind sweeps through the trees, prelude to a frigid night. Knowing she will not live until morning without shelter, Ruby hopes they will turn back soon. Or worst case – Ruby prepares herself for the possibility – the Old Ones have a plan for the night, one that

considers human needs and an old woman's limits. Briefly she
wonders why they didn't call someone younger and stronger.
Maybe they did. Maybe she was fifth or sixth on the list of
people who might be crazy enough to come.

In late afternoon, the steep switchbacks at the beginning
of the trail give way to long upward slopes punctuated with
dips and folds set into the mountainside. They are walking just
inside the tree-line. Treeless, open space is visible above, a
place of dry rocks and shale, moss and lichen. Evening falls
early, the sunlight blocked by the surrounding mountains.
Colors fade. The red leaves of dying Oregon Grape look much
the same as this year's new growth. Rocks and roots on the
path are hidden. Brush becomes the round shoulders of a bear,
a crouching animal.

Another creek and it is the dark shimmer of the water
that guides Ruby to its edge. The wind has stopped but cold
rises from the damp ground and falls down the mountain from
the glacier above. Her feet are numb. Ruby wishes it was her
back and hip instead.

As she drinks, a familiar smell catches her attention, a
smell not suppressed by the cold or the dominance of
evergreen. In fact, the rich funky smell is distinctive and hard
to suppress by anything. With a rush of affection, Ruby
recognizes *Skunk Cabbage, Bear Medicine* – an old friend. It likes
muddy alcoves, the swampy places where water overflows and
the light filters through trees. The smell is so strong, it can't be
far. Bear Medicine will stop the cramping muscles
foreshadowed earlier, the pain she knows will fill the night
when they finally stop. She splashes upstream listening to the
predictable staccato of grunts behind her. They have not
touched her yet and she hopes it stays that way, though she
feels their distress rising in her body. One of them follows. He
seems younger; certainly he is smaller and lighter-boned than
the others.

The place isn't far. Ruby finds it when her foot sinks into
the deep mud deposited by the creek during spring floods and
kept damp all year by melting snow. Carefully she pulls her

foot from the sucking mud so as not to lose a boot. She persuades her swollen knees to bend, squats at the edge of the muck that Bear Medicine loves. The Old One following has stepped across the creek. He bends forward watching. By feel she locates the long slick leaves. They tear easily and the thick spine down the middle snaps. Ruby tears the leaves close to the ground to get as much of their length as possible, whispers her thanks. This is a rich bed of old plants and her arms fill quickly. *Skunk Cabbage*, preferred by Bears; releases what is finished; the end of one season and the beginning of another. Innocence.

The Old One beside her murmurs softly but Ruby does not understand what he is saying. Does he know the use of Skunk Cabbage? Perhaps. If bears use it, why not the Old Ones, too? Though collecting the Skunk Cabbage takes only minutes, by the time she feels her way back to the trail, it is fully dark. The old woman's impatience is clear in the rumble of her voice; she turns abruptly, her long stride leading upward again. The lighter shade of her gray bulk keeps Ruby from stumbling into the forest.

She is nearly asleep on her feet. When the old woman suddenly stops Ruby almost runs into her. She takes two long steps backwards distancing herself from the reputation of the Old Ones for violence, and keeping the cushion of distance from the three-dimensional and concrete reality of the Old Ones. Until now they'd existed only in someone else's stories. Not that Ruby doubted her sister's friend or her grandmother, but believing someone else and having the experience yourself is not the same, or even close.

The Old One makes a sharp right and turns directly into the forest. Urging her legs to walk faster, Ruby tries not to lose sight of the old woman's guiding bulk. She weaves between the trees and Ruby carefully repeats her exact path so she won't trip, blunder into the brush or off the edge of a ravine. The strange little group arrives at the edge of a clearing, or it may be the edge of the tree line. In any case, the forest ends. Ruby looks up to see stars appearing and disappearing in the gathering fog. One, brighter than the others, sits exactly above

Epilogue

In a tall building in an office defined by elegance and rare objects, sits a man. He wears a fine gray suit. In fact gray seems to be his favorite color because everything from chairs to the art of the wall is in shades of gray; all chosen carefully to reflect his power, as if anyone allowed to enter his office would have the smallest doubt. He is behind a desk of polished stone, but it has no drawers, no pens, only several phones and more than one computer. This is not a place for documents. The man does business, communicates with his allies in other ways, never in writing. It is to one of these, his allies, that he is talking now. Actually, the person on the other end of the line is not so much an ally as a messenger. The phone is secure. No one will hear who is not supposed to. Or at least not by technological means.

There is a problem and the man on the other end is making a report. The messenger says, "We lost them in California, but we knew where they were going so we watched the roads near the old man's place." The question the gray man does not state is how they could lose a vehicle they were tracking by satellite as well as following on the ground. "I don't know how we missed them but they are there now – with him."

The man asks one more question, "How many were in their car?" The messenger hesitates, uneasy about acknowledging more failure. "We don't know. The sisters, for sure."

Important, the gray man thinks, but not what he most wants to know. He knows the sisters are forces tied to the power he seeks, but is not exactly sure how. The people he answers to say little to fill in the gaps, but he has picked up some gibberish about bloodlines and mantras. Actually, as he thinks about it, he shouldn't be calling it gibberish. After all, the highest levels of his group talk in similar terms.

He hangs up, calls another number. Of all the numbers he knows, and there are many; the numbers of bank accounts, codes to trigger networks into action that, once initiated, can't be stopped. Of all those numbers this one is the most secret. It is a number he earned; he still doesn't like to remember what "earning" it required of him. He takes a deeper breath to shake off the unfamiliar flutter of anxiety.

The man he wants to reach is not in an office, nor even in a big house. Instead he lives simply, but his reach is everywhere, even into the dimensions of spirit. Especially into the dimensions of spirit. He cannot be reached directly but only through several intermediaries, one of which answers the phone now.

"Yes. He says to make your report to me." And so, the now sweating gray man in the office does; he is at the moment acutely aware of the cost of his luxury, his immunity from ordinary difficulties. The cost is in knowing that failure is not tolerated and could cost his life. Not that the group takes such extremes often; after all it wouldn't be a solid sales-pitch for recruitment. Not that many are ever asked to join; and it is uncertain whether if asked, one could refuse.

"We missed them on the road, but picked them up near the mesa. They are there now," he says, waits for the consequences.

"Yes, we saw," comes the answer. "We've brought all our most powerful groups into the effort."

For a moment, the gray man feels envy. He is not a member of one of these central groups. Like the man who called him earlier, he is only an intermediary, though of higher rank. Not that he doesn't have training, and he even might have the necessary bloodline, but he is only allowed to participate at the edges, not much more than a servant, really.

If you are thinking of these groups the man envies as groups of chanting monks, you'd be wrong. Not that they don't sometimes chant, but the basic strata of their power in this world, and the other, is fed by rituals so dark we will not speak of them. This group, these people, knows about old arcane things; they know about the sky and the secrets of the earth. They know how to bring correspondences into form, the focus required to build power, contain it, and then wield it toward their purposes.

Until recently, its members would have said they knew everything important, but then they learned this wasn't true. To their chagrin, they learned that they'd only tapped the edge of enormous possibility. Chagrin led to anger, as if somehow they'd been cheated. As if their bloodline had been deprived of its rightful privilege by a tiny group of cultural dinosaurs.

Since learning what they had, their primary focus has been to wrest this power from its hidden places, from its caretakers. No, it is not known how they found Charley, learned of the old people who help him guard what is hidden in the mountain. But they did learn and it will not be easy to divert them, to stop them. No, it will not be easy.

Between the two on the phone a long silence stretches. The man in gray is sweating even more and admits to himself that he is afraid. Sometimes he isn't sure if the men he works for are altogether human. He is no longer confident he knows exactly what "human" encompasses. But, to his surprise, the answer on the other end of the phone is somewhat reassuring. "We think that perhaps the old man does not know what help he called, what it will do. There may yet be a moment when we can reach it, make it our own. That red creature from the sky says the moment will come. He is stronger now, restless and hungry." What the man doesn't add is that the reptile is becoming insistent, demanding, seeming to give orders to people not used to taking them.

He also doesn't add that he, and a few others, are not worried about failure, but about success. Some of them are fearful of what they've called. At first, the group had only intended to call the red power, to use it, but the red power had told them more was possible. It said they could also claim the sky spirit sent to prevent their efforts. That, in fact, they must. So, for now, the group focuses on the freed snake in Blue's care. Later, maybe they will do more than that.

This group, this alliance of groups, has always been able to direct power. They don't want to think about what would happen if this new power they've called wielded them instead.

That is, all but a few avoid thinking about this possibility. The man on the phone thinks of little else, he and a few others. Why not leave well enough alone? For centuries his group has done well with no more than they've always had. But greed and hubris demand more. They always do.

Confident again, the gray man hangs up the phone, turns his attention to the cabin beside the mesa. He mustn't let the people there escape again. A few women, an old man! They will not be so difficult to capture, not for a man who can control governments, the secret machines of war.

About the Author

June O'Brien lives in the northwestern corner of the United States. A member of the Nansemond Tribe, she is a dream consultant with degrees in psychology and counseling, and has published two books of poetry.

She is from a culture in which seeing spirits, visiting with them, and being summoned by them is not unusual. She knows the spiritual medicine of wild plants, gathers them and makes medicine for the body and for the soul.

When in the forest, or the mountains gathering medicine, she knows that sometimes a spirit comes. It may seem only a sudden shift of the light, a spooky shiver, or a shadow between the trees.

Or, if you are fortunate, you may see a spirit-creature fully revealed. If that happens, it may follow you home, tell you a story. Maybe you will have no peace until you've written what it says. Maybe it will change your dreams, send your life in a strange new direction.